I0667964

LONGING

LEGATUM - BOOK 4

LULU M SYLVIAN

GRIFFYN INK

Copyright © 2018 by Lulu M Sylvian

All rights reserved.

No part of this book may be reproduced in any form or by any electronic or mechanical means, including information storage and retrieval systems, without written permission from the author, except for the use of brief quotations in a book review.

❀ Created with Vellum

To everyone who helped along the way.

PROLOGUE

Bright lights assaulted him first, then pressure in his privates. He whined and twisted. There was something in his mouth, down his throat.

"Someone get that animal back under." He heard the order, though it sounded muffled, as if his ears were full of cotton.

The pain came next. Pressure followed by stabbing pain.

Coughing and biting at what was in his mouth, he rolled onto his paws. Paws...oh no. He shouldn't be in this form. He always got in trouble when they caught him in this form.

Vomiting the tubing from his throat, he shook his skin back into place. Hands and knees replaced paws as he crouched on top of a stainless steel table. The pain was still sharp. He reached down and, not quite feeling the blade, pulled the scalpel out of his upper thigh. Warmth trickled down his leg.

The voices and the bodies surrounded him. He stabbed the first one who reached out to him. The knife sank into the man's forearm; the man screamed and pulled back. Shane was off the table and running. Sort of. His feet were not quite working. He could only half feel them as they hit the floor.

He entered the hallway and suddenly was aware of his nakedness. Ducking into the first open room, he hid in a pile of laundry. His nose wrinkled, and he flinched back from the stench. Vampire. Stuffing down his revulsion, he pulled on a shirt from the pile. He couldn't show up in Lucy's room naked. Voices passed the room, and then he staggered out of his hiding place; he needed to get to Lucy. She would help him. She would take away the pain. She always did.

Shane sat bolt upright. Pain pierced his skull. Sweat slicked his brow, his breathing shallow and fast. He fumbled with the blankets to check his thigh for blood before he settled into reality. It was a dream. A nightmare of a very bad memory. There would be no blood; there never was any blood, at least not now.

He pulled the blankets from his legs and paced around his room for a moment, trying to settle his nerves. It was nights like these he was glad he lived at Mission Run and not alone. There would be someone up somewhere in the compound; there always was

He pulled jeans on and began roaming the house, finally making his way to the game room. The blue glow of laptops illuminated the faces of a group of teens playing a marathon session of some online RPG. Shane opened the drinks fridge and grabbed a beer.

"Warcraft?" His voice felt like sandpaper in his throat. He must have been screaming again.

"Uh-huh. You play?" The teen never took his gaze from the monitor in front of him.

"Nope, I'm more a single-shooter kind of guy. Mind if I just hang?"

"Whatever."

Whatever was enough for him. Whatever around a

group of kids who were not trying to castrate him was better than sweating through a PTSD episode alone. He'd call Melinda in the morning. She was a therapist, she'd said he could text her at any time if it got bad. So far it had never gotten so bad that he couldn't hang tough until morning.

1

"**M**om!" Lucy flinched as her son thundered down the stairs yelling for her.

"What did I say about yelling at me from upstairs?" she yelled back.

Justin ignored her. "I can't find my jersey, and it's team day," he whined.

Lucy continued to pull together items for today's lunches. "Did you check the laundry?"

"Did you wash it?"

"No, J, I didn't. Remember you are responsible for your own laundry. And if you needed a clean jersey for today, you needed to wash it. Besides..." She turned around to face the frantic tween. "Did you tell me you were going to need a specific shirt for school today?"

Justin wilted. He was still young enough that disappointment turned into tears before it turned into undirected anger. Lucy saw his lower lip begin to quiver.

"Do you have to wear this year's jersey? Do you have to wear your soccer team jersey?"

Justin stared at the floor, frowning.

"Hey, dork, you gonna cry over a stupid shirt?" Stacey entered the kitchen and swatted her brother's sandy blonde hair.

That broke the dam, and Justin's undirected anger now had a target. He leaped for his sister, but never made contact. Lucy grabbed him around the middle. Soon he would be bigger than her, and she wouldn't be able to over-power him so easily.

"Stacey, not helping," she growled.

"It's spirit week. Banners have been all over the school for like two weeks. He's lazy, he didn't tell you, and he didn't bother to do his laundry." Stacey's tone had thick neener-neener, tattletale tones to it.

"Justin, is this true, that you've known about this for two weeks?" Lucy still had her arms wrapped around her son.

He answered with a low, defeated, "Yeah."

"Go grab one of your dad's hockey jerseys." Lucy pushed him out of the kitchen.

"I wish you wouldn't call your brother 'dork.' He's too young for his brain. And high school is hard, especially being younger than everyone." Lucy raised her eyebrows at her daughter.

"I'll go apologize to the dork." Stacey grabbed an apple, then headed back upstairs.

"Stacey!" Lucy yelled after her in exasperation.

Geoff grabbed his insulated lunch box from the counter.

"I'm off," he announced.

"What, no coffee?" Lucy asked. She pointed to the fresh pot she'd made. It was the second week in a row Geoff had left without coffee, and she didn't drink it. But she had to make it; if she didn't, he would get cranky. And cranky wasn't fun for anyone.

"Sure." He grumbled and grabbed a travel mug from the cupboard. "I'll be home late, no dinner for me."

And he was gone, out the back door.

Lucy sighed. "Have a good day. Call me when you get the chance. I guess I'll just make the pineapple shrimp tomorrow. I've got my appointment this morning, so I won't be home until after lunch. Bye, honey," she said to the door. Lucy had been saying her morning monologues to the door more and more, instead of actually having a conversation with her husband. He was her husband, wasn't he? She hadn't had a normal conversation with him in—she couldn't remember how long. And when was the last time he had actually been home for dinner?

Justin came back into the kitchen and made a bowl of cereal. He wore a red and blue Canadiens jersey. It was too big on him and hung almost to his knees.

"Better?" Lucy asked.

He nodded.

Stacey followed him in wearing a different hockey jersey she'd grabbed from their father's closet. She had knotted the blue and gold jersey at her back with a hair tie, so that the shirt fit snug to her hips.

"What other spirit items might I need to be made aware of?" Lucy asked as she watched her children eat.

Stacey nodded, her mouth full of milk and cereal. "Crazy hair day," she mumbled.

Lucy lifted her eyebrows.

Stacey swallowed. "Sorry, crazy hair day. Do you think we could dye my hair green?"

Lucy stared at her daughter's frizzy curly hair. She wore it natural. The texture and the volume of her daughter's hair indicated the girl had African heritage in there somewhere.

Stacey had been almost four when Lucy and Geoff were

finally allowed to take her home. The adoption process had taken what felt like forever. Only later did Lucy learn that they had actually had a rather quick adoption, especially since they had gone through the state. Justin's adoption had been easier since she and Geoff had already been in the system. A processing glitch in their favor had granted them adoption of an infant boy ten months after the judge made Stacey their daughter.

Lucy began running her fingers through Stacey's hair. Playing with the strands, feeling the texture. In a mutual decision led by Stacey to take control over her hair, they'd stopped regular visits to the hairdresser earlier in the year, and stopped the relaxer treatments altogether. Stacey's obsession with research on the Internet had provided her with the information she felt she needed to maintain healthy, natural hair.

Lucy nodded. The hair felt good and strong, not dry and not greasy. "Sure, why not. We can try."

"Oh, can I get my hair green too?" Justin asked cheerfully, all traces of this morning's sullenness gone.

"No, you can't, copycat."

"Since Stacey is going to be territorial over the green, why don't you go for blue or fire-engine red?"

"Can I, Mom?" His wide brown eyes looked at her eagerly.

"I've got my appointment this morning, so I'll stop by the store on my way home, and I'll pick up what they have. If they don't have green, will you survive a different color?"

Stacey nodded.

"Good, now go. I hear the bus coming." Lucy gave each child a bear hug and walked them to the front door.

She leaned against the doorjamb as she watched them hike their backpacks on as they made their way to the bus stop. Lucy did not leave her perch until they were on the bus and the door was closed.

The house was quiet. It felt like such a drastic change after the cacophony of the morning rush.

Lucy returned to the kitchen, placed the cereal bowls in the sink, and wiped down the table. She returned assorted items to their places before making her way back upstairs and into the shower.

She had just over an hour to get ready and drive downtown to the specialist for her appointment. She was two weeks late for her infusion, and she felt the symptoms sneaking in: constant fatigue, inability to sleep at night, weakness in her limbs, neuropathy in her toes and fingers. It wasn't bad yet, barely noticeable. If she went much longer, it would get worse and she could add flu-like symptoms to the mix. The longest she'd managed to go without an infusion was twelve weeks, and she had been extremely ill by that point.

Lucy would have liked to completely separate from her past and her birth family, but this need for blood every six weeks was a constant reminder of what she really was.

A child of vampires.

Not that she had ever been a vampire. No. She ran her tongue over her filed teeth. They had made sure she was aware of her own limitations. She hadn't been allowed to keep her fangs. She was the daughter of a vampire, a daywalker, and had lived by their rules and followed their habits.

But not just any vampire. Her father had been a particularly sadistic coven master. Her mother, a blood slave, died giving birth. There had been no love between them, and certainly no love from them for her. Lucy had left that life behind as soon as she could escape. Her father's violent disappearance provided the opportunity she'd needed when she was nineteen to completely break ties with her past and disappear. Without the protection of her father, and as his daughter, she'd faced a future of slavery. Her future would have been that of guard dog, blood slave, and rape victim. At least she would never be able to bear children for those monsters. That was one small consolation.

She would never be able to escape what she was. Every six to eight weeks she needed blood. All daywalkers did. She didn't need to hunt for blood like a true vampire. She didn't need to consume it, though that would provide for her needs. A blood infusion was easier, cleaner. And certainly tasted better. Lucy's tongue did not like the taste of blood. Drinking it for the first half of her life had been more than enough.

But she wasn't a vampire. Vampires do not shop at Walmart or any place that ends in -mart. They do not clip coupons, or wonder if pizza two nights in a row will stunt the kids' growth. Vampires do not worry about bedtime. They stay out all night and take the first train home in the morning. They do not concern themselves with carpools and balancing part-time work and full-time family. Vampires barely know what work is. They invested their money wisely and have unfathomable amounts of wealth. Lucy did miss the money. But now she was a mom and her life was completely different.

Her phone pinged with a text. She smiled.

Just wanted to say hi. I need to swing down there soon for a visit. I have some stones for you.

Shane always brought her the best gemstones. He never told her were they came from, always hinting at nefarious dealings. Lucy liked the idea that her oldest friend was a bit of a gem smuggler, as long as he didn't get into trouble smuggling anything more dangerous.

Blood and Shane, two reminders of what she really was. Blood she wished she could live without. Shane? She was glad he had tracked her down and stayed in her life.

Shane heard Joe push the door to the apartment open. It wasn't locked. He stepped inside, his footfalls almost silent. But not to Shane's ears. Joe was probably thinking one of the kids had broken in on a dare and was hiding. The rapid *bam-bam-bam* of video-game assault rifles should let him know whomever it was, they weren't hiding, at least not from him. A few more steps into the apartment and Joe would see a first-person-shooter video game dominating his TV screen.

"So this is where you've holed up?"

Yep, people were looking for him. Joe's apartment was the safest place in the meantime. Of course he could always ditch town. That would be the fastest way to make sure no one could find him. And the fastest way to never being trusted again.

The reply he gave Joe from his position lying back in the recliner was a grunt.

"Wanna beer?"

Another grunt.

Joe made his way to the small kitchen, which he rarely used, since he typically ate up at the house. It made sense to Shane—why cook for yourself when Connie was a master chef and fed everyone? Joe's refrigerator, however, was always stocked with beer.

"What are you doing here, Shane?"

As if that wasn't obvious.

The game figure on the TV screamed, and red splattered across the screen as if the viewer had been brutally shot.

Shane tossed the game controller on the table and grabbed the open beer Joe had set down for him.

"I'm shirking my responsibilities. You gonna nark on me?"

"What?" Joe chuckled. "The mighty Shane is in hiding 'cause he don't wanna?"

"Damn straight," Shane responded humorlessly.

"I'm not gonna narc on you, you are going to turn yourself in, or I have it on good authority that Connie will cut you off."

"Threatening me with food; that's low even for Morgan," Shane smirked.

Joe nodded. "Yep. My understanding, it's Honey's idea. That woman has a mean streak."

"Well, she has to; she's playing with wolves. Anything to gain advantage over us, right? Between you and me, I don't think she plays fair."

"So you gonna call in?'

Shane stood, groaning. "I'll do one better. I'll go up to the house, put on my big-boy pants, and deal with this."

Joe snorted at the term *big-boy pants*.

Shane shot him a glare. "I know, I know. Honey's terminology is rubbing off on all of us. But Morgan's never been happier. Can't really deny him that."

"No, but I swear it's getting a little scary around here. Morgan, then Julia. Mates. Hell, even Dante got married. Dante."

"Naw, I wouldn't begrudge any of them their mates. That's something special there, man. You should be so lucky to ever find your mate. When you do, you'll do anything for them." Shane felt that reality deep in his gut. He tipped his beer in thanks to Joe, grabbed his hat, and then headed out the door.

"As if you have," Joe scoffed.

I would do anything for her. Shane let the door close behind him. *Including not being with her.* And that was the part that hurt the most. The few days after his last visit to Lucy he had identified the five stages of grief as each one hit him freshly in the face. Denial: this wouldn't be forever. Anger: for an instant he held blind hatred for Geoff. The hate was never directed at Lucy for picking Geoff, but always at Geoff for being the one available for her. Bargaining: he could handle knowing she was safe, loved, and cared for, even if she wasn't his. Depression: this was the hardest to get past, and some days he didn't. Acceptance: this was his life, and while Lucy left a big hole in the middle, he still had her in it. Melinda had introduced him to the concept during one of his brief conversations with her. Leaving someone you love can be just as painful as having them die. Lucy loved her husband, and Shane died a little more each day. Unrequited love sucked.

And what Morgan wanted of him also sucked. Shane had a choice, to continue to hide from his duties or to suck it up and face this. To everyone else it looked like he had to man-up against his personal prejudices. For Shane it meant facing down his past. It meant daywalkers and vampires.

People who had never treated him as anything more than a target for their anger, their torture. The vampires were the worst of them. Something in their nature, their violent need of blood. Or maybe it was simply that Lazarus was a sadistic bastard, and Shane had been unlucky enough to be born in the wrong place and the wrong time.

He had gotten out. Of course at the time he hadn't

wanted to leave Lucy behind, but he had to. Living on the street as a teenager certainly hadn't been easy, but with his natural skills as a shifter it had been a whole lot easier than staying as a slave in the coven's compound in Las Vegas.

He trotted down the stairs from Joe's apartment over the car barn into the vast space that housed the Palatines' vehicles: family cars in the middle, personal ones to the left, and on the opposite side of the garage, the bike collection.

A beautiful orange and green custom build-out chopper sat gleaming, waiting to be ridden in the golden hills of Northern California. He could turn right at the bottom of the stairs, get on his bike, and... And what? He wasn't a coward. The family considered him to be one of their top men, an alpha even. Some alpha he was turning out to be, afraid to have a single meeting with a woman. Not just any woman, but a woman who represented everything he hated about his past.

He turned left. He knew what Morgan wanted of him. Time to deal with it, get it taken care of.

"Let's get this over with," Shane announced as he approached Morgan. The taller man was attempting to review several documents and feed his infant nephew at the same time. It did not appear to be a successful attempt at multitasking.

Morgan nodded, picked up his cell phone, and placed a call. He smiled at his wife when she entered. He began speaking into the phone with low tones.

Honey, tall with golden curls pulled into a messy ponytail, strolled in and picked up the baby. She cooed as she wiped orange mushy food from the baby's face. The baby cooed back at her and grabbed handfuls of her hair.

"I think he was winning this round." Shane nodded to the boy in her arms. She looked down at the papers spread across the table in front of Morgan. "I agree, but it's good practice for him." She tipped her head toward Morgan, keeping her voice down while he was on the phone.

Shane's brows shot up.

Honey giggled. "No, nothing like that. Not yet. Hopefully sooner than later." She sounded a bit wistful. She leaned in and began whispering conspiratorially. "Honestly, I think Julia will get knocked up before I do. You know how she is about timelines and schedules."

Shane huffed a chuckle.

Mates, babies. Yeah, this place was becoming scary, but in the best way possible. It was only scary to know that he wouldn't ever join in the happiness his friends knew.

Morgan set down his phone. He stood and took the baby back from Honey. "I said I would watch Ethan today. You and Caro are supposed to be off." He smiled at his wife.

"I am. I just came over to let you know we were leaving, and get a kiss." Honey leaned in and kissed him. "See you after dinner."

Honey wiggled her fingers in a happy good-bye wave.

"You trust those two together?" Shane nodded his head after Honey.

"My wife and my sister? Hell no," Morgan chuckled. "That's why I'm staying out of their way." Morgan adjusted the baby on his shoulder. "I think it's a ploy to get my biological clock ticking for one of these. Spend time with an adorable baby, and I'll be jonesing for one of my own."

"Is it working?"

"Not at all. I have to change his diapers. That is a vile prospect."

As if he knew they were talking about him, the baby raised his head to look around before closing his eyes and falling asleep on Morgan's shoulder in a post-meal nap.

Shane chuckled quietly. Babies weren't his thing. He didn't mind kids. He had a couple that he was particularly fond of and would put up with, but babies, not so much.

"Truth, I'm ready whenever Honey is." Morgan began patting the baby. "We have a confirmed lunch meeting with Del Fuego tomorrow. You gonna go into hiding on me again?"

"No, I'm good. What time we have to leave?" Shane asked.

Morgan looked at the papers on the table next to him. "Let's say..." He dragged the word out, calculating in his head. "Meet you in the barn at ten. Business attire. Suit, tie, the whole bit."

Shane nodded.

Suits, ties, vampires. It was going to be an uncomfortable lunch.

2

Sitting across from Cyan del Fuego, Shane had to admit to himself that he harbored great resentment toward her kind. She had been nothing but charm, beauty, class. He had nothing against her personally. In fact he had nothing against most of the daywalkers he had met, personally. Only a small few—hell, one, just one fucking vampire did this to him. One colored his world in such a negative manner that he now had to remind himself to get over his prejudices so he could have lunch with this woman.

Cyan del Fuego, head of the Cyan Group, a highly successful business entity, and daughter of the West Coast's lead coven master, ran her own string of boutique hotels and managed her father's affairs and kept the peace.

Shane twisted his head, wiggling a finger between his collar and neck. The tie strangled him. He hated the things, but Morgan had insisted.

A formal lunch in San Francisco. Shane should have anticipated the players involved. It wasn't going to be hamburgers and fries with some construction workers.

This was far from it.

When he'd followed Morgan into Cyan Group's lobby, he was not surprised to find Morgan's sister, Julia, and her mate, Roman Aventine, waiting for them. The Palatine and Aventine families had recently ended a feud that began in prehistory with Remus and Romulus, the founders of Rome. Not myth to their families, but the basis of the conflict between their families. Romulus killing Remus while arguing over which hill they should found their city upon had kicked off a case of extreme sibling rivalry. Roman, the Aventine's newly elevated primary alpha, was now mated to Julia, a rare female alpha. They set the definition for power couple. The region's top dogs, literally, were all here.

What did surprise him was that lunch was catered and served in a chic, modern, yet formal dining room. Cyan did not cater in boxed lunches to eat around a conference table; no, a menu with a full selection of choices was presented. Waitstaff dressed formally in black bow ties and long white aprons. If he asked, Shane expected a resounding "yes" from Cyan about lunch being prepared by a celebrity chef. He did not ask.

He swallowed hard and forced down all the resentment that rose with the bile in the back of his throat.

"I know this can't be easy for you, Mr. Vincent." Cyan had a voice that sounded like a lover's purr. The soft lilt of her accent lured Shane in. Only stubborn resentment kept his back ramrod straight.

"Shane, please. Mr. Vincent is some unknown man in a phone book with a good last name." His guards back in place, Shane offered a small smile.

"Your friends care for you. They have effectively put off our meeting until there was no other option," Cyan continued.

Shane grunted.

"Shane, you know why we had no other choice, right?" Julia smiled one of her new dazzling grins at him. A tough businesswoman, Julia had been prone to glower to maintain her hard-ass attitude. That had all changed a few months previously when she came home from a conference and announced that she and Roman were mates. The happier Julia was no less a business force to be reckoned with; she just did it now with a smile.

Julia's smiles scared Shane more than her glares. Before, if she was going to go for the jugular, he could read it on her face. Now she was just as likely to comment on a beautiful flower as she was to eviscerate her victim.

He felt as if they were all set up to tag team him into submission. Except for Roman—he had no friendly advice to offer since the two of them had no history together. Roman was here because this involved Lazarus. And everyone here knew Shane was the one with the connection, the history, with Lazarus.

Shane should have insisted a second come with him. Today Morgan was in primary-alpha mode, and not best-buddie, I've-got-your-back mode. Well, he would show them. He would be able to do this without a PTSD breakdown over the soup.

"Ms. Del Fuego, I try to ensure that my past does not dictate my prejudices. But there are times that I fail miserably. I would like to be able to do nothing more than trust you based on the recommendations of my alphas, Morgan and Julia. Your track record with them should speak for itself, but—"

Cyan cut him off. "But you have a hard past. One that I am sure you would like nothing more than to forget. And my kind were directly responsible for the pain of your past. I am not asking for forgiveness for daywalkers as a group, or even the vampires. I am asking that you give the Del Fuegos a chance. We are all here to work toward a common goal. Lazarus has proven to have returned. His people have already made attempts on Morgan's life, and they had Roman targeted. His reach is insidious; his people have contacts in places we don't expect."

Shane listened as Cyan ran over Morgan's kidnapping and two-week disappearance, and the failed attempt by a vampire and a Canadian wolf on Roman's life, as if she were reciting a shopping list. Neither seemed like they should be items jotted down on a scrap of paper, with a line scratched through after they were discussed.

Morgan had been kidnapped by a daywalker and a rogue wolf, a Smith, working together. In what could have only been an initiation activity, following the directions of a voice on the other end of a phone referred to as His Lordship, an ex-boyfriend of Morgan's wife was ordered to shoot him. In a twist of fate that brought Cyan into the entire mess, Maplecourt, the ex, worked as an accountant for her firm. Maplecourt, thinking he was working for the Russian mafia, had stumbled into a situation that was substantially above his pay grade. No one had ever asked Cyan what happened to the man. They only knew he would not be found in the concrete footings of one of Morgan's construction projects.

During that abduction, Morgan had been propositioned to kill the Aventine alpha, an offer Morgan refused. He'd escaped, but it had taken him two weeks to find his way back home.

No other known attempt had been made on Morgan's or Roman's lives, or that of Roman's father. It wasn't until Julia discovered that her roommate for a genetics conference was not the chemist from Toronto she thought she was, that the threat against Roman had reemerged. The imposter had been seduced by a vampire who had a tap on Julia's office phone. Julia found transcripts to the phone recordings that implicated the scientist's imposter and a vampire in an attempt on Roman's life. Fortunately that threat had been eliminated; unfortunately no one was able to gather more details from the vampire other than that he too worked for His Lordship.

His Lordship. Shane shivered. That was a phrase he could have gone the rest of his life without hearing.

Shane leveled his gaze on Cyan. His Lordship, Lazarus, once ruled the vampires of the West Coast, and substantially more areas farther afield. That was his problem, his mania, and his eventual downfall. Cyan's father, Alejandro del Fuego, had swept in from South America, stopping the madness the vampires had unleashed. He started by destroying the mess that was the infection started by Lazarus. Everyone thought Lazarus was dead. Everyone including Shane.

"So what do you want from me?" Shane asked. He followed Cyan's gaze to Morgan. Shane drooped. No. He knew what they wanted. And he did not want to involve her. "Not Lucy."

Morgan's expression was grim as he nodded. "Yes. We need you to just check in on her and make sure Lazarus hasn't reached out to her."

"Lucy left that life; she is not in his realm of control anymore. She's..."

"We know, Shane. But since he is back, we need confirmation. As far as anyone here is aware, Lucy is a non-threat," Julia explained. She leaned in close. "Look, I know you went to Peru; that means you brought back a few or more"—she paused as if to collect her words—"pebbles.

You always save the best for her. Have you taken them to her yet?"

Shane grunted. No, he had not. He'd never needed an excuse to go see Lucy and the kids before, and Julia was right. He did have a few choice "pebbles" to deliver.

"What did you do last time when you visited?" Morgan asked. "You did stop by on your way to see those kids in Arizona, right?"

Shane nodded. "Said hi, stayed a few days, played with the kids, rattled her husband's cage. The typical brother-comes-to-visit activities."

"And that is all we are asking of you this time," Cyan added. "Only, this time see if she mentions anything about her father. Does she seem to suddenly have more anxiety, or more paranoia? She was also his victim; we are aware of that."

"Information gathering only. You don't even need to let her know what's going on," Julia soothed.

"Actually, it's probably best that she not know what's going on. If she is unaware that Lazarus has resurfaced, her ignorance could be her best protection. Is there any reason to believe he would contact her at all? From what I've gathered, there was not a strong father-daughter bond between them to begin with," Roman commented.

"There wasn't," Shane growled. His memories of the past too close to the surface. Lucy had been her father's pride and joy, a cherished, loved child whom he lavished with gifts and her heart's desire. Until it became clear she was not what he wanted of her. By then he would lash out just as quickly as he would send her off to Paris for a week. When the hitting was no longer balanced with the gifts, when the barrage of abuse became constant, Lucy finally left. No, she would not seek out her father, but he might come looking for her.

"Fine. I'll go check in on her. I'll hang out for a few days, and when I come back, I'll tell you what I'm telling you now: she's not going to have had any contact with her father."

3

Lucy's head throbbed. She wanted to go back to sleep. Sleep where her world was not falling apart. Sleep where there was no pain. She groaned and pressed a hand to her forehead, trying to keep her brain from exploding out of her eyes. Crying oneself to sleep gave a crapulence feeling worse than drunk-hangover head.

Now there was an idea. Was it too early to start drinking? Maybe she should leave the kids at their Aunt Jen's for the day? They were already spending the weekend with her. Lucy could get totally blitzed, then deal with all of this tomorrow. Lucy stumbled into the bathroom. She squinted into the cabinet, looking for pills. "Hello, gorgeous," she crooned to the three blue gel pills before popping them into her mouth and swallowing.

She leaned against the counter. Geoff's shaving cream sat at the other end. Quietly, without a plan, Lucy picked up the garbage can and began filling it with all his items that were left in the bathroom. Razor blades, shaving cream, muscle rub, foot powder, hairbrush, toothbrush, toothpaste, nose spray. She finished cleaning out the cabinet and counter; she cleaned out under the sink and in the shower. After tying off the garbage bag, she tossed it down the stairs.

She climbed into the shower and let the warm water bring feeling back into her numb body.

Dressed in jeans and a T-shirt, with wet hair causing damp spots on the back, Lucy began cleaning the presence of Geoff out of the bedroom. She padded downstairs and got a box of large black garbage bags from the garage, then returned to the room.

That stupid red dress was the first thing in the next bag. Geoff had planned a nice dinner out, just the two of them, since the kids were at his sister's. She had worn it to feel beautiful. The red set off her pale skin and black hair. It had been too long since she had actually seen the man, let alone gone out on a date with him. Geoff had been hit hard by the big four-five. Middle-aged. Even though it really wasn't. She had planned on reminding him that forty-five was not old.

How long had she spent digging in the back of her closet looking for something that wasn't black or taupe? Her closet wasn't the gloriously large walk-in type she'd had when she was a spoiled brat. It was slightly deeper than two hanger's widths and as wide as half the bedroom. She had known in the depths there had to be a sexy red dress. The clothes pressed against her back and felt uncharacteristically heavy. She should have taken that as a sign. Instead she'd walked right into his trap dressed in that stupid spaghetti-strapped velvet sheath dress.

She hated the sheets—they were a color Geoff had liked, so they used them. Off the bed and into the garbage bag. She swept the top of his dresser on top of the sheets. There was no finesse to the removal of items.

Lucy grabbed her phone and dialed her sister in-law.

"Hey, Jen, sorry it's so early."

"What?" the groggy voice at the other end of the line asked.

"I'm sorry if you had any plans today, but I need you to bring the kids home. They won't be staying the rest of the weekend."

Jennifer grumbled rather incoherently about the kids staying.

"Yeah, I know. You need to speak to your brother about that. Did you know he was leaving me? Is that why you took the kids?"

The shock and outrage she heard in Jennifer's voice at least let Lucy know that Geoff hadn't told his sister before he told his wife. Ex-wife.

"Lucy, do you realize it's like stupid five in the morning on a Saturday?"

"No, I didn't realize it was this early. Sun is up and I couldn't sleep," Lucy answered.

"Do you need the kids now?"

"No, no, go back to bed. Late morning is fine." Lucy hung up the phone and continued to empty Geoff's closet into garbage bags.

Each full garbage bag she sent down the front stairs.

He had a booth in the back. Geoff looked up. His smile didn't fade. It vanished.

Lucy held out her hand to the other woman. "I'm Lucretia, Geoff's wife." Typically she wouldn't have bothered with her relationship to Geoff; that should be obvious. Typically, she would have said, how do you do *or* nice to meet you*. Hell, she would have called herself Lucy. But something in Lucy's gut redirected her words. And the name Lucretia was a threat in and of itself.*

"I'm Chrissie." The other woman smiled nervously.

"I'm not staying, am I?"

Each bag down the stairs, another memory tainted by

his hand around the hand of that young woman with the shiny shoulder-length brown hair that swayed as she moved her head. She was thin, with augmented breasts and a vapid grin.

Lucy ran out of garbage bags before she ran out of items to put in them. It wasn't until that moment she realized it was just past six a.m., and she had been cleaning out her room for almost an hour. Home improvement stores open early for all those construction workers, she thought as she put on shoes and headed out to buy a few more boxes of black garbage bags.

He claimed to have already moved a few things out, necessities for the time being. Well, she was moving the rest of his stuff out. He was giving her thirty days to find a place and move. That was not going to happen, not if she could help it. And she needed a lawyer for some meeting he already had set up for Tuesday to go over the details.

Lucy had no concept of time as she bagged up her life with Geoff, and began hauling it out the front door. She paused and watched as her sister-in-law's SUV pulled into the drive.

"Mom, what's going on?" Stacey asked as she got out of her aunt's car. Lucy was pulling another garbage bag onto the front lawn.

"What happened, Mom?" Justin sounded panicked.

"I'll explain in a bit. Go in and help me drag the bags out here." Lucy's tone was eerily calm. "Hi, Jen." She addressed her soon to be ex-sister-in-law with a brittle grin.

"Lucy, what's going on here?" Jennifer asked.

"Well," Lucy began, "your no-good cheating, lying, asshole, scum-sucking thunder douche cunt of a brother introduced me to the woman he is leaving me for last night.

And that fuck weasel, jizz-gargling troglodyte is trying to unadopt his children."

"Language!" Jennifer gasped in shock.

"Language? What? I'm taking it easy on the twat-monger. Be glad I'm insulting his flat white ass with words and not fingernails and high kicks to the groin. Right now my anger is fathomless. Tell him he has until one to remove his belongings from my lawn or I will set them on fire. I can't call; I believe he has my number blocked."

"Lucy, are you sure you want to do this?"

"No, I don't want to do this. That bastard is having his name expunged from the adoption records. This is not a want; this is a need. I want to be up there in bed." She pointed toward the upstairs windows. "I thought I was going to be up there in flagrante delicto with my husband, not moving his sorry ass out. Not trying to figure out what I'm supposed to tell my children, and not freaking out because I don't have a lawyer and can't afford one. I'm about to get screwed with a rusty barbed-wire dildo in a divorce I didn't see coming," Lucy shouted.

"I'm sorry to hear this, Lucy. I'll call Geoff." Jennifer nodded and got in her car. Lucy turned to face her children. They stood slack-jawed and wide-eyed.

"I guess you heard all that, huh?"

Stacey nodded mutely. Jason's lip began quivering.

"Oh, babies, I'm so sorry." Lucy rushed to the children and pulled them into an embrace. "That's not how I wanted to tell you."

"Dad wants to divorce us too?" Stacey's voice had a hitch. She may have been too young to remember details about her adoption, but somewhere deep inside she still had fear over being wanted. This was going to send her back into counseling.

"Dad's just being stupid right now. He's mad at me for whatever reason. I don't know what it is. He's got this new girlfriend, and I guess they are going to get married. I don't know anything more than that. We only had a brief meeting, and it ended when I poured wine all over them in the restaurant."

Jason started to laugh. "You poured wine on them?"

It had been glorious. She'd stood there poised with a glass of red wine in her hand. She told the waiter to get some towels, and before anyone figured out what she meant, that woman was shrieking as Lucy upended the glass of red wine all over her front. And before the shock set it, Lucy picked up the nearest glass and tossed its contents into Geoff's face.

Geoff had roared.

"Hush, darling, you don't want to cause a scene."

"Uh-huh, not particularly mature of me, but your dad picked the restaurant so that I wouldn't make a big loud fuss. I wasn't loud about it. I just dumped my drink on Chrissie—her name is Chrissie. Then I dumped another drink on him and left."

Lucy continued to hug her kids. "Look, I'm supposed to meet with Dad and his lawyer on Tuesday. I'll know more then. Any questions you have for Dad, you can try to call him, or you can write them down and I'll take them with me on Tuesday."

"Are you really going to burn his stuff?" Justin asked.

"Maybe not," Lucy chuckled. "That was the anger talking. But I will ask the garbage guys on Monday to take it, or pay them extra, whatever, to haul it off. He's not playing nice. I'm not going to let him think he's getting away with anything. So I will not be playing nice either. I'm fighting tooth and nail."

She broke off their embrace. "C'mon, there are still more bags to haul out. Then let's go see a movie. I'm in the mood for watching shit blow up and burn."

"Mom, language," Stacey said, obviously mortified at the words her mother used.

Lucy grinned. "It's not like you haven't heard me use that word before. I know you've heard worse."

"Well, yeah, but just not from you."

4

Lucy wrung her hands. She tapped her foot. She paced. She looked at her phone and sat. She was not going to let Geoff beat her in this. She looked at the phone again and was out of the seat and pacing once more. Her teeth worried at the already painfully short nail on her thumb. A flicker of light bounced off the lobby doors, and her breath caught.

Her gut roiled with nerves. If she was prone to digestive issues, today would have her in knots. As it was, she fluctuated between wanting to throw up and needing to cry. She smoothed the fabric of her skirt one more time before sitting again. She crossed her legs. Her right foot bounced back and forth of its own accord.

Another suited man walked through the lobby. She settled long enough to not be a spectacle as he passed through the room and out the double doors. Her knuckles turned white as she clasped her fingers together in a clench. She looked at the phone again. The time hadn't changed. How could that possibly be? She had been here, in her mind, forever, but according to the phone less than five minutes had passed. She wanted to puke.

"Mrs. Asher?" A sharply dressed receptionist approached her.

Lucy paused. Panic flooded her system. Her skin felt sharp, as if she had been stabbed by a thousand pins all at once. The pain subsided, leaving her cold. "Yes?" Her heart pounded in her throat.

"Your attorney called and requested we have you wait in one of our offices so that you don't accidentally run into Mr. Asher when he arrives. Will you please follow me?" She held out her arm, indicating the direction they were to proceed in.

The tension in Lucy's neck melted at the words *your attorney*. Bentoncourt had gotten her message and was going to be here.

Calling him had been difficult. It meant returning to the people she considered her abusers. People who had worked for, or were controlled by, her father.

She had no idea if he would be able to represent her, whom he would send, or if he could let her know what had become of her money or even if she had any left.

The receptionist led her into a small windowless room, a table and four chairs. It looked more like a holding cell than it did an office, but she didn't care. Half of her nerves were over having to see Geoff before she was ready, before she had the comfort of a lawyer with her.

She couldn't sit. Her nerves were still too dance-happy with fear.

She closed her eyes and pinched the bridge of her nose. She had barely slept last night. Geoff had set her up for today. He had given her less than two full business day's notice. He'd counted on her not being able to find a lawyer over the weekend.

He never really had believed any of the stories she

shared of her past. She hadn't lied to him. She had grown up ridiculously spoiled and rich, and abused. It was a nasty combination, and one that was difficult to leave. To anyone not deep in the trenches of the life, it always seemed like it should be so easy to just walk away from a life of abuse, but that was so far from the truth.

Lucy didn't know how to take care of herself, and the year away at college hadn't taught her anything beyond balancing how many classes she could skip and still pass a course, which bars carded girls, and which bars the rich men hung out at.

When she met Geoff, she'd been clueless and rapidly running out of money; cut off and alone. He had been her knight in shining Oxfords. She didn't even have a checking account at that time, forget about knowing how to balance one.

She was back up and pacing in the small space. What was going to be required of her? There wasn't a local coven, one of the reasons she lived here. Would Bentoncourt be associated with the coven in LA, and if he was, would they let him come here today without there being strings—no, chains—attached? Was she willing to do what they asked in order to win this fight with Geoff?

She willed images of her children into her mind's eye. Yes. She would do anything for Stacey and Justin. Even if that meant flaying the skin from her back, she would.

A memory flashed in her mind. How many times had they done that to Shane over something she had done? It was a miracle he wasn't covered in scars, but then again he had healing skills she did not possess. She was a fast healer, faster than most of her kind, but nothing like Shane.

The door opened.

Lucy let out a small scream and jumped, knocking over a chair.

"I know I can be frightening, but I didn't think I had gotten that ugly." A kind-faced, older, Santa Claus of a man entered the small room.

"Bentoncourt!" Lucy cried out and threw her arms around the man's neck.

He was here. That meant she was saved. She began crying.

"Now, Lucretia, is it really all that bad?" He placed his case on the table and helped her into a chair.

Lucy couldn't speak between the sobs that racked her frame. Relief and anger rolled through her system.

Bentoncourt handed her a linen handkerchief. "When you're ready."

He stepped out of the office. When he returned, he was followed by the receptionist and two glasses of water. He sat and placed a hand on Lucy's shoulder.

She sniffed, took in a deep sigh, and slowly let the air out of her lungs. She dabbed at her eyes and blew her nose before giving the lawyer a weak smile. "I am so pleased you were able to come." Bentoncourt Roberts had been one of the daywalkers who helped to manage and run her father's empire. She shouldn't have wanted to see him, but Bentoncourt had the particular job of overseeing the estate, and that meant managing her finances and her life.

Bentoncourt had worked for her father, there was no doubt about that, but he had served Lucy. And helped her take care of Shane. That counted for quite a lot in her book.

Lucy clomped down the gangplank on the new cruising yacht she had finagled Daddy into paying for. He was never around, so why couldn't she have a little fun? He had cut her off from any more trips to Paris.

Daddy waited for her on the dock. He was out early tonight. The sun had only been down for about twenty minutes. She sashayed up to him expecting his typical chilly reception, a fake hug and a sneering endearment. Instead she received a sharp slap across the face.

Lucy cried out and placed a hand over the stinging cheek. Daddy snapped his fingers, and a muscled brute threw a bloody Shane at her feet. All thoughts of Daddy and the slap were replaced with wondering what she had done this time.

"Are you all right?" It was a stupid question. Of course he wasn't. The skin above his brow was split, and his eye was swollen shut. Dried blood caked his lips. He looked like a boxer having gone eight rounds without gloves on.

She glared up at her father. "What did I do this time?" She knew not to cry when she saw Shane like this.

She wanted to shrink from the glare he leveled on her. He turned and left.

Various followers appeared from the shadows and trailed behind in her father's wake as he left.

Lucy returned her attention to Shane. She shouldn't have left him alone, but Vegas was so far away, and if she had brought him along, he would have gotten a beating for not being on the compound. "What did I do?" she whispered.

Bentoncourt, her keeper, was suddenly by her elbow. "Come, Miss Lucretia. I have ice bags and antiseptic waiting for him in the car."

Lucy let herself be lifted back to her feet. Another muscled assistant lifted Shane. He was so thin he looked like a child in the other man's arms.

"Do you have painkillers for him?" she asked.

Bentoncourt shook his head. "He needs to shift to speed the healing."

Was Shane even strong enough to shift?

The security guard gingerly placed the beaten Shane into the car. Lucy followed him in, Bentoncourt followed behind. He was a lawyer, but he knew how to clean wounds, and stitch skin. Lucy stroked the smooth skin of Shane's shoulder while the other man cleaned his injuries.

"Why did it happen this time?"

"This has been going on for two days. Miss Lucretia. Your father expected you for dinner and not out gallivanting on your boat. Each day you did not return, well... This." Bentoncourt indicated the beaten young man partially on her lap.

She knew he was beaten when she misbehaved, but she had been good. She made sure to not do the stupid stuff her father typically disapproved of. She knew Shane hadn't been beaten because of her in over a year. She hadn't gone gallivanting, as Bentoncourt said. She had her nanny. She never went anywhere alone anymore. Shane should have been safe.

Her glance darted to the glass that separated them from the driver, and to Bentoncourt. She mouthed. Help me.

Bentoncourt nodded.

Lucy blinked to clear the current tears from her eyes. He had helped her back then, and he was here to help her now.

"I wasn't sure if you would be able to come, or if you were going to send someone. I'm so glad you'll be able to help me."

"Hold on a minute there, Lucretia. I don't know what I'll be able to do. I haven't had a chance to begin digging up your records. Have you accessed your trust fund?"

Lucy looked at the man, her eyes widened, and she began struggling for air. "I don't even know if that money still exists. Can I even gain access to it? I can't pay you without that fund. I have practically no money. Geoff locked me out of all accounts yesterday. I don't even know how I'm going to buy groceries or put gas in the car."

"Sh, sh, sh. It's okay. I didn't mean to set you off. These are just things we need to think about. Don't worry about fees right now."

A soft tapping on the door preceded it being opened by the receptionist. "They're ready for you now."

"Give us a few moments please."

She nodded and stepped back out.

"I am here to help you. Let's get through this meeting today, see what the man wants, and then go from there."

Lucy nodded.

"Good." Bentoncourt opened the door and asked the receptionist to please show them the way.

Lucy followed behind.

The conference room they were led into was large and walled in glass. Light flooded the room. Where Lucy had privacy to cry in the small enclosed office, there was no privacy here, not from the other people in the conference room, not from the people outside of the conference room. She felt like a goldfish in a tank. She half expected someone walking by to tap on the glass and make funny faces at her.

Lucy sat next to Bentoncourt on one side of the large table. Geoff and his lawyer, Thomas French of French and French and Associates, sat across from them with a series of documents already spread out on display.

"Put your papers away, gentlemen. We are not signing anything this morning," Bentoncourt announced before he even sat down.

Geoff shot French a concerned look. French didn't seem to notice anything at all. Lucy immediately did not like him. Even if he wasn't representing her husband—no, her soon-to-be ex-husband—she wouldn't like him. Something about him oozed slime. His hair was thinning and slicked straight back. He had a weak chin. He looked like he wanted to look like a shark in human form, but he had missed. He had little teeth.

"My client is here to listen to your terms. We would like to hear what you have to say, and then I will present a few demands that will be met this morning before we leave this office."

Lucy clenched her fist in mini triumph under the table. French might be slick, but he wasn't Bentoncourt, who could talk an alligator out of his skin and have him sew a pair shoes for you from his own hide. He was that canny and smart and had a talent for finding loopholes in contracts. At least he had when she was younger.

Geoff began to make those ridiculous huffing and rambling noises as he geared up to being angry and indignant. How had she ever thought them cute? He was blustery and a caricature of frustration.

French held up his hand to halt Geoff.

"Well, that is not the intention of this meeting." Even French's voice felt slippery to her ears.

She shivered from the unexpected tactile sensation from the sound.

"What exactly am I here for then?"

"Since your client, the respondent, did not file a response to the original petition, we are here to agree to the division of assets and to finalize the resolution of adoption in the case of Justin Patrick Asher and the emancipated youth status of Stacey Yolanda Asher."

Lucy jumped from her chair, knocking it back. She leaned heavily on the table. "What?"

Bentoncourt placed a hand on her wrist, possibly to calm her down, maybe to prevent her from climbing across the table and strangling Geoff.

"Mrs. Asher, will you please calm yourself? You had

thirty days to respond to the divorce, and you took no action. Since there was no contest, we proceeded with the equal division of assets and belongings. The petitions for the dissolution of adoption and for the emancipation of the aforementioned youth have also already been filed."

"How is this legal? Geoff only told me about all of this on Friday. Friday, that is not thirty days ago!"

French ruffled through a file folder. He produced a document with an image of Lucy holding a folded document. He pointed to the image and the time/date stamp. "This documentation shows that you received the served documents almost five months ago."

Lucy turned to Bentoncourt, her brows furrowed into deep ridges, her mouth open. Words stuck in her throat. "I'm asleep in that picture. How is this even legal?"

Bentoncourt sat back and crossed his hands over his ribs. "It's not." He leveled his eyes on the lawyer across the table from him. "Lucretia, dear, they expected you to show up here today without any recourse. They expected to be able to bully you into signing documents that would lay any wrongdoing firmly in your lap. And to remove any custodial situation from being part of the divorce proceedings. That's not going to happen now, is it, gentlemen?"

"She was served. She accepted the papers," Geoff responded. "I have a witness who will testify that we spoke, and you willingly took the papers."

Lucy closed her eyes and counted to ten. She sat down. Her hands held a firm grip on the edge of the table. "You damn well know I talk in my sleep. You used to get a good giggle out of recording entire conversations that I had no recall of, because I was asleep. That was a dirty move, you bastard." She spit the words between her teeth.

"I agree, a dirty move. However, since nobody here

wants to drag this divorce out, and my client would love to expedite the process as well, we are going to let you get away with that."

Lucy turned to Bentoncourt. "What?"

"This can be over in three months if we agree to this sneaky move, or we can say no and it's another six months minimum, Lucretia," he explained.

"Oh, okay. I'd rather get this over with. But I will not agree to anything about the kids. He does not get to unadopt to get out of custody."

"They're your kids, Lucy. I never wanted them."

Bentoncourt's large hand descended on her wrist again. "Let's table that issue for now. As you can see, my client has been caught completely unprepared for any of these claims. What else are you planning on surprising us with?"

"None of this would be a surprise if your client had paid attention when she was served," French slimed.

"As we have established, my client has no knowledge of those proceedings, as she was asleep. Now what else have you got?"

"Retirement, investments, and savings funds will remain in my client's name. The respondent does not have claims to these funds as the accounts were established prior to marriage."

Lucy's mouth turned to desert. Her spit was sand. Her heart dropped into her gut. She'd walked into that marriage with nothing, everything was Geoff's, and he was manipulating the system so that he owed her nothing. He was even trying to unadopt his children so he wouldn't have to pay child support.

"An account will be set up in my client's name before you leave this office, and you will transfer in—" Lucy's ears began ringing as they discussed figures. Geoff would pay alimony. A set figure would be agreed upon at a later date, but for now a figure to be paid bimonthly into the newly established account was agreed to.

The next blow came when she was presented with an estimate of their house's value and the demand that she pay half of the current value to Geoff within thirty days or move out. In the ten years they'd lived in that house, its value had skyrocketed. She thought it would be a more reasonable request for her to buy him out at the rate their mortgage was at. The new value was insanely overinflated.

She shook as she left the conference room with Bentoncourt. "I should really be getting half of the retirement account. After all, I spent years contributing to it."

"I have no doubt, Lucretia, but if he is going to claim all accounts prior to marriage as sacrosanct and off-limits, then we will agree." The lawyer was firm.

"Bentoncourt," Lucy almost whined.

"Think a minute, Lucretia. All accounts prior to marriage." He enunciated each word slowly and deliberately.

Her mouth dropped into an O. She nodded. "Yes, right. I agree. And purchase of the house should be no problem then."

"Are you still going around telling people you were some rich heiress whose money was locked away from her? Huh, Lucy? That's not a good game to play, especially with your lawyer." Geoff sneered as he passed her, leaving the offices of French and French and Associates.

"Don't worry, my girl." The lawyer patted her reassuringly on the shoulder. "We'll get you out of this marriage with your dignity and your finances intact."

5

S hane stared out the glass window looking over the freeway. His fingers tapped against the coffee cup in his hand. "Tell me being here isn't admitting some kind of defeat."

"Strong men survive horrible things all the time. It doesn't mean they aren't affected by it. And being strong doesn't mean getting over it. I'm tired of you big macho types saying that you have to deal with it or face it down or..." Melinda flapped her hand around in frustration. "You are here because you are strong and you want to survive this. Talking to me about it does not make you weak. It makes you human. And you have a better chance of surviving by talking with me. I'm glad you found a method that helps you cope, but if you are ever stuck, reach out, no matter the time. I will do my best to respond as soon as possible."

"I should be able to handle this better on my own." He walked behind the couch, constantly in motion.

"You keep this up, Shane, and I'll make you sit in on a group session. Maybe if I get a bunch of you man-holes all in a circle, you might hear how stupid you sound. You endured something no one should ever have to face, and you did it at a very young age. It's a minor miracle you are as mentally solid as you are. This would have fractured the psyche of most people."

"I haven't had the nightmares in a long time. Why are they back? Why now?" He paused and looked at Melinda.

Her head was cocked to the side, and one eyebrow shot up. "What's been going on? Who are you having to deal with?"

As an extended member of the Palatine family, Melinda was well aware of what he was dealing with. As the best friend to the secondary alpha of the family, Julia, Melinda was more privy to situations the family tried to quietly manage to not cause a panic. As Shane's therapist, she knew exactly how everything impacted him. She had a better grasp of the big picture than anyone else he would be willing to talk to other than Morgan. But she had the training and the tools to help Shane learn, cope, deal. And that was something Morgan did not have.

Shane walked around the front of the couch and sat with a huff. He stared into the cup for a long few minutes, thinking.

"It's because I have to deal with the Del Fuegos."

"You can do better than that," Melinda prompted.

"I miss her, Melinda. I miss her every day, and Cyan del Fuego wants me down there to spy on her. Morgan even agreed to it. They want me keeping tabs on Lucretia as if she would have anything to do with any of this." His nostrils flared with anger.

The problem was, he wanted to see her, needed to see her. Shane was like a junky. Only after the last visit, he'd thought maybe he should go cold turkey and never see Lucy again.

Maybe that was the only way to get over her. The mate glow wasn't some predestined one and only. But it was rare to get a second mate. That wasn't to say it didn't happen, just that most wolves, when they saw that glow, they held on for dear life. Of course it only worked when the mate also held tight.

Not Lucy. She'd stopped holding on to Shane a long time ago.

"We both know that Lucretia isn't why your nightmares are coming back. Do I need to confront Morgan about this, tell him it's too much?"

"You're my therapist, not my mommy. You don't get to write a note to the principal's office telling him I'm sick and can't do my homework. That's not how this works. Doctor-patient confidentiality and all."

"Yes, but I can drop hints. The Palatines need you whole, not about to have a mental collapse. Morgan values you and your sanity. If pushed too far, you could snap, and who knows how that will play out and how many people you'll end up taking with you." Melinda kept her tone even.

Shane knew where she was going with this. If he lost control he could become incredibly violent. Who knew if that violence would be limited to self harm? Or would he lash out and hurt those around him who cared for him; who he cared for?

"I won't spy on Lucy, but I will go and keep her safe."

"From who?"

"Damn it," Shane spit. "I will keep her safe from her father, the vampire who tortured me."

≈

Shane walked in the front door. He never knocked, not here. Not at Lucy's. He hadn't knocked for years. This was family. He knew he was welcome.

He caught sight of her before he called out.

She sat staring at the floor. The look of sheer hopeless loss on her face felt like a bucket of ice water. Instantly he was by her side, kneeling down so he could look up into her face.

"Hey, Luce, what's wrong?" His hand ran up her arm.

With a sob she was in his embrace. Her entire body shook from crying.

Shane looked around the room for any hint or clue as to what was upsetting her. Not even a cell phone on the coffee table.

He shifted so that he could lift her, and then he sat holding her on his lap like a small child. How many times had she held him like this? How many times had she soothed his inner turmoil? Lucy would tell him when she was ready. That was always her way. He just needed to be here for her while she cried it out.

She clutched so fiercely to his shirt, Shane was afraid of what she would tell him.

"Are the kids all right?" he asked in a quiet voice.

She nodded but continued to cry into his chest.

He stroked her hair. "As long as they are okay then." He made soothing sounds and continued to stroke her back.

Eventually her sobs leveled out and her crying turned to the soft, even sounds of sleep.

Shane stood. He braced himself as he realized his foot had fallen asleep. He shook it while trying to not jostle Lucy in his arms. He smacked it against the floor a few times, and finally feeling stable enough, he climbed the stairs.

Her bedroom looked as if it had been completely tossed.

Things were missing. He wasn't familiar enough with this room to be able to identify exactly what was gone. It was more of a gut feeling than anything else, and a visual emptiness. He laid Lucy on her bed and pulled a blanket over her.

He was playing on his phone in the living room when the kids burst through the front door.

"Hey, Shane," Stacey called out before heading over to give him a hug.

Justin yelled and jumped onto the man, still full of small-child exuberant enthusiasm.

"Dude, when did you get so tall?" Shane ruffled his hair. The blond was starting to turn dark with age.

Shane followed them into the kitchen, where they began rummaging through cupboards looking for an after-school snack. Even though this was their kitchen, in their search for food they looked more like they had no idea which doors the food was kept behind.

"Guys, if you don't know, I don't want to upset you. But—"

"Mom and Dad are getting a divorce," Stacey stated. Her tone was even and cold.

Shane listened. Taking it all in. He knew how much Lucy loved Geoff. At first their relationship had hurt Shane like a red-hot knife straight into his heart, but he'd learned to live with it. And eventually Shane came to accept Geoff because he loved Lucy and she loved him. Lucy's happiness and well-being were all that mattered to Shane. End of story.

"Fuck." The word was out of his mouth before he remembered his audience.

"Language!" Justin corrected.

"Yeah, pretty much." The look on Stacey's face spoke a

thousand words. She was angry, beyond pissed off at her father.

Shane reached out for her and pulled her into a hug. "I'm here for you guys. Your mom, and you too, okay? If you need anything." He released Stacey and looked her in the eyes. "Anything."

She nodded and angrily swiped at a tear.

"How long are you staying?" Justin asked.

"Well..." Shane turned to the boy, who now held a super-sized bowl full of rainbow-colored cereal, with milk sloshing over the sides. He laughed. "Not sure. I thought I was cruising through for a quick trip, but it looks like I might need to stay for a bit. Let me see what I can work out."

"Cool." Justin turned and carried his snack out of the kitchen. He turned back around. "Hey, I've got all this homework I have to do. Wanna play Assassin's Creed when I'm done?"

"Sure thing, J-man."

Stacey held a mug with a tea tag hanging from the side. She sat at the table and looked up at Shane. She glanced after her brother, then back to Shane. "Dad is trying to divorce us too. Mom told us he's being a jerk, but then she talked to me separate from Justin." She leaned forward and hissed at Shane. "He doesn't know how bad it is, and he's not gonna find out from either of us, right?"

She was threatening Shane to protect her brother. He wanted to laugh at her fierceness, he was so proud of her at that moment.

Shane nodded. "This is between you and me." He pulled out a chair and sat at the table across from her. If Geoff did anything to hurt these kids... Shane breathed in deeply. Lucy's well-being extended to her children. He would do anything for the three of them. At one point Geoff would have been in that protective circle. Well, not anymore.

Stacey took a long sip of her tea. "Mom wants me to go back into therapy. She said this thing with Dad is about to get really ugly." She stared out the sliding glass door for a long minute. When she faced Shane again, her eyes were rimmed with the dark pink of tears, and pain. So much pain. She sniffed.

"Dad filed emancipated youth papers on me."

For a second time that day Shane had a crying Asher woman in his arms. Any kindness he'd ever felt toward Geoff evaporated in that moment. How dare he file emancipation papers on Stacey? Shane had witnessed, from the sidelines, her years of therapy. In the four short years before her adoption she had accumulated a lifetime of abandonment issues in her tiny little body. Did that asshole have any idea what kind of damage he was doing to the girl, all to get out of paying child support?

"I don't want to go back into therapy. They treat me different at school when I'm in therapy. He's gonna make us move. I just know it." Stacey pushed out of Shane's embrace and wrapped her hands around her mug. "Mom's been a total mess all week."

"When?"

"He told her on Friday. They met at the lawyer's office on Tuesday. Wow, that was only two days ago. It really seems like a whole lot longer than just two days. Mom is real manic. She is either so angry I swear she spits fire, or she is so sad I'm afraid she'll just stop breathing."

"That's how I found her when I got here today. So less than a week?" He rubbed the back of his scalp. "Fuck. Sorry." He apologized the second the word left his mouth.

"Mom's been saying a lot worse. I've even started saying

it. Never realized how useful of a word it was until now." She sighed heavily and looked into her empty mug. "I've got homework too. Hey, how are you with World History? I have a test and..."

"Sure, I'll help you study. Then we can figure out what to do for dinner and let your mother take it easy."

Shane was quizzing Stacey on the US involvement in Vietnam when Lucy padded into the kitchen.

He set down the flash cards and wrapped Lucy in his arms. "The kids filled me in some." How could he tell Lucy he was here to fight for her now? She just needed to say the word, and he would take care of Geoff.

Lucy pushed out of his arms. She patted him on the chest. "It's been a bit of a mess. I'm a bit of a mess." She stepped back and began playing with Stacey's hair.

"Mom." She batted at her mother's hands.

"Sorry." Lucy straightened up and opened the fridge.

"I told him not to tell Justin," Stacey said.

"Okay, good." Lucy closed the fridge door. "Should we have spaghetti for dinner?"

"We had that last night," Stacey answered.

"Oh, right."

"Hey, Luce." Shane stood in front of Lucy. She wasn't acting like she was all there. He lifted her eyelids one at a time and peered into her pupils. "What did you take?"

"Nothing, just a Xanax."

"Lucretia?" All he said was her name, but the question was loaded.

"I took a Xanax with a Jack chaser. This is the hardest part of the day to get through, when everyone is coming home and he doesn't. The doctor gave me a prescription after I had a panic attack on Tuesday. I'm having a hard day." She sniffled and slumped against Shane's chest. "He doesn't love me anymore, Shane. What am I supposed to do?"

Shane managed to wrap an arm around her before Stacey hugged in on the side. He adjusted and held on to the two of them as their world dissolved, and he was helpless to stop it.

He wanted to kick himself. He could have been down here days sooner, only asshole had to drag his heels. He hadn't wanted to face her because it would break his heart, but maybe if he had come down here sooner, he could have helped Lucy hold it together. He could take care of the kids while she slept, he could cook, he could... he could pick her up from the floor every time she fell and was too weak to get back up by herself.

6

Shane considered his options. Lucy was all tucked up in her bed. The kids were fed and finishing their daily chores. He really was proud of them. He knew, as typical teenagers, they were never the best at completing their chores without constant reminders. He had stood in this very kitchen time and time again while either parent groused at them for not having done some basic house-keeping job or another.

But tonight they moved with task-oriented precision. Justin even vacuumed the living room and the TV room without prompting.

"Can I help?" Shane asked. Usually he assisted Lucy with the dinner cleanup. It gave them a chance to catch up.

"No, you made dinner. It's only fair one of us does the cleaning." Stacey turned her attention back to loading the dishwasher.

"So there's nothing I can do?" He didn't like feeling help-less, but in times of crisis the kids stepped up to the plate. And with Lucy upstairs snoring, he really wasn't needed for anything.

"Um, yeah. If I give you a list, could you go grocery shopping? We are out of a few things. And I can't drive, and…" Stacey bit her lips into her mouth, hesitant to continue. "I don't think Mom has any money right now. I overheard her on the phone complaining to some lawyer guy that Dad had only put two hundred bucks into some account, and how were we supposed to live off that."

Shane nodded. He pulled the magnetic notepad from the front of the refrigerator and scrounged a pen from the ubiquitous junk drawer. Every kitchen had one.

"Okay, what do we need?"

Stacey provided him with a well-thought-out list that would cover school lunches for the next week. As she rattled-off foods, they discussed what meals they would want. By the time they were done, Shane had an extensive grocery list.

"And one last thing." Stacey wouldn't look up, and her voice got quiet. "I need girlie stuff."

"Not a problem," Shane said. "What do you prefer, or do you want to come shopping with me?"

"Ew, I can't believe you are actually talking about that with her! She is such a freak." Justin interrupted as he came stomping into the kitchen, dragging the vacuum cleaner behind him.

"Shut up, nerd. It doesn't make me a freak, so cut it out," Stacey yelled back.

And there were the kids Shane knew and loved.

"Why? It's not gross. It's what female bodies do," Shane explained.

"But you're a dude, and she's a girl, and"—Justin tossed his hands around—"it's not something I ever want to deal with."

Shane looked at the kid. That was a standard reaction he noticed among the younger boys at the school at Mission Run. And so, he was going to give Justin the same standard response they did at the school.

"You think you're going to have a girlfriend when you're older?" Shane asked.

"Yeah, I'm not gay," Justin responded in an overly defensive tone.

"Chill, J-man, and listen. You plan on living with and dealing with women in your life in your future. Girlfriends, a wife maybe. Kids? You think you might have kids? What if you have girls? This is a part of their biology. The sooner you learn that it's not gross or freakish, the easier your life will be."

"But—"

"But nothing. You plan on sticking your fingers in your ears and singing lalalalala every month for the rest of your life? No, you don't. So you might as well start now." Shane stared at the boy, daring him to contradict him.

Justin looked pained. He sighed and pushed the vacuum cleaner into the pantry. "I still don't wanna know."

"Look." Shane caught the kid around the waist and pulled him to stand in front of his chair. "There are plenty of things you can be grossed out about, like your sister's fashion sense."

"Hey!" Stacey called out.

"Or her taste in music. But there are things you never pick on someone about, and those are the things that they can't control. Would you ever harass me or Stacey about our darker skin color?"

Justin looked terrified at the prospect and shook his head.

"So you don't pick on girls for being girls, and that includes this."

Justin stared at the floor for a minute. He smirked and looked Shane straight in the face. "Ha, you can't even say it."

"What, menstruation? Of course I can. I just figured if I threw that word out there too much, you might pass out from sheer fright. I'm trying to take it easy on you while getting a message across. You don't need me to repeat this while incorporating the words 'menstruation' or 'period' more, do you?"

Justin looked green around the edges.

"J-man, you and me are going to have to have some serious man conversations. I think your dad missed a few lessons with you."

"Oh my God, you are not going to talk to me about my dick? No." Justin ran from the room.

Shane looked up at Stacey. She had stopped loading the dishwasher and watched openmouthed. Her head turned, and Shane followed her gaze.

Lucy stood, bleary-eyed, leaning against the wall where the hall transitioned into the kitchen.

"Thank you. He needed to hear that from an adult male." Her voice was raspy from sleep.

"That was brilliant. The little twerp usually makes fake throwing-up sounds whenever it comes up," Stacey giggled.

Shane huffed. "So what am I adding to the list? What are your preferences?"

Stacey answered in a rush, "Tween pads, rainbow box. Um, yeah. Okay, I'm done here." She left the room in a hurry.

Lucy staggered to the table and sat with a thud. "She really just asked you to pick up product?"

Shane nodded.

"I'm sorry, I've been so out of it. I'm not being mentally here for my kids." Lucy rested her elbows on the table and ground her face into her hands.

"You are doing your best. You were dealt a pretty harsh blow."

Lucy let out a sharp laugh. "Like discovering the man I thought was my husband has been schtupping some chick almost half his age. She's twenty-three, Shane. Twenty-three. She's closer to Stacey's age than his. And I come down here and listen to you calmly explain to my jerk-boy son why he needs to learn to deal with his sister's period. And I realize, Geoff never did that. He usually said something equally jerk-boy about throwing chocolate at her and running. Thank you. Thank you for that. I'm really starting to think my son has not had a man around to actually teach him how to be a man." Lucy's focus drifted off.

"I'm going to have to reevaluate everything, aren't I?" Lucy pulled the shopping list to her. She picked up the pen and crossed a few things off, muttering that they were in the pantry, and she added a few things too.

"Stacey said you have a lawyer."

Lucy sighed. She stood and crossed the kitchen. "Yeah, I do. About that." She pulled a coffee mug from the cupboard, pressed it against the water nozzle on the front of the fridge, and placed it in the microwave. She opened another cupboard, pulled out a tea bag, and added it to the mug. Once she pushed the buttons and the microwave started, she turned to face Shane.

"I had to call Bentoncourt Roberts."

Shane felt his blood pressure rise. His pulse suddenly thrummed loudly in his ears. Roberts. Bile burned the back of his throat, but he knew he kept his expression passive. Maybe even too passive.

"I didn't know who else to turn to. I don't have any money of my own." Lucy looked frantic. "Say something, Shane. Don't just stare at me like that. I know that look, and you are judging me and plotting something."

Shane closed his eyes and released the breath he was inadvertently holding.

"You could have called me."

"No, I couldn't, and you know that. This is my problem, not yours. You don't need my problems destroying your life anymore. I'm surprised you still come around."

Shane stood up. Lucy looked small and lost wrapped in her robe, curled into herself on the kitchen chair, cup of tea steaming in her hands.

"You never hurt me." He walked from the room.

Lucy pushed open the window from Justin's bedroom and crawled out onto the roof. She knew Shane hadn't left the house, and he wasn't blowing things up with Justin on his video game. She figured he had crawled out to this spot. It was isolated and gave a great view of the sky.

She would come sit out here for hours and watch the stars. And when the kids needed a place to hide but still have the safety of home at their backs, they would be here.

Shane's arms were crossed and resting on his knees. She perched next to him.

The moon wasn't quite full tonight. A line of coastal fog hid the ocean and the horizon. City lights twinkled a bit brighter than the stars in the sky.

"You know, when I was a kid, I always thought the moon

was my friend. It always followed me around. Sometimes it would be a smile in the sky, just for me. And I could count on it, It would always come back to a happy full moon every month. Reliable." She glanced at Shane. "Like you. I could always count on you to be my friend when things got hard, and it seemed like no matter how hard it was, there you were. Then I got older and I'm the one who outgrew the moon, and I'm the one who outgrew you. But both of you came around to check on me. And here I am realizing, things are shitty in my life again but I still have my very best friends with me." She nodded at the bright moon above them. "The moon, and you." Lucy sniffed back tears.

Shane moved closer to her. Lucy laid her head against Shane as he wrapped a protective arm around her shoulders.

"Geoff wants me out of the house, or I have to buy his half from him at current market rates. This is the kids' home. This is my home. I don't want to leave it. But there is no way I can pull that kind of money out of my ass right now."

Shane nodded, his expression still stoic and blank.

"If it were just me, I'd cut and run. Take the few things I need to keep working, or not. I could walk away. But it's not just me. Stacey has had a hard time with school. She's so smart, but getting her to focus and absorb has been really difficult. Last year she started passing all her classes by midterm. I can't put her in a different school where we would have to start all over again. Same with Justin. He has friends, and he's not getting bullied."

A low growl rumbled in Shane's chest. Lucy patted his forearm.

"Exactly. I have to take care of those two. And Geoff won't. I didn't really realize how much Geoff wasn't parenting until that conversation just now. That's something that should have been said to Justin at least a year ago or more. And now"—Lucy ground the heel of her palm into her eyes, crushing away the tears—"their father doesn't want anything to do with them, and I walk in on you being a real man for them, and… and… Okay, maybe I should have called you first."

"What did Roberts tell you?"

Her eyebrows tried to pinch together in the middle of her forehead. Her cheeks felt tight as she squinted up at Shane. She rubbed at her facial muscles, getting the tension to ease. "Nothing. I mean, apparently I still have money out there. I didn't even realize that I would. I figured after I ran away that my father would have cut me off completely. Bentoncourt told me he was going to have to see if he could tap into my accounts. I have accounts, Shane. Apparently he made sure they were locked down when I took off. He also told me that we weren't going to fight Geoff's lawyer over the illegal way documents were served. It would actually work to my benefit to let him get away with that. Why? What should he have told me?"

Shane nodded, his gaze still focused out somewhere in the night sky.

"So Bentoncourt Roberts doesn't want you to do anything for him? How much of your trust fund is he expecting in return for helping with the divorce?"

"Shane, I know you don't trust him. But he was on our side back then."

"No, Lucretia, he was on your side. Only you were on my side. Only you." He turned to face her. His dark eyes glowed with an inner intensity.

She hadn't seen his eyes do that for a long time, a very long time. He was angry, and this time it was at her. She flinched back and shifted away, out from under his arm. She thought she saw him jerk out toward her, but he stopped before he hardly moved at all. She blinked to clear her vision. It must be tears and the dark messing with her vision.

"Shane, I..." She stopped. There were never enough words to convey the guilt she still felt over his misuse and abuse. She swallowed. Until he brought up the past, she needed to respect his choice to not speak of it. It was his pain to deal with how he chose. "I called Bentoncourt because he had been a friend when I didn't have any. And he's a lawyer. I figured he would know how to help me. I can't let Geoff destroy the kids the way he is trying to."

"Okay, but the second that man wants you to do anything that brings you back into that life, you tell me, and I will take care of everything."

Lucy huffed. "I'm not going to take the kids and go into hiding. I talked to him. Bentoncourt has been out in the human world for years. He doesn't have ties with the daywalkers anymore. I certainly doubt he knows any vampires."

"I just want you to be careful, that's all."

"I know you do, I know."

"Look, if this is about money, I can give you what you need, and you can tell Bentoncourt to get lost."

Lucy chuckled. "Not for the kind of money we're talking about. If it were only a grand or two, I might be willing, but this is significantly more zeros than that. Significantly. My trust funds have been sitting doing nothing but earning interest for twenty years. There should be a ridiculous amount in each one. Bentoncourt assured me my father didn't clean them out before he died. And after he died, I was the only one who had access."

Shane began to make growling noises.

"Bentoncourt is concerned those accounts are being watched. I can't imagine that anyone is keeping an eagle eye on them anymore. I hope I can gain access without any fuss. I'd rather not touch anything that came from my father, but that money will make all the difference right now."

7

S hane stood in the middle of the living room, his duffel bag at his feet. He rotated his hat through his hands. Leaving this house was always difficult. His heart lived here. But today it was even harder. He needed to check in with Morgan and Cyan, and while truthfully that could be done over the phone, ever since Julia discovered her phone had been tapped, everyone was a little too paranoid to conduct important business in any form other than face-to-face.

He had put off leaving until the kids came home from school. He didn't like the idea of taking off without saying goodbye. There were already too many adults leaving them. He wasn't going to add to that list.

"You have everything you need?" Lucy asked for the tenth time. She sat on the arm of the couch looking at him as he checked his phone for his flight check-in code.

"I'm good. My ride should be here in about twenty minutes. So that's plenty of time once the kids get home." He knew he fidgeted. He would be back at Mission Run late. Morgan would ask for a complete debriefing, and then they would drive into San Francisco tomorrow or the next day, and he would repeat everything for Cyan. And then he would begin looking for an excuse to come back, so he could be here for Lucy, for the kids. And he would stay until Lucy told him to go away.

Shane fished deep into his front pocket. "Hey, I actually did come here with a purpose yesterday."

"You mean you didn't show up just so everyone could cry on you?" Lucy was joking about it; that was a good sign.

"Maybe I knew you needed me, and that's why I really came. But no, I was in Peru, and I picked something up for you." He extended his hand to her and deposited three rectangle emeralds.

"Oh, Shane, these are beautiful. Why were you in Peru?" Her hand flipped up in that universal stop motion. "No, don't tell me. I know you can't."

You wouldn't believe me if I did. No, Lucy would never believe him if he told her it was an excuse to run away from a threat he did not want to face down. She may have seen him at his weakest, but she would never see him scared and vulnerable again. And she really wouldn't believe him if he told her that he'd traveled to Peru to consult a breeder on some alpacas that his boss wanted to get his wife as a present.

She stared at the gems in her hand. "You always bring me the best stones. Thank you." She tilted her head to the side, listening. "Kids are back."

A minute later they came bursting through the front door.

"I thought you said you were staying?" Justin whined.

"I couldn't get things worked out man, but I will be back. Promise."

They said their goodbyes, and Shane got one last hug from Justin, something he knew was rare and wonderful, since the kid would probably hug him less and less as he got older. The sound of a car pulling into the driveway made Justin freeze. Stacey's eyes went wide, and she looked panicked.

"Hey, it's probably my driver, a little early." Shane balanced his trilby on the back of his head.

"No," Stacey whispered. "That's Dad's car."

She grabbed the back of Justin's shirt. "Let's get out of here."

The kids ran upstairs. Shane looked at Lucy. She had gone pale as well.

The doorknob rattled as it was opened.

Shane faced the new person. He crossed his arms and puffed up a bit.

"What are you doing here?" Geoff was barely inside the house before he snarled at Shane.

Shane smirked. Geoff could snarl and bark and even try to bite all he wanted. He may be fit, but he wasn't as tall, as broad, or as genetically strong as Shane.

"He's here because he knew I needed him to be. The real question is, why are you here?" Lucy crossed the small distance between where she sat and where Shane stood.

He placed a protective arm around her. He was caught slightly off guard when she wrapped one arm around his waist and slid the other one up and across his chest. She plastered herself to his side. He was too pissed at Geoff to fully enjoy the feeling of her. He could only focus on the looks of fear on everyone's faces when they heard the car pull up.

"I came to get a few things." Geoff glared at the two of them embracing and blocking his path into the house.

Lucy stepped out of Shane's arms—damn, she belonged there—and advanced on Geoff.

"You picked up all your stuff last weekend."

"Well you forgot to pack"—he sneered the word *pack*, and Shane wondered what had happened—"a few things. I came to get them."

Lucy threw up her hand to stop him from taking a step farther into the house. "No, you will provide me with a list. I will pack the remainder of your items, and let you know when they will be available to pick up."

Shane growled, "You need to leave."

Lucy stepped back to him and ran her hand up his chest. What was she playing at? "It's okay, baby. I can handle him. I did for years. He's easy to manipulate. His new girlfriend must have figured that out by now." Lucy's voice had a false high-pitched quality to it. Almost as if she were speaking through clenched teeth.

Shane grabbed Lucy's caressing hand. He needed to focus and not be distracted. No matter how much he wanted to be distracted.

"You need to leave, Geoffrey. You heard what Lucretia had to say. Send her a list and it will get taken care of."

Geoff glared at him. If he could have shot lasers from his eyes, Shane was certain Geoff would have burned him where he stood. "That's an awfully friendly arm you have on Shane there, Lucy. I thought you told me he was nothing to worry about, that he was basically your little brother."

"Oh, you have no idea just how not basic our relationship is, do you, sweetie? You honestly thought I'd keep a man around who is this fine, and not—" She cut herself off with a cackle.

Lucy turned into Shane, reached up and pulled his head down. She knocked his hat off.

He closed his eyes when her lips plastered against his. He knew he shouldn't have, but Lucy was kissing him. It wasn't the soft, tentative, first-time kiss from a new sweet-heart. It was full-bore passion with aggressive tongues from a longtime lover. Shane growled deep in his throat and pulled Lucy closer into his chest. If she was going to finally kiss him, he was going to kiss her back. He poured years of longing into that embrace, and then his brain turned back on, and he kicked himself hard in his metaphysical balls. Lucy was kissing him to piss off Geoff, not because she suddenly had feelings of this type. He forced his ardor to wane while letting Lucy continue to kiss him. Let her have her show of power.

Her lips stayed on his until he heard cussing and the door slammed closed.

Lucy blinked up at him as she pulled back from the kiss. She looked as confused as he felt. Her eyes were open wide, and her brow crinkled. Maybe it was horror, not confusion he saw on her face. She wiped at her mouth with the back of her hand. And there was his clue. This had been an act.

"Sorry about that. It just popped into my head as the fastest way to piss him off."

Shane pulled back and quirked his eyebrows at her.

Lucy continued. "In the sixteen years we were together, he never fully believed that there hasn't been something going on between us. He doesn't understand there can be bonds of friendship and love without sex, or sexual interest."

Shane picked up his hat and blinked at Lucy. He took her in with his gaze: her sleek black hair, her clear blue eyes that had a slight slant that hinted at mysterious origins, her sharp little chin, and those delicious lips. *I have waited my entire life for you to kiss me like that.* He smiled at her and pulled her in for a substantially less than passionate hug. "I'm here for you, Luce. And I get it. I do." *I don't want it, but I have it.* He balanced his hat back on after she stepped from his hug. Damn, she was glowing again.

Two sharp beeps from a car horn brought him back to the reality that he was leaving. "That's my ride."

～

Lucy sat at her worktable. The stones Shane had given her sat in the middle of a piece of paper with sketches on it. She had two stones and five different designs. She picked the stones up and rolled them around in her hands.

He had stopped by for a typical brief visit to hand her pretty stones, this time emeralds. Only instead of thanks and laughter, this weekend she had handed back a cartload of baggage. And he had taken charge of the cart, and the horse pulling it.

When he left, it felt as if he took away her worry. Not that he was the cause of it, but he had shouldered that burden for her. Even Stacey seemed calmer in the wake of all the turmoil Geoff's leaving had stirred up.

Lucy mindlessly traced her pencil around on the piece of paper, waiting for inspiration to strike. She never planned a piece before getting a stone. The stones had to speak to her.

The sketches she had were flat and boring. She didn't like them; the energy she read off the stones didn't like them. Lucy huffed, as if she could read energy from the pretty sparklies. Sometimes she wondered.

In every handful of gems that Shane gave her, one or two never wanted to be made into jewelry. Whenever she held those particular stones, she felt calm, as if they wanted to be held. As if they were the gift stones Shane had given her, and the other stones were meant to be used in her jewelry.

It was stupid. She shook her head and tried another drawing.

This time it was hard to ignore the sadness in the design. Jewelry design therapy, that's what she was doing. She would design her feelings out and craft them into sterling silver and copper. She placed the emerald squares over the various designs. One mentally stuck.

The one stone seemed to want to be in that sad design. Well, artistic intuition or whatever force it was behind her creations, told Lucy to do that design, and it would sell. The pieces that included the stones from Shane always sold the best. Always. She briefly wondered if people could sense the connection between her and Shane and if that transferred into the jewelry. Or was it that she simply did better work so that he would feel it was worthwhile to keep bringing her stones?

She pulled out her collection of other stones. She held the different colors and let them glow up at her. Shane had supported her "little hobby" from the beginning, while Geoff had scoffed and rolled his eyes. She'd had to prove to Geoff that this would pay for itself, and be a money earner. He'd agreed to invest in the tools she needed, but she needed to pay him back out of her earnings. At the time it seemed logical; of course she would pay for the supplies out of money earned from selling her work. Only now she realized it wasn't particularly supportive of him. As her husband why wasn't he willing to support her endeavors? Shane always supported her.

She had put up with many of Geoff's foibles, but how often had she turned a blind eye?

No, she didn't need to think about this now. She didn't need to think about this at all.

She opened the drawer where she kept loose stones and

tossed her collection back in. She slid open the drawer where she stored the sheets of sterling, and pulled out a few pieces until she had what she needed.

The phone rang. She would finish breaking down the design into traceable templates later. She crossed the room to pick up her phone.

"Lucretia." Bentoncourt's voice rumbled through the phone.

Lucy sat back down.

"Did you find anything out?"

Shane paced back and forth. He didn't like having to wear a suit and a tie. It wasn't him; it made him feel confined. He was aggravated that Morgan kept insisting on it. They were meeting with Cyan at Cyan Group offices again, and it felt like a cheap ploy. He could be just as serious in clothes he was comfortable in as he could be in a suit.

Morgan sat with one leg crossed over the other, reading his phone while they waited. Shane knew the man hated suits just as much, but there he sat in dark pinstripes and a gold tie. He would bet money that Honey now controlled Morgan's wardrobe. His friend's sense of fashion had certainly improved once Honey was in his life. Shane expected that she would have an eye for dressing Morgan better than he dressed himself, especially since she was a retired fashion model.

Shane snaked a finger under the knot of his tie. He worried the silk fabric back and forth. Pausing to watch the street in front of the office his hand took up the lack of movement and continued to slide side to side, something he only realized after the knot slipped out of the tie and was completely undone. Shane continued to free his neck from the confines of today's clothes. He unfastened the top two buttons on his shirt. He rolled the tie up, and shoved it in his pocket when Cyan stepped into the meeting room.

"Mr. Vincent, thank you for coming back to let us know what you found." Cyan extended her hand to him. Her fingers were tipped with claw-like nails painted almost black. "Morgan, a pleasure to see you again."

Morgan stood and exchanged two cheek kisses with the woman.

"Sit please."

Shane sat and began rubbing his thumb over his fingertips. He didn't have a pen to play with. "I need to go back. And I need a reason to be down there for more than a few days, or Lucy will know something is up. I don't think she'll accept that I can just take off work to hang out right now."

"You found something?" Cyan sounded excited, if that's what the lift in her voice indicated.

Shane shook his head. "No, I didn't. But I want to make sure that I didn't."

Morgan sat forward. "Lucretia Asher is apparently in the middle of a divorce. She is in a vulnerable position regarding her funds; access to any accounts has been limited or cut off by her own decisions. Now, it looks like she might need to tap into those funds."

Shane grunted and shifted uncomfortably in his chair. He did not like Morgan talking about Lucy as if she weren't dying inside. He needed to be there for her, and if Cyan Group was interested in funding his stay, then that's how he would play it.

"She's contacted a lawyer who was in her father's employment. I remember the man, and he seemed to be fond of Lucy. She trusts him, at least enough to find out what she needs in order to proceed with her divorce."

"And do you trust him?" Cyan's voice lilted over Shane.

"I never trusted anyone who had anything to do with Lazarus."

"But you trust her," Cyan purred.

"That's different. Lucy was a victim too," Shane snapped. He shoved up out of his chair and returned to his initial pacing.

He paused in front of one of the windows and faced the outside world. Shane closed his eyes and breathed deeply.

Lucy shoved her hand deep into the fur at his neck. She leaned into his side and whispered into his ear, "You need to run, get out of here. I will be all right. He won't hurt me."

She had been wrong. The vampire served her father, and somehow thought that meant because her father hit her, he could as well. Shane had seen the bruises the first two times and had not been present for either beating. He still wanted to kill the man, almost as much as he wanted to kill her father.

The vampire approached Lucy. She shoved Shane away from her. But he wouldn't leave.

Shane stood between Lucy and the man approaching her with intent to harm.

The rest of the memory was hazy at best. There was blood everywhere, and it tasted wrong. It stung the inside of his mouth. He wretched everything from his system.

Lucy hadn't screamed once. But the vampire had.

Lucy was covered in blood, but not her own.

She had a knife and was plunging it into the man over and over again in the places where Shane had torn flesh, and in the heart. Destroying it.

Shane nosed up to Lucy, wanting her to bury her hands into his fur again.

She shoved at him. "Go, you must go. Now is your chance to leave and never come back. Shane, you have to run. I will be fine. They won't do anything to me. I'll tell them I did this. Now go. Go."

He didn't want to leave her. She was the only home he knew, the only caring he had ever received. He needed to be here to protect her from her father's wrath.

"You are the brother I never had, and I did not take care of you properly. Please now let me help you. You need to go. I love you. Go." She pushed on him until he ran away.

He wasn't strong back then, he had mostly limped, but he had escaped.

No, Lucy was the one person, the only person from his past he could trust. "Yes, I trust her."

"Even though she called someone who worked for—"

"She only called him because her ex is putting her in a bad position and is playing dirty. This has nothing to do with her father. Nothing." Shane growled as he cut Cyan off.

Ease up, man. You need her to want you in San Diego. Chill, let it happen.

"Now that Bentoncourt Roberts has entered the playing field, we think it's best that Shane set up temporary residence in the area. He can keep an eye out on both the lawyer and on Lucretia." Good, Morgan agreed and brought the plan forward.

Shane suppressed the urge to smirk.

"What is it exactly that you do, Shane?"

"I stand around and look pretty."

Cyan chuckled at the smart-ass retort. "I don't think we can sell your friend that you are in San Diego on an extended modeling contract. If you don't want her to know you are keeping an eye on her for us, what would your excuse, your cover be?"

"As far as Lucy is concerned, the form of employment I think she bothered to pay attention to of mine was when I was a courier. As far as she knows I still am, I just transport different items."

"Courier, as in smuggler?"

"I won't need a cover. I'll simply allude to my nefarious actions as I typically would, and I'm sure Lucretia will pretend to know nothing about it. She already thinks I'm a gem smuggler."

"Those little baubles you always buy her?" Morgan asked.

Shane nodded.

"I will go and keep an eye out on Roberts and Lucy, but I'm telling you now, nothing is going to come of it. She is not working for her father. She hates Lazarus as much as I do."

8

Lucy pulled into the driveway. Her sister-in-law's familiar red SUV was already parked. Jennifer sat on the stoop waiting.

"Why are you here?" She didn't want to deal with anyone who was currently on the Geoff side of this debacle called her life.

"Hold up, I'm not here on my asshole brother's behalf. I wanted to get a chance to talk to you." Jennifer followed her into the house.

Lucy dropped her purse on the catch-all chair at the bottom of the stairs.

"Want some tea?" Lucy continued through the house into the kitchen.

"Please."

A few minutes later Lucy slid a mug of steaming tea in front of Jennifer and sat across the table from her. Anything her sister-in-law had to say, Lucy was prepared to take with a salt-lick.

"My brother is a stupid asshole," she began.

Lucy's eyebrows shot up, and she snorted with laughter.

Stupid and *asshole* on their own were under statements. The combination of the two words still didn't even begin to touch how horrible Geoff was being about this whole situation.

"Well, we agree on that."

"Not only is he being stupid, he is being hurtful. He gave me a brief overview of what his plans were, and I..." Jennifer shook her head. "I have a relationship with my niece and nephew, and I don't want Geoff to dick that up. If you're okay with it, I want to still be in their lives." Jennifer wiped at her eyes. "I can't tell you how pissed I am at him, at what he is doing to you, at what he is doing to those kids."

Lucy relaxed. Tension that she'd held in her shoulders melted to the floor. It was good to know the kids still had some adults on their side. Their father may be giving them the shaft, but so far no one else was.

"I really appreciate that, Jen. I'm trying to not vilify Geoff too horribly in front of them, but—" Lucy closed her eyes and breathed. "I'm not particularly good at it. It's just... he makes me so angry." She took a sip of her tea. "He blocked their phone numbers, and last week we got notification that he discontinued their contracts. I had to scramble and find a carrier that would work on their phones. That's actually a lot harder than you would think. Not all cell carriers work on phones that have been chipped by someone else. He has effectively cut them out of his life."

"Our parents would be so ashamed of him." Jennifer looked mournfully into her cup.

She looked up. Her eyes locked with Lucy's. Damn. Jen had the same piercing blue eyes as Geoff. Eyes Lucy used to love so much.

"I don't know what's gotten into him, and as much as I would like to think he'll wake up one day and pull his head out of his ass, I don't think that's going to happen. I... God, Lucy, I didn't even think. You aren't expecting to be able to fix this and maybe reconcile, are you?"

Lucy huffed and shook her head. "No. I mean, maybe I might have. I don't know. I don't think so. Not any more."

Lucy stood and wandered into the central part of her kitchen. She opened the refrigerator door.

"Geoff made it pretty clear by making his big announcement with that bitch present that this wasn't open for negotiations. You want chicken for dinner?" She asked the question as she pulled a defrosted whole chicken from the fridge.

Jennifer sighed. "That sounds lovely. How can I help?"

By the time the kids got home from school, Jennifer and Lucy had chopped, sautéed, and assembled everything necessary for chicken cacciatore, which now simmered in a large Dutch oven.

Lucy sliced a long loaf of French bread, and Jennifer creamed together garlic, butter, and some basil.

"What's for dinner? That smells good." Justin stopped in his tracks when he entered the kitchen. Stacey, fast on his heels, crashed into him.

"Is Aunt Je—" She stopped and stared wide-eyed at her aunt.

The kitchen plunged into uncomfortable silence.

"Um, hi, guys." Jennifer finally broke the silence. "Can I get a hug?"

Justin looked panicked, and his gaze shifted back and forth from his aunt to his mother.

Lucy nodded, and he rushed into Jennifer's embrace. Stacey followed, with noticeably less enthusiasm.

"Jen is gonna stay and have dinner with us. We've made a big Italian feast, and we're all gonna talk."

"Talk about what?" The sullen tone in Stacey's voice was thick and unhappy.

"Everything, including your dad."

Stacey crossed her arms and glared at her mother.

"Okay, let's try this: Jen and I will talk; you may join in if you like. But, you will listen."

Stacey was taking the breakup the hardest of the two. At least on the surface she was angry with her father, but Lucy knew those wounds ran deep. Hopefully their aunt willing and wanting to be around would help.

"Fine, I have homework." Stacey turned and walked out of the room.

"How soon is dinner? Can I have a snack?" Justin rummaged through various cupboards.

"Dinner should be ready around six, so not a huge snack."

"Okay," he mumbled around some crackers he had already shoved into his mouth.

Pretty soon he would be eating twice as much and growing like a weed. Lucy expected his growth spurt to hit any day now.

Dinner prep passed in a blur, and soon they were all sitting down for dinner.

"So typically when a couple gets divorced, the whole family tends to break up. I don't want that to happen." Lucy watched as Jennifer began to explain her thoughts.

Justin eagerly shoveled a forkful of sauce-covered noodles into his mouth. Stacey tried hard to look bored.

"I don't have a lot of family left, and my bro— your fa—" She turned to Lucy. "What do I call him?"

"I know a few things we could call him."

Lucy suppressed a laugh. She was not going to chastise Stacey because she was not wrong.

"How about we just call him Geoffrey. It's his name, and in our heads we can add whatever expletives or descriptors we want." Lucy couldn't believe how diplomatic she was being. She had a long string of descriptive cuss words she would prefer to use. But the kids. She let out a heavy breath, not quite a sigh.

"Okay." Jennifer nodded as everyone else made affirming noises. "Geoffrey has decided to remove himself from what family he has left. I don't want him to take that from me. I don't want him to have the power to take you from me."

Lucy felt the stinging prick of tears again.

"So do you still talk to Dad?" Justin asked.

Jennifer nodded. "Sometimes. But not like every day. I don't want to become a go-between, or some kind of courier, but I will tell him about things you want him to know about. He is being really, really dumb. And it's going to bite him on the butt."

"I say let it bite him, like a freaking shark." Stacey stood and placed her dishes in the sink with a loud clatter.

"Honey, I know you are mad at him. But I hope you aren't mad at me." Jennifer turned in her seat to follow Stacey's movements.

"But you still talk to him." Stacey crossed her arms and leaned heavily against the counter.

"He is my brother."

"So you're choosing him over us?" Stacey pursed her lips and tilted her head to the side.

"Jen doesn't have to choose between you. She is allowed to have her brother and you in her life. I'm sure she isn't going to attempt to make you see him, or vice versa. This is about you and her, not you and him," Lucy tried to explain.

Stacey sighed heavily and rolled her eyes. "Fine, but I

don't want to have to *accidentally*"—she made air quotes around the word—"run into him as some kind of setup. He wants to be done with us, then I want to be done with him. Understand?"

Lucy closed her eyes. The pain rolled from Stacey in waves, she was trying to be so tough, but all she really wanted was to not hurt. Lucy stood and approached her daughter, pulling her into an embrace.

Stacey shrugged away from Lucy. Lucy wanted to shatter and cry for her daughter. The pain she felt over Geoff announcing they were over was easier to bear than the sharp-edged pain he was causing their daughter. Her daughter. He wanted nothing to do with any of them.

"Look, Stacey, I'm not going to do some kind of stealth reconciliation against your will. I want us to be able to have our weekends like we used to. I want to see you on more than just Christmas and your birthdays. I want to be able for us to go to LEGOLAND like we had been planning. I don't particularly like my brother right now. I think he is a grade-A jerk."

"Dad can go suck a bag of dicks. Can we still go to LEGOLAND?" Justin asked.

"Justin!" Lucy tried to come up with the words to convey her surprise at the unexpected, yet fully accurate sentiment.

"You aren't going to 'language' me, are you? I mean, come on, Mom. You have been saying a whole lot worse."

"I know, I know." Lucy threw her hands in the air in defeat. Any chance at curbing her children's cussing was long gone the second Geoff announced the divorce.

Jennifer chuckled. "Okay, so cussing is on the table now?"

"I guess we are realizing its usefulness in certain situations." Lucy scratched the back of her head. Yep, it was definitely more and more useful these days.

"Yes, we can still go to LEGOLAND."

Stacey gestured toward Jennifer. "Yeah, but you still talk to him." Her hand flopped back into being crossed over her chest.

"Please don't make me choose between you," Jennifer pleaded.

"Why? Because I'll lose?" Stacey huffed.

"No. I will."

Lucy's days began to regulate into a routine. Mornings were pretty much the same, only she no longer made a pot of coffee. She still talked to the closed door, but now, it wasn't because Geoff had walked out in a rush as she tried to let him know what was going on. She found that it helped her to remember her schedule.

Stacey sorted through the fruit bowl looking for what Lucy could only guess was an apple of a certain shade of green. Justin shoveled cereal into his mouth. At some point that boy was going to have to learn how to eat like a human and not a caveman.

"Hey, I have my appointment today, so you'll be home before I am."

Her announcement was met with grunts.

"You have your key, Stacey?"

She lifted her ID lanyard and jingled the key in response.

"I hear the bus," Lucy announced. She followed the scampering kids out the front door. "Remember, don't kill each other before I get home."

She laughed as she watched them step up and disappear into the darkness of the bus. The new rule of not arguing when an adult wasn't around was actually working. Well, or it wasn't and the kids were cooperating about the collective lie. Lucy expected that it was working simply because, on the days they beat her home, she walked in on a quiet house, only to have the peace shredded when they started screaming at each other the second they realized she was home.

She needed to take a shower and head downtown. She was proud of herself. Her life was falling apart, but she'd remembered to make an appointment for a transfusion in a timely fashion. Even though she couldn't really afford the appointment, she couldn't afford to skip treatments right now; she needed her strength and senses about her.

Lucy focused on the drive home. Traffic seemed worse than normal for this time of day, then again the afternoon commute started earlier and earlier it seemed. The conversation with Bentoncourt had not gone as hoped. Nothing from Geoff for days. She needed him to make another deposit soon or she wasn't going to be able to afford gas. This was ridiculous the way he was holding her financially hostage.

Of course having to wait on the account transfers was equally annoying.

It was her money, but because they had sat dormant except for the interest-earning part, the bank was requiring all sorts of identification checks, and she was pretty certain they were going to request her to put on a show that involved her doing backflips through flaming Hula-Hoops while riding on the back of a perfectly white pony.

She opened the front door. Silence. Today had been full of bad news. At least the kids weren't trying to kill each other. The silence was filled with a thundering of running feet.

"Don't be mad, Mom." The words were out of Justin's mouth before Lucy was all the way inside.

"What happened at school?"

"Nothing, it's not school, I promise."

"No, he's right; it's not school. And I don't want you to get mad either, it's just..." Stacey trailed off.

"It's just what?" Lucy asked. She hung her purse on the back of the chair at the bottom of the stairs. Turning to her kids, she folded her arms and gave them the give-it-up-I-already-know-what-you've-done-but-it's-better-to-confess mom face: eyebrows up, lips pursed.

"Well, since Dad doesn't live here anymore—" Stacey began.

"We thought maybe we should get a dog or something..."

"A dog?" Lucy tilted her head to the side. They hadn't discussed this, and she really wasn't in a good mental place to take care of a dog right now. She huffed.

Justin grabbed her arm and began pulling her toward the kitchen.

"You do not have a dog in the house." It was a statement, not a question. She was not going to agree to this.

"No, no. We left him in the back. He's sweet and would make a great guard," Stacey said.

Justin continued to pull Lucy through the kitchen and onto the back patio.

"I'll walk him every day, and we'll clean up after him, and—"

"Okay." Lucy cut him off. "Where is this dog?" she asked, expecting to see a medium to small fur ball barreling at them any second.

Stacey pointed.

Sweet he was not. Small he was not. Guard dog, he was perfect. Skulking around the edges of her yard, between the redbuds and the wood fence, an insanely large, dark gray wolf lurked.

Lucy crouched down to be closer to his level. "Hi there," she said, a smile in her voice.

The creature loped toward her.

Stacey screamed as the wolf reared up, placing its paws on Lucy's shoulders and knocking her back.

"Holy crap, I thought he was attacking or something." Stacey breathed out in relief.

"It's all right. It's definitely or something." Lucy laughed between licks to her face. Her fingers sank into the thick fur at his neck. She pushed him back. "Get off me, you brute. What are you doing here?" she asked as she sat up.

In response the wolf rolled onto his back, exposing his belly.

Stacey and Justin knelt down and began petting him.

"See, Mom, he's really a good dog. Can we keep him?"

"Can we?"

The kids pleaded.

Of course they could keep him; they already had. The question was, would he keep them?

Lucy looked into the familiar dark eyes. "What are you doing going all submissive in front of me, huh?"

"What should we call him?" Stacey eagerly asked.

"Let's call him Wolfy."

Stacey smacked her brother on the back of his head. "Don't be lame. Wolfy. Ew, no. He needs something big, something epic."

Lucy smiled to herself. Shane. That was epic.

"Desmond." Justin suggested another name.

"Dude, no. We are not going to name him after your lame video game."

"It's not lame." Justin sniffed.

"Cut it, you two. Yes, we can keep him, as long as he stays. But you are going to have a hard time keeping a beast like this fenced in back here."

"Get real, Mom. It's not like he can jump out." Stacey used her I'm-smarter-than-you voice.

Lucy just smiled. That child knew so little.

"Can he sleep in my room?"

"No, he's going to sleep in my room."

"He's not sleeping in anybody's room; he can have the couch." Lucy gave the beast a direct stare, making sure he heard her.

"Ow, I wonder what caused this. Poor guy." Lucy looked at the scar on the dog's leg that Justin trailed a finger over.

"Don't do that, honey." Lucy snatched his hand away from the dog's inner leg. "He probably doesn't like that." She couldn't take her eye from the scar. The wound that caused it had been deep and ragged and had scared her.

There had been so much blood.

9

He was covered in blood. She couldn't tell who was more scared, Shane or herself. He crashed into her room, his eyes wide with fear and something else—at the time she did not know it was the sedation drug still in his system—and he was bleeding.

Shane didn't cry, at least not anymore, but he was gasping and panting and whimpering. A combination that pulled Lucy fully awake.

"Did you come to curl up with me?" She was confused. Typically when Shane wanted to 'play puppy,' as they called it, he would climb into bed as soon as he sneaked into her room.

But not tonight. Shane held on to the door as if it were holding him up. His noises were barely audible and full of distress.

"Shane?" Lucy threw back her covers and crossed the room to him. That's when she saw the blood; that's when she realized he was naked underneath the long T-shirt he wore.

He was bleeding from his boy parts.

"Oh no, oh no, oh no." Lucy panicked. "How do I make it stop?"

Lucy scanned the room around her as if her bedroom held answers. Her gaze landed on the television. What did they do on TV?

"We have to apply pressure." She ran to her dresser and pulled out whatever was on top. She returned to Shane's side and dropped the clothing on the floor. She helped him to sit on her bed. In the back of her head she knew she would get in trouble for the blood, but right now she had to help Shane.

She picked up a handful of the clothing and shoved it into his hand. "You have to apply pressure." She pushed his hand toward his groin. She was being brave, but she wasn't brave enough to touch down there, and she was pretty sure he was bleeding from his balls as well as his leg. She pressed a T-shirt into his upper thigh.

It looked bad. "What happened?"

Shane whined. It was the closest to crying she had heard from him in years. "I woke up. Table. I shifted. I wasn't me; I was the wolf. They were operating on the wolf." He moaned in pain.

Lucy pulled the T-shirt back and peered at the wound. The bleeding had stopped. There was a cut from his sac into his thigh. It looked deep. It was long. She wanted to throw up. She held her mouth together and breathed through her nose until the feeling passed.

"I think you're going to need stitches." But there was no one at the compound who would help Shane. Not the boy they kicked and treated like a dog, so much so he started turning into one. Well, that was the explanation her nanny had given her.

Her nanny thought she was stupid. As if Lucy didn't know she had useless fangs because she was a broken vampire, a daywalker. And Shane was clearly a werewolf. What she didn't know was why hadn't he been able to turn earlier? He had only started shifting this year. And he could shift whenever he wanted. Now when they played puppy, he could turn into a real puppy.

Lucy sneaked out of her room and creeped down the hall to where her nanny slept. It was a hard house to be sneaky in, someone was up all hours. Her father never slept at night, only during the day. He was a real vampire, something Lucy would never get to be.

Nanny kept a sewing kit in a tin that used to have cookies in it. When Lucy asked her why, she had answered that that's just how her mother had kept her sewing kit. The woman snored loudly. Lucy could hear it in the sitting room. Nanny had two rooms, while Lucy only had her bedroom. It didn't seem fair; then again a whole lot about her life wasn't fair. She would be blamed for all the blood in her room, but it was someone else who had cut Shane. And that person wouldn't get into trouble. No, she would, and then Shane would. Shane always got in trouble for her.

She spotted the cookie tin, grabbed it, and ran back to her bedroom.

She chewed a hole in her lip from biting it so hard as she stitched Shane's thigh back together. He had tried to be brave, but it had hurt, and he had made noises. She squinted and pretended she wasn't touching his boy stuff, but she put a stitch in there too.

God, they had been so young. Too young to know what Shane was capable of, too young and no guidance. Neither of them had known then that if he had shifted, he would have sped up the healing. He had hurt too much to change. Lucy had managed to hide him in her room for almost a week. By then the damage had been done, and the scar would be permanent.

"Look, it goes right up into his ball sac." Justin's voice felt overly loud as his twelve-year-old Captain Obvious skills kicked in.

Lucy's gut clenched. Yes, it went all the way up into his privates. She had been uncomfortable looking at them when she was twelve; she shouldn't be looking at them now.

The wolf quickly flipped around and stood.

"It's not nice to point those kinds of things out, honey," Lucy said calmly.

"But Mom, look." Justin gestured at the animal's male anatomy. "I mean, he's freaking huge."

"Stop looking at the dog's junk, you weirdo," Stacey teased her brother.

The wolf barked. It was deep and menacing, a roar of a sound. Everyone froze and listened. A car had pulled into the driveway. The engine cut off. They heard the thud of doors closing and indistinct voices.

"Dad's here." Justin's entire being sank, his posture folded, and his voice sounded shaky.

Lucy went to pull him into a hug, but the wolf lunged between them and sailed over the back gate. Justin bolted after him. "Holy crap, did you see that?" He opened the gate and ran after the dog.

Stacey stood. "I'm gonna try to catch him too. I really don't want to see Dad either."

Lucy nodded. "I understand. Don't be disappointed if you can't find the dog. I'm sure he'll come back here when he's ready. Hey, Stace, I think you should call him Fang or Magnum."

Stacey paused and looked at her mother. "Oh, how about Remus or Sirius?"

Lucy chuckled. Shane now being associated with the Palatine family, he would not appreciate a connection to Remus. Not when his adopted family was a direct line of descent from Romulus, founder of Rome. Even though that's not the Remus Stacey was referring to.

"Definitely not Remus, and not Sirius. He's not black, he's gray. Go on. I'll deal with your father."

Lucy stood as she watched her daughter tear after Justin

and the wolf, usually known as Shane. Lucy slid the glass door closed behind her. And followed the shrill sound of Chrissie's voice into her living room.

"We're gonna need new furniture; you can let her keep this old junk. I don't—"

"Get the fuck out of my house." No greeting. Lucy came straight to the point.

"This isn't your house, Lucy." Geoff started to posture and puff out his now seemingly meager chest. She'd been hanging out with Shane too much lately. Everyone was small compared to him.

"Bullshit it isn't. You left us; the property is in my possession. Get out of my house." Lucy stood still. It took all her control not to shake. Damn Shane. Fine time to run away. She could use his strength right about now. Like he had so many times in the past, he would press against her legs while she gripped his scruff and found strength and comfort from his warmth. A low, menacing growl wouldn't go unappreciated either.

The front door burst open, and framed in the afternoon glare stood Shane in all his muscular human glory. The mirrored sunglasses were a beautiful menacing touch. For a split second she wondered where he had hid his clothes to have gotten dressed so fast.

Lucy did not miss Chrissie's inhale of fear, nor how she shifted behind Geoff.

"Gee-off." Shane mispronounced the name in a way he knew that irritated the other man. Lucy smiled. Good guard dog. He took three long strides straight up to Lucy and twirled her into his arms, pinning her tight against him.

She knew exactly what he was doing, and she loved it. Showing off, oozing sexual prowess, flexing his muscles, and pushing every last one of Geoffrey's buttons, from the mispronunciation of his name to continuing the ploy that there was something between her and Shane.

She ignored the slight butterfly flip that pulled at her core as a release of fear, as the rush she sometimes got from a fresh infusion, and nothing more.

"Hey, baby," Shane purred in a deep rumble. He nuzzled Lucy's ear. "Do I have to play nice?" he whispered.

"Not at all." She laughed. She could feel the heat of Geoff's rising blood pressure from where she stood. The combination of fear and attraction rolled off Chrissie in such thick waves even Lucy could smell it. The smell was tangy and full of rich blood. Shit. She pushed out of Shane's grasp as senses she tried not to engage took over. Chrissie had the very distinct smell of...

"She's fucking pregnant?" The screech tore from Lucy's throat as she lunged for Geoff.

Shane caught her around the middle and held her tight. "Lucretia." He said her name in a calming tone. He had to repeat it a few times before Lucy heard and stopped thrashing in his arms.

"How does she know, Geoffrey? We haven't told anybody yet." Chrissie's voice was small, scared.

"She doesn't know. She was just guessing. But you basically just told her." Geoff snapped at his girlfriend. He held his hands out as if to calm Lucy down. "Look, Lucy, we just came to check out a few things. I wanted Chrissie to see that the place is plenty big. She wants to start picking out colors so she can—"

"She can't do anything. This is my house." Lucy seethed and spit the words from between her teeth. She struggled against Shane's viselike arm around her like some super-human belt-of-steel muscle.

Shane chuckled. "She can leave, and she can take you with her. This is Lucretia's house."

"You can't stop me in this, Shane." Had Geoff lowered his voice to sound more menacing? Middle management was no match for six feet of solid alpha brute muscle.

"You gonna try me?"

"Come on, Geoff, let's get out of here. We can come back some other time."

Lucy glared daggers as the couple finally began to leave.

Before she could say anything, Shane cut in, "That wouldn't be a good idea. I heard they got a nice big guard dog who will rip out your throat at the drop of a hat. And I'm changing the locks tonight. You won't be getting a key."

Geoff started toward Shane, it was a brief twitch of movement in the wrong direction before he caught himself and guided Chrissie out the front door.

Lucy relaxed, her muscles melting into lumps.

Shane released her.

"Thank you. Your timing…" Lucy sighed, unable to put her feelings of relief at not having to face Geoff and Chrissie alone into words.

Shane reached out and lifted her hand in his. "I will always be here when you need me. I promised you that a long time ago. It still holds true."

Lucy sniffed and threw herself into his arms for a comforting hug. "You always have my back, don't you? Looks like I'm gonna need you to be my rock for a bit."

"Shane!" Justin tackle hugged Shane and his mother. "When did you get here?"

Shane reached out and ruffled the boy's hair. "How've you been, man?"

"Eh," Lucy heard the false bravado in her son's voice. "I was kinda watching for Dad's car to pull out. I didn't see you though. You must have showed up while I was off chasing the dog. Oh, Mom, did you tell him about the dog? She said we could keep him." Justin's excitement took over, and his words rushed out.

Shane stepped back from the group hug and smirked. "A dog, huh? What are you gonna call him?"

"Dogstar," Justin announced triumphantly.

Shane cringed.

10

———

"Where are you now?" Morgan asked.

Shane wiggled the earpiece to hear better.

"I'm sitting in a park watching the waves, why?"

"I thought you were down there to keep an eye on Lucy, not to take a seaside vacation."

"I am keeping an eye on her. I don't have to stalk her. I'm already at her house more than I am not."

"So she knows you're there? What did you tell her?" Morgan's gruff voice gave away some angst that he typically didn't demonstrate.

"Dude, what is going on? Are the bloodsuckers breathing down your neck or something? Why are you so tense about this?" Shane let his gaze follow the actions of a young woman in professional work clothes as she biked past him. A smile twitched at the corner of his mouth. She came back.

He gave the woman about a quarter of his attention while he focused on his conversation with Morgan.

Morgan growled. "I'm your alpha, and—"

"And you are being a complete asshole. You sent me here

to do a job, and now you are micromanaging every action I take. We basically had this conversation yesterday. Not a whole lot has changed. Or do you need me to start providing information on my bowel movements? What gives?"

The young woman put the kickstand to her bike down and bounced—she didn't walk—up to a food cart vendor. The vendor stepped out from behind his cart and pulled her into an embrace, spinning her in a circle. After he set her down, she scratched the ears of a golden retriever.

Morgan was not forthcoming with an answer.

"What did you tell Lucy, Shane?"

"I told her I had an opportunity in the area, and I wanted to be around for her and the kids in case this divorce got any uglier. She seems to think that her son could use the influence of a real man these days, and his father isn't stepping up to the job."

"So that's it? You're going to step in and what? Mentor the kid?" Morgan's tone changed yet again as soon as kids were brought into the conversation.

"I am going to be a positive male presence in his life. Now are you going to tell me what the hell is going on with you?" Shane demanded.

Morgan sighed. "It's Honey." Then silence.

"Is she okay?"

Nothing.

"Morgan, is she okay?"

"Shane, dude, she is really tetchy and cross, and it's seriously wearing on me."

Shane snorted. "I thought she was all 'I'm ovulating perform for me now,' and now you're telling me she's moody?"

"Moody as fuck."

Shane roared with laughter.

A few pedestrians turned to face him. The young couple he was watching didn't notice. They were too far away.

"Your wife is pregnant, man. Congratulations."

Morgan was silent on the other end of the line.

"Are you still there?" Shane stood up as the young woman got back on her bike. He was walking south on the path that would circle back toward the street when she pedaled past.

"Morgan?"

"No, no, I don't think that's it. She hasn't had a positive test yet. Honestly, I think that's what's setting her off. Not being pregnant yet. I had no idea that women could be this driven when it came to getting knocked up."

"You're too used to making sure that's not what happens. Look, Honey has been in foul moods before, and it hasn't rubbed off onto you. I think this is some kind of hormonal connection between mates, and you are experiencing her mood swings or something."

"Or something," Morgan muttered. "Are you walking?"

"More like a light jog. Look, do you want a full report or a blow-by-blow of my afternoon?" Shane continued following the lady on the bike, quickening his pace.

"Fill me in on what you currently have."

"Currently I have a whole lot of nothing. The ex is being a serious asshole, and he's got Lucy over a financial barrel. She's broke. I had to buy groceries for them again last night. You already know her lawyer is a daywalker. She's supposed to meet with him this week, but she isn't giving me her day-by-day schedule, so I'm keeping tabs on his office. His secretary type person seems to be having an affair with a local hot dog vendor."

"How is that helpful?"

"It's not, but I've been tracking her today to get in some practice. And on the off chance that I might actually learn something." Shane continued to jog past a single-story bungalow where his tracking subject was now walking the bike in the front door. The sign in the front yard indicated this house was Bentoncourt Roberts's law offices. Shane kept running.

He slowed his pace half a block away.

"I'm looking for patterns, habits, weaknesses. Any indication that this guy is in bed with anyone suspect, any bloodsuckers, or..." Shane swallowed, the name brought bile to the back of his throat. "Lazarus."

"What have you learned?"

"Not much, but the only people coming to his office are normal people. Not us, not daywalkers. I haven't begun trailing him at night, mostly because the few times I've tried, he doesn't do anything. On the surface he is a boring upper-middle-aged man, who has small dogs and watches TV at night."

"See if you can go to one of the meetings with Lucy. Hold her hand, be supportive," Morgan suggested. "Get into his office. Maybe you can sniff something out that way."

Shane was shaking his head even though Morgan couldn't see it. "He knows me. That's not a good idea. If he is working for Lazarus, seeing me there would... No, that would put me on their radar, and that's something I have avoided for over twenty years. Let's just not go there." Shane ran his hands over his face. This job required delicate balance, and right now he was feeling neither delicate nor particularly stable enough to be balanced. Lucy was hurting, and all that mattered was figuring out a way to make that stop as soon as possible.

"Look, go pay attention to your wife. I will let you know as soon as anything of interest happens down here."

Morgan made noises agreeing and ended the call. Shane picked up his pace and began running again, this time to clear his head. He hated that he couldn't just be here for Lucy, that it was expected of him to keep tabs on her and her activities. He didn't like it at all.

Lucy sat with one leg crossed over the other. She had dressed up today, wearing her best business attire, which meant she was in the same houndstooth-checked skirt and black blouse she wore to the offices of French and French and Associates. However, this office was nothing like that steel and glass fortress of money and power downtown.

Bentoncourt's office occupied a small, humble, stucco house tucked into the upper-scale neighborhood of La Jolla. It was a far cry from what she had expected of him. In her youth, he had always worked from the compound, so she hadn't really formed an opinion of what his offices probably looked like now. It wasn't until they met at Geoff's lawyer's office that she had assumed he practiced in a similar setting.

She didn't know what to expect now. Lucy closed her eyes and shook her head. She had to get rid of preconceived notions. The temperature was more regulated here by the presence of the ocean. Even in her own neighborhood the temperatures would soar, while the coastal areas stayed relatively moderate and comfortable.

Also, there was something entertaining about visiting a lawyer across the street from a surf shop. Maybe she would stop in after this meeting and find out about lessons for

Justin. Geoff would never commit to them, and they lived too far for Justin to find his own way down to the beach. They still lived pretty far, but he was older now and she needed to be able to trust him to get around.

Her thoughts snapped back to the task at hand when Bentoncourt stepped into his office.

He wasn't in the corporate-approved suit she had last seen him in. He wore relaxed slacks and a Hawaiian shirt. He looked like Santa on vacation.

He let out a loud sigh as he sat and sorted through a file of papers.

"Okay, Lucretia, this is what we have." He slid a printout of a spreadsheet across to her.

Rows and columns of numbers. Big numbers.

She gulped.

Bentoncourt circled the first three columns. "I knew about these accounts. There were in place when you were nineteen. This one was where all your college money was coming from." His pen, functioning as a pointer, indicated the first column. He moved to the next two columns. "These two accounts you weren't allowed access to until you turned twenty-one."

Lucy felt her eyes widen. That was a lot of zeros. She could not only buy Geoff out of his half of the house, she could pay it off completely. And buy a new car. And a beach house. And...

Bentoncourt's pointer continued across the tops of the columns. "These two are direct inheritance. And this last one"—he looked up, making eye contact—"has had money withdrawn from it recently. I have concerns."

Her forehead tightened as her eyebrows tried to meet in the middle. "Concerns?"

The older man leaned back in his chair and nodded his head. "No one should have access to that money. Technically the owner is your late father, or you as his only descendant."

He shifted uncomfortably in his chair. "Lucretia, I can get you into your trust funds immediately. You are alive, I have signature cards and can provide fingerprints and DNA evidence—yes, I locked those accounts up tight when you left, for when you decided you needed them again. I cannot easily get into these other accounts. I have started the process, but your father did not die cleanly or with much evidence. We have no hard-and-fast paper trail, no magic passwords, and no key to be able to waltz in and claim the money as yours. We do have processes that we can go through that document and prove you are his heir, and thus access those funds for you. As I said, two of the accounts have you listed as the inheritor."

Lucy shrugged. She didn't see that as any big deal, especially compared to the totals in her personal accounts. That was more money than she could have ever guessed, ever realized she had walked—no, run—run away from. "So why the concern then?"

"Lucretia, there are only two people who should even be able to gain access to that money. You are one of them." This time he emphasized his words carefully. Only two people.

Lucy felt like the chair she sat on disappeared and the bottom fell out of her world. Her vision went splotchy with absent gray areas. She couldn't breathe. The sound of the traffic outside was suddenly cutting through her skull. And sharp shrill screams somewhere in the distance made the other noise feel dull and throbbing.

A cool cloth rested on her head, and someone patted the back of her hand.

Lucy pushed the washcloth from her and opened her eyes. Light, soft muted colors. Bentoncourt's worried face. She blinked a few times and pushed into a sitting position.

"Go slow; you had quite the shock."

The leather of the couch squeaked beneath her. Her head lurched, and she decided being horizontal was better at the moment. She lay on her side and tucked her feet against the back cushion.

"Do you mind telling me what happened?" She peered up at Bentoncourt.

His expression slowly shifted from worry to relief.

"Simply put, you passed out."

Her head throbbed. "I remember there was a god-awful noise, like a train hitting the building."

"That was you screaming and falling out of the chair." Bentoncourt's perky blonde assistant handed Lucy a bottle of cold water.

"Thank you, Celine." Bentoncourt gave the young woman serious side-eye.

Lucy realized she knew nothing about this man. She had called him in a panic because he had tried to help her when she was younger, and when she ran away, thinking he might be in a position to help her again. But what did she know of the Bentoncourt of today? "I'm sorry, she…"

Lucy waved him off and then pinched the bridge of her nose. "Why did I pass out? What were you telling me?"

"You passed out because you are a smart woman. And you put two and two together rather quickly."

"So you did insinuate that the only other person who should technically be able to touch that money was Daddy?" Lucy made a disgusted, almost groan noise as she pushed into a sitting position.

She rolled the cold water bottle up the side of her neck.

"If I touch my money, will he be able to find me?" Her tone was as cool and as even as she could keep it. She didn't want that man to know where she was. She didn't want him to know about her life, her children, anything.

"With your permission, I can start moving your accounts around. Into shell corporations, through the Caymans, and basically create a smoke cloud that can't be traced."

"So, you're saying I can't take my money right now, aren't you?" She buried her face into her hands.

A large, but gentle touch landed on her shoulder.

"It probably doesn't mean anything. Someone probably found a dormant account of a dead man and found a back door into it. Hell, it could have been any number of his followers, or even Yves Marat's followers. It doesn't mean your father is mysteriously back from the dead."

"Did you see his body? No, from what I understand nobody did, just that poof, he was dead in a bloodbath, nothing left. He was the kind of bastard to find a way back from the grave." She flashed an angry glare at Bentoncourt. "It could be you for all I know. So why isn't it?" Her accusation was loud and angry.

Bentoncourt gave a quiet chuckle, and his chest bounced with the action. "I left shortly after you did. You helped me to see that I didn't need a master simply because I was born into a situation of servitude. I had my own money. I had an education. I did not need to waste any of it on playing survival games. There was a time under your father's command that I would have never thought anything like that. I am a daywalker, I was created to serve, as were you. We were all brainwashed." He glanced at the door to the small sitting room, got up, and closed the door. Keeping Celine out.

"Your father became more and more paranoid. Things were not going as planned. You were not as planned. He distanced himself from his advisors, let Yves Marat into his inner circle. Suddenly he became more violent. More wolves died in his experiments. I'm pretty sure he had even begun experimenting on blood slaves, because they never lasted very long. Marat fed his illusions.

"He would either rail with anger that you were not around and demand that you be found, or he would assume you were away at school.

"I still don't know how you managed that. For him to allow you out of his sight to go away to college." He shook his head. "By the time you had disappeared, a few of us appeased him by reminding him you were away at school. He had become a senile old man. Most of us understood that the vampire condition is not one of immortality but extreme longevity. We figured he was at the end of his life span. I never knew how old he was."

He looked off to the side. Lucy focused on his face, and realized he had been as much of a pawn as she had been. Son of a blood slave, no choice in his life. Probably sent to law school because he showed an aptitude above and beyond being a strong arm and a dull brain, like most of her father's bodyguards had been.

He ran his hand over his face. "Let's see... I passed you some money, and that was the last I heard from you. I knew you were no longer attending classes. And your father's spies had not been able to set eyes on you for several weeks at that point. I knew you had made it. Marat and your father were at each other's throats more and more.

"I packed my documents, and I slipped out one day and never looked back. Marat staged a coup shortly thereafter. I made sure to distance myself further from the community. I think it's a fortuitous coincidence that we both ended up in the same city. A city that happens to not have an active coven."

Lucy blew air out through her nose on a huff. "LA isn't that far away if either of us needs access to a coven. But, no thank you. They may have helped me out as I transitioned from one life to another. But"—she shook her head and grinned sardonically—"they were still embroiled in all the drama and politics of that world. They still perpetuated dominant species doctrine and spewed hatred for others. No thank you, I don't need a coven."

"Precisely my thinking. Besides, I have discovered that while I do need more sun protection than the average person, I enjoy the beach and the sunlight. I have no desire to live the night life or to work for those that do."

"But you kept your name," Lucy pointed out.

"And you yours," he countered. "By the time I was far and away, the bloodbath at the Vegas compound settled, I figured there was no one left who would think twice about me. I figured no one really knew me, no one would be interested I was gone, and I needed to be able to continue with my profession. I already passed the bar in California, and I didn't feel like doing it again. I was a very low man on the totem pole there."

"But you were in charge of me." How could he be lowly? He had been one of her keepers.

"I was your babysitter. Think about that. My job was to keep you essentially out of trouble and financed to do usually whatever you wanted. But close by enough that when your father demanded an appearance, you were available."

"But you were a lawyer." Lucy knew she whined. How could her father have put a lawyer as her keeper, and have that be considered a babysitter?

"Yes, in case you got into trouble. I was able to legally act on your behalf, or your father's behalf for you while you were a minor."

Lucy let out a sardonic laugh. "My perspective is all skewed, isn't it? I wasn't the all-important child, was I?" She looked up at Bentoncourt. His expression told her what she thought. "No, I was just some spoiled brat. With a nanny and a lawyer looking out for me because Daddy couldn't give me more than a few backhanded slaps and money. Was it as bad as I thought?"

Bentoncourt shook his head. "It was worse, so much worse."

She looked at him, confusion tensing her brow.

"How many people do you know who actually grew up with a whipping boy? How many?"

Lucy shrugged. "They had them in ancient Rome all the time, and probably right up through the end of slavery."

"Lucretia, you had a whipping boy in the twentieth century. It's probably more common than we realize, but honestly. How many people do you know, or even know of? Hmm?"

"I didn't..." she began to protest, and then reality slapped her hard. She did; she knew she had. She knew his beatings were almost always a direct result of her actions. She knew, she just had never really put a definition on it. Why didn't he hate her? Slowly, she nodded. "Shane."

Bentoncourt's eyebrows were raised toward his hairline. "Exactly." He reached over and handed her a small square of a handkerchief.

In all the shock of the afternoon, it didn't surprise her that tears were leaking out of her eyes without her noticing she had begun crying. She dabbed at her cheeks and blew her nose.

"So what do we do now?"

"We move your money so that whomever has accessed that account does not try an attempt at your accounts."

Lucy nodded in agreement.

"We continue with the process to access your inheritance, prove who you are, and that the money is legally yours."

"Okay, once the money has been all shuffled around, what happens? Do I get a big suitcase of non-sequential bills? What?"

"Once the money has been transferred out of the reach of the original account holders and shuffled a bit so they can't trace the funds, you will have a nice new secured account, or three, or four. And you shouldn't have to worry about anything financial again."

"And the rest of the accounts?" She felt numb. This was on the verge of being too much.

"We'll do the same thing."

A light knock sounded on the closed door.

"Come in," Bentoncourt called out.

Celine cracked the door open. "Your next meeting is here. I put them in your office and have a pot of coffee started. I just wanted to let you know. Anything else you want me to do?"

Bentoncourt shook his head.

"Oh, could you grab my purse and bag from his office?" Lucy asked.

"Already taken care of. I have your things up front for when you're ready," Celine answered.

"Thanks."

The door closed.

Lucy leaned back into the couch with a sigh. "How soon before I can access my money so I can buy Geoff out and stop relying on him?"

"Two weeks, three? It's been a while since I've done anything along these lines. I no longer have the nefarious connections I used to, and I kind of don't want to either. So... I will keep you posted, and I will show you how and when your money is being moved. You know I'm not doing this to defraud you. I'm doing this so that there is no trail."

Lucy nodded; she understood. She didn't want there to be a trail to her either.

She stood with the help of a hand from the lawyer.

"You know, only two people call me Lucretia anymore. You and"—she paused—"Shane."

"You still see him?"

She nodded.

"He always was in love with you. Never blamed you once for anything. That's good then. And for the record, only you and the bar association call me Bentoncourt; it's Ben."

Lucy hugged Ben and then stepped into the sunshine outside his front door. She would have sworn the weather turned dark and gloomy like the oppressive cloud that hung over her. Still no money to call her own. She was stuck relying on the no-good, whoremonger of a not-soon-enough ex-husband, daddy issues that any psychotherapist could base a career on raised their ugly head, and Shane. What exactly had Bentoncourt mean, that he had always been in love with her? They had been each other's only friends for the longest time. At one time her best friend, and then he was her brother to protect. And then he had been gone.

But he always came back to her. Always.

Shane could have run away so many times, but he didn't. And when he finally did, he would come back to her time and time again. She groaned. Her chest felt weirdly hollow and tight at the same time. She placed her hand on her chest and forced a deep breath. Shane.

11

Lucy tossed her purse with her keys on the chair like always. She stopped and looked at the empty living room. She was fighting tooth and nail for this house. Why? It didn't have a foyer, it didn't have a pool, and it didn't have a wet bar upstairs. No, it had memories, and it was where her kids were growing up, and while it wasn't the biggest or the fanciest, it was hers.

She passed her jeweler's bench and walked into the kitchen. Stacey's butt stuck out from the open refrigerator door.

"Hi, chica," Lucy said.

"Oh, hi, Mom. Just grabbing a snack. I'm gonna head over to Abby's house if that's okay."

"Sure. Where's your brother?"

"He and Shane are upstairs playing video games. Is it okay that he comes over here all the time?"

"Why wouldn't it be?" Lucy asked. "He's my oldest friend. He's part of this family."

"I dunno. Something someone said at school got me thinking."

"Got you thinking what?" Lucy crossed her arms. "Has he done or said anything, ever, for you to doubt him?"

"No, but..."

Lucy leveled a mom quality stare at her daughter.

"Some kids said something dumb about how you're getting a divorce and now some guy is always hanging around our house, even when you're not home. And he practically lives here. And..."

"And what did you say?"

"I told them to shut up and stop being stupid." Stacey shrugged.

"So what should I say to you?"

"Shut up and stop being stupid?" Stacey scrunched up her face and nodded.

"Look, honey, Shane has always, and I do mean always, just shown up whenever he feels like it. He moves in for a day or a week, and then he's gone."

"Yeah, but he's still here this time," Stacey pointed out.

"Why do you think that is?"

Stacey shook her head, no answer.

Lucy sighed. Bentoncourt's words flitted through her brain. *He always was in love with you.*

"He's here because he thinks we need him."

"What do you think?" Stacey clearly needed to hear it from her mom before she could safely make her own decision.

Lucy let out a small laugh. What did she think? She thought she needed Shane, but now she wondered why. For a big, strong shoulder to cry on? For the feel of his thick fur fisted in her fingers to give her strength? So she could kiss him again to piss off the man she had once thought she was in love with?

Lucy leaned back heavily on the counter. How quickly

had she gone from love to hate? She no longer cared about why Geoff had done what he had. She no longer cared that he had an affair. She did care that he was being a selfish asshole and making everything about her life miserable. She did care that he had their daughter second-guessing everything she knew about those in her life.

"Shane is here because your father isn't. He's here because he loves us and wants to take care of us and make sure we are happy. Is that good enough? Next time your friend at school says something stupid, don't worry about it. You know what they are saying is stupid."

Stacey crossed to her mother and kissed her on the cheek. "I won't be home for dinner."

"You and Abby going to moon over that guitarist all evening?" She teased her daughter.

"No." Stacey rolled her eyes. They probably were. After all she had just put up a new poster of him in her bedroom. Lucy wouldn't admit it out loud, but her daughter had good taste. He was attractive with shiny long hair and full lips. But she could admit to liking his music whenever Stacey played it in the car. "We have this big history report and will be doing a lot of research. Abby's mom said she'd take us to the big library downtown if that's cool with you."

Lucy nodded. That was why she was fighting for this house—no, this home. Because Stacey had posters on her bedroom wall, and she had friends down the street.

Stacey grabbed her backpack and left out the sliding glass door, and out the back gate.

The air around Lucy felt odd this afternoon. Her world was in disarray, that was all. The words out of Bentoncourt's mouth still shook her. Someone was accessing her father's accounts, and Shane loved her. She climbed the back stairs, passing through the bonus room over the garage. She glanced at Shane and her son playing a video game. She thought about stopping and watching, but she wanted a chance to think, to take a shower and change.

"Hi, boys," Lucy said as she walked past.

"Hey, Mom." Justin didn't look up.

With a chuckle Shane said, "Hi, Mom," also.

She climbed the rest of the stairs to the second floor and continued into her bedroom. The shower didn't ease her thoughts or quiet her mind. She could hide from that first bit of news, could ignore it. She could tap into her own accounts and call it good. Honestly, she had no need to access the rest of her inheritance. If she were smart and made sure the balance of those accounts was properly invested, she could get away with never working again. She may have grown up surrounded by lots of money, but as an adult she had lived without any, and with just more than enough. She didn't need to be able to swim in a pool full of it.

But what he had said about Shane? Of course Shane loved her. She was being stupid. She loved him. They were best friends, and friends loved each other. But she knew that's not what he had meant. She also knew that most men didn't bend over backward the way Shane had for her for years. No, stop it. Shane did not love her at that level. He had considered Geoff one of his good friends until... he had been awfully quick to take sides. There wasn't a second of hesitation; he hated Geoff as easily if not more than she did, on her behalf.

Shane.

When she returned to the bonus room, now in jeans and her wet hair coiled into a top knot, it looked like neither of them had moved. Justin still lay back in a beanbag chair, and Shane sat forward. Both had game controllers and were leaning back and forth, and side to side, as they controlled the actions of their characters on-screen.

Lucy perched against the back of the couch. She wondered if there was a plot, or if this game was just run, run, kill, run, run.

Shane's avatar stopped running.

"Dude! What are you doing?" Justin yelled as blood splatter indicated Shane's character had been mercilessly massacred.

"I'm out." Shane's voice sounded gruffer than normal. "You keep at it."

He stood. Lucy looked up at him when he brushed his hand along her upper arm. It made her skin tingle in a way she wasn't used to. No, Shane didn't have feelings like that for her. She needed to not think of him that way. Not while she was still trying to get over Geoff.

She leaned over and ruffled Justin's hair before leaving.

"Mom," he complained.

She followed Shane down the stairs and back into the kitchen. She instantly melted into him when he pulled her into a hug. He had hugged her thousands of times before. Why did this one feel different?

She was tired. She was overthinking things. She pushed out of his embrace.

"You looked like you needed a hug."

She did. She wanted another one. But she was confused. She was mixing up her feelings for Shane all over a casual remark from her lawyer.

"I saw Bentoncourt today." She began rummaging in the refrigerator. If she was physically doing something, she wouldn't think about hugging Shane again.

A chair squeaked along the floor as he pulled it out.

"I need to put pads on the bottom of that chair. Will you remind me?" she commented absentmindedly.

Onions, peppers, she could chop. Chopping was good. Chopping wouldn't stop her from talking, but it would stop her from imagining his arms around her again.

"I'll fix the chair," Shane commented. He flipped the chair and placed the seat on the table as if it weighed nothing. "What happened at the lawyer's?"

He told me you were in love with me.

"He showed me the accounts." She blinked back tears as she sliced into a potent onion. "We're going to be okay. There are several trusts in my name, and a couple of accounts I should inherit. We have to jump through a few flaming hoops to gain access to the inheritance. Proof of death and some other issues like that. But I don't think I really need that money."

"It's better to gain access to what's legally yours than to let it sit around as free money for the banks." Shane rummaged through the junk drawer. He found what he was looking for and returned to the chair.

Lucy didn't want to watch him as he examined the foot of the chair with a thoughtful expression. She didn't want to see how deftly he moved. She cast her gaze back to her chopping.

"I'll be right back," he announced as he passed out to the garage.

Flipping a hammer in his hand, he came back in. She started breathing again.

"It's going to take a while to gain access to those accounts either way. Maybe years even. I'm not sure it's worth the struggle."

"What about your own money, the trusts?" He didn't

look up, all his focus on his task of prying the current foot from the chair.

"Bentoncourt said he has to do some transfers and move the money through a few shell corporations."

"That sounds like money laundering. The accounts are legally yours. Why does he have to do that?" The piece popped off from the chair, and Shane began working on the next foot. If she weren't talking to him about this, about her money, they could have been having any normal day-to-day conversation about anything. She breathed in and took their situation as a sign. There was nothing to worry about, nothing to freak out over.

"It's less about money laundering than it is about creating a smoke screen. He doesn't want anyone who is watching those accounts to be able to find me."

Shane put down the hammer. Lucy could feel his gaze on her, but she continued to focus on chopping the vegetables in front of her.

"Who would be interested in finding you, Lucy?"

She ignored him. "I won't have access to my own damned money for at least another week. Possibly more. And Geoff hasn't made a deposit since last week. I'm tired of never knowing if I'm going to have gas money. I can't keep asking you to buy our groceries."

"Lucretia." Shane crossed the kitchen to where she worked. He reached in front of her and took the knife from her hand, turning her to face him. He held her with his hands on her upper arms, dipping his head down to be able to look her in the eye without her having to tilt her head.

She wiped at her face. "Stupid onions."

"Talk to me."

"Someone has accessed one of the accounts. Only two people should be able to do that. I'm one of them, and I currently don't have bank clearance." She tried to turn away from him, but his grip held her in place. She began talking faster. "It's probably just some hacker or someone trying to see if they can break into someone's dormant accounts."

"Shit." Shane dropped his hands. Before she had a chance to hiccup, she was engulfed in his embrace. He was warm and so strong. He felt safe. There had been a time when she was the one with the protective arms wrapped around him. Had she felt safe to him then?

"I don't want any of them to find me," she whispered through her tears. "I don't want to ever go back."

Shane murmured against her hair and stroked her back.

She sniffed and looked up at him. His face hovered above hers. Their eyes locked. Her insides did a flip. She wasn't certain if he tightened her against his chest first, but she raised up on her toes just enough and pressed her mouth to his.

Shane's lips were soft and slid gently against hers. She closed her eyes and sighed into his mouth. She licked her own lips and flicked her tongue across his. Shane moved his hands to hold her face. His lips danced across hers. She trailed her tongue back across his mouth, and suddenly their tongues were dancing. Lips consuming each other.

Hands were everywhere, stroking, caressing, touching. He lifted her and placed her on the counter. Now her face was slightly higher than his, and she tilted her head down to meet him.

Shane's hands bit into her thighs as he pressed into her.

Lucy fisted her hand into the back of his shirt, pulling him tight. He tasted like nothing she had ever had before, like something she had been missing her entire life. There was no Geoff to piss off. This kiss was for her and her alone.

"Hey, Mom!"

Shane jumped back from her, and she slid off the counter as Justin's feet abused the stairs into the kitchen.

Shane's back was to her, fussing with the chair again. She sliced the pepper in front of her as if nothing had happened, as if her entire world was as even keeled as it could be while in the middle of a divorce, and finding out your abusive, sadistic father might be out there and not dead, and that your best friend was the best fucking kisser ever. Ever.

"What's for dinner?" Justin asked.

"Ya know, I have no clue. I just started chopping, and I have no plans here." She focused on Justin, hoping he couldn't see an embarrassed flush across her face. "What kind of homework do you have?"

He shook his head. "Nothing. It's all done."

"Okay. Look, I have no clue what to make. Stacey is eating with Abby. How about we just go get some tacos, huh?"

Justin's face lit up. "Awesome, so do I have time to go play another game?"

"Yeah, sure. It's too early to go eat now."

With a handful of some packaging that crinkled, Justin headed back upstairs.

Lucy let out a relieved sigh. She opened a cabinet and selected a container. She finished chopping what she had started. Shane finished pounding new feet onto the chair in front of him. They worked in silence.

She put the chopped veggies into the fridge and closed the door. Shane was there. He reached out for her.

She flinched. "We shouldn't. I can't. I'm still married."

His hand caressed the side of her face. "You don't love him anymore, do you?"

"I'm still technically married." Her nerves were

bouncing around so hard she expected them to be picked up by the city's Richter scale downtown.

"Are you, Lucy? Are you still married here?" Shane placed his warm hand over her heart. "Where it counts?"

She wanted to melt against his touch, to lean in and have him caress her. Lucy shook her head no.

"Then we'll let the paperwork catch up to us." He lowered his head, gently pressing his lips back to hers. Tasting her with soft, tentative kisses. Each kiss grew a little bolder, lasted a little longer.

Lucy reached up and cupped the back of his head, holding his lips to hers, deepening and lengthening the kiss.

12

Shane dropped Lucy and Justin off, and made his excuses to leave for the night. He would return. He returned every night as Dogstar.

As soon as Lucy had found out he was renting an efficiency apartment by the week, she made him bring everything to her house. She saw no reason for him to rent what was basically storage for his bag. He could leave it in her closet and change and shower after the kids left for school. She was a demanding woman, and he was happy to do as she commanded. They both knew it was a waste of money, especially since Dogstar first appeared, he had spent every night at her house.

He didn't know how he was going to pull this off much longer. He couldn't be a pet forever. Well, he had started off as her pet, and he would happily remain her pet. As long as he could also be her lover.

Damn, that woman could kiss. Clearly her displays of affection around Geoff had just been bad acting. There was a difference in her kisses, a distracting difference.

He couldn't keep doing this. He ran his hand over his

face up and back over his head. His priority was to Lucy and the kids. But damn it, he had a duty to Morgan. And this was big news.

He pulled the Dodge Magnum he'd purchased second-hand into the school lot where he would leave it for the night. He wiggled the earpiece in and hit call to connect to Morgan.

"Palatine," the voice on the other end of the call announced.

"Okay, boss man, you cannot say I'm slacking. I don't think this is small. Lucy's lawyer found someone has tapped into one of the accounts that should be locked up all nice and tight because he hasn't yet been able to provide proof of inheritance or some such bullshit."

"What does that even mean?" Morgan asked.

Shane explained what Lucy had told him regarding the acrobatics required before she could legally gain access to the money she was entitled to inherit. "It means that either someone has discovered a back door into a banker's vault, or Lazarus has someone accessing his accounts on his behalf. I seriously doubt he's tapping into them on his own."

Morgan made noises deep in his throat. "Okay, I will pass this along. Tell me, how was Lucy with this news? How did she tell you? What's her status?"

"Her status is she is in the middle of getting screwed by her ex, her lawyer seems to have her best interests at heart, but I'm still not certain of the guy. She very much didn't want to tell me."

"Trying to hide it?"

"No," Shane all but barked. "Hoping it will all just go away. She's scared. She's managed to live away from daywalkers and bloodsuckers for a very long time. I don't think she has any interest in going back to living under a coven's control."

"Are you sure there isn't a way she's the one accessing that account?"

Shane huffed. "Morgan, she's broke and struggling. She doesn't want her kids to know how bad off things are right now. This morning she had me make a payment to PG&E before they cut her electricity off. Her ex has walked away from all responsibility, placing all the burden on her, knowing she is not in a position to financially shoulder any of it. If she was tapping into that account, I seriously doubt I would have been paying her power bill."

"Fine. Anything else on the lawyer?"

"No, nothing new."

"Okay, fine. I'll be in touch tomorrow."

Shane ended the call. He tucked his phone and wallet into a hidden lockbox behind the passenger seat that he had installed. The car would have to essentially be stripped before his belongings were located. A simple break-in would get the thief a car radio and some loose change.

He opened the door a crack and shifted. A large dark gray wolf nosed the car door shut. He arrived at the house at the same time Stacey returned home from studying.

"There you are." She scratched behind his ears and called him a good boy.

He was going to have to figure this double life out sooner than later. He ran up the stairs into the bonus room where Justin was still playing video games.

"J, it's bedtime," Lucy yelled from the upper hallway.

Shane's tail thudded against the floor a little faster. Stupid tale, giving away his racing heart.

"But Mom, I'm in the middle of this— Hey!" he yelled

when Dogstar nudged his controller, causing him to lose control of his character and end the game.

"Well hurry and die already." Shane's exceptional hearing heard her mutter, "What a messed-up thing to tell your kid. Oh the joys of video-game moms."

"Never mind, I'm dead." Justin glared at the wolf next to him.

Shane trotted up the stairs after Justin. He nudged into Lucy's bedroom. Would she let him sleep in here tonight after this afternoon's kiss?

She had told the kids the dog couldn't sleep in their rooms, but she had succumbed to having him in her bed after only one night. She had held tight to the thick mane of fur at the scruff of his neck and cried herself to sleep. She had done that more nights than he cared to remember when they had been younger and he began shifting. She cried when he hadn't been able to.

He began shifting shortly after his mother's death. Of course he didn't know she had died for months after the last time he had seen her. He wanted to cry, but by then he had forgotten how to. Curling up with the young Lucy had been the only comfort available to him. She was his shining star. That soft glow began shimmering around her at about the same time. After she saved his life, he vowed to himself that he would always protect her, always be there for her. He hadn't known what the aura indicated for years. Lucy still shone with the mate glow when he looked at her. This afternoon it had been dazzling.

He leaped up into the big bed and made a nesting area next to Lucy's side of the bed.

She stepped from the bathroom, toothbrush in her mouth. She looked at him.

He cocked his head to the side, asking permission.

"Puppeh?" she asked around a mouthful of foaming toothpaste.

Shane thudded his tail in response.

She grabbed her pajamas and disappeared back into the bathroom.

Shane waited with his muzzle resting on his paws.

Lucy slid into the bed beside him. Shane shuffled closer to her. She laced her fingers into his scruff.

"You have always been here for me," she whispered. "Thank you. I think I need your strength now more than ever."

Shane wanted to shift, to wrap her in his arms, but he knew the rules. *Puppy* very specifically meant he was welcome as long as he was a wolf. He wouldn't chance it, not while she was still fragile, and not with the kids around.

He huffed and let Lucy's warm breath caress his fur.

Lucy sat. Sat and wondered just what was she doing here. Watching the clock did not help. It seemed to make time go even slower.

Two hours ago she had been nervous and felt like she was going to throw up. One hour ago the nausea reduced to a swarm of angry bees in her midsection. Thirty minutes ago her senses were heightened with expectation. And now. Now she felt like a fool.

Cyan del Fuego was late.

When Bentoncourt told her he had been contacted by the Coven Master of the West Coast, Lucy wanted to cry. Miraculously enough, she didn't. She had been in fear of the other shoe dropping for days, since he had first told her someone was accessing her father's accounts. This felt like the other shoe dropping. She had braced herself, lashed metaphorical steel girders to her spine, and agreed to a meeting.

Why had she agreed to a meeting?

What did she know about this woman she was meeting? Cyan del Fuego. An Internet search gave Lucy a list of business holdings and endeavors. That was different, and legal. Typically coven masters were out of the eye of the general population. At most Lucy should have been able to find hints and suggestions regarding this person, not the name and address of her company in San Francisco.

When Lucy had run, she'd tried to distance herself from the dark world of vampires and daywalkers. The group in LA that took her in, promised to hide her from Yves Marat after he supposedly slaughtered her father. She'd thought she had made real friends. Well, she'd thought Lyric might be. A few years younger, so completely goth, and being groomed to be a lifelong blood slave. At sixteen the young woman seemed to have it more together and figured out than Lucy and all her father's wealth had ever prepared her for. Lyric had been the only one who had shown Shane any kindness when he showed up looking for Lucy. He hadn't hung around long. He'd been sixteen himself, and all angles and height. A lanky kid, he hadn't started to fill in yet. He had been nervous, a lifetime in the compound and two years on street; no wonder he'd been constantly looking over his shoulder.

The rest of them had been far from kind once they learned who her father was. The abuse she'd suffered at their hands had been humiliating. Body slave. Escaping from their clutches had taken longer than she cared to admit. And she was out of there before Marat's short rule was over.

She'd successfully distanced herself from the LA coven and moved farther away from all things vampire.

She had heard a rumor that an Argentinean vampire had swept in and stabilized the region, and began collecting the loyalties of covens along the coast. Del Fuego.

How exactly did Cyan fit into all of this?

Bentoncourt had provided her little guidance. He wasn't surprised that they both had been under light surveillance the entire time. They never would be truly free, but Del Fuego had let them live their lives, so how bad could she be?

Lucy didn't have the physical strength that most daywalkers possessed. She was considered to be as weak as a human, and therefore she was treated poorly by others of her kind. Especially if they knew her parentage. She was a weak daywalker whose father had been a murderous fascist. If she had been watched, then the Del Fuegos knew who her father was. Did this mean they also knew who was accessing her father's money?

Was Cyan being late to show her dominance? After the first forty-five minutes Lucy wondered just how long the vampire was going to drag the psychological toying out. Lucy had planned an extra hour for this little game, but she had not planned for, or even remembered how tortuous waiting could be. It was worse than waiting at the pediatrician's office with a sick baby.

Neutral ground, not sacred or holy, just neutral. The main library downtown was both sacrosanct and neutral. Vampires considered knowledge to be extremely important, but not so important as to be sacred. Unknown to most humans, the library had been built on an ancient ritual site. The land had been leveled and developed long before anyone seemed to pay attention to the archaeological importance of the region. Yet the ground remained sacred.

The blood, souls, and beliefs of the ancients had seeped into the soil, and they rose into the buildings over them.

This led to a heightened creepy factor about the library to begin with. Add to that the near death silence of a practically empty library in the late evening on a Wednesday night closer to the winter solstice than the fall equinox. The sun had set, and the library was going to close soon. The special collections room, set apart on the roof of the building, felt as if it absorbed sound and energy.

She should have told Shane where she was going. Her gut clenched with nerves. Figures moved outside the windows.

Lucy looked up at the soft whoosh the door to special collections made as it opened.

In walked a tall, glamorous woman. She could only be Cyan del Fuego, flanked by bodyguards, boy toys, and a small woman who must be her personal assistant.

Cyan's long, pointed nails trailed along the top of the glass display case. They looked sharp enough to cut glass. Cyan didn't walk or strut so much as glided. Black hair, pale skin, red lips. She was the epitome of vampire, yet she wasn't one. Daywalker.

Lucy's gaze kept returning to one man among the bevy of beautiful men that traveled with her. The fae-looking one to the back was too pretty to be muscle. Anyone else might peg him as her toy du jour, but Lucy figured of all the men surrounding Cyan, he was the real bodyguard. He was the only full vampire.

How ironic. Daywalkers had been bred to protect the vampires, and here was a vampire protecting a daywalker.

He was incredibly familiar looking. He had a similar look that Stacey tended to admire, ethereal and pretty. That had to be the connection.

Cyan slid into a chair opposite of Lucy while the men positioned themselves around the collections room. The only real danger here was the setting sun, and that had already sunk beneath the horizon.

The lithe, beautiful man sat next to Cyan. His long limbs folded, and he had the attitude that this meeting was at his behest. Did that mean Cyan was a front for him?

Cyan lifted her hand, and the small woman handed her a tablet.

"Lucretia Khalid Asher, why are you back?"

Lucy squinted and felt the pinch of confusion between her eyebrows. "Excuse me?"

Cyan tossed the tablet away from her and leaned back, crossing her arms. "You have been off our radar for years. Of course we have kept an eye on you when it seemed likely to expect you to resurface, but you didn't. Until now. You have lived without access to your personal accounts, only to access them in one foul swoop."

The fae-looking man leaned forward to pick up the tablet. He settled back and seemed to be studying what it displayed.

Cyan turned and snatched the tablet out of the man's hands. "Nando." His name was an admonition.

Nando. Lucy's brain was distracted by the man and not focusing on Cyan. There was something incredibly familiar about him, and she could not figure it out. Lucy forced her focus back onto Cyan. "I'm not back, I'm broke."

"You've been broke before. You were homeless for six months without touching your funds. Why now, when Lazarus is back?"

Lucy's throat went dry. She blinked. The room tilted, and Lucy clutched the edge of the table.

"Excuse me. What did you say?" She couldn't have heard what she'd heard.

"Why now?" Cyan's tone held annoyance.

Lucy shook her head. "The other, you said La... Laz..." Lucy had to fight to say the name. She couldn't. "My father is dead."

"Lazarus has returned, Apparently he is not dead," Nando drawled.

Lucy stared blankly ahead. She focused on not throwing up. Her brain wasn't a swirling mass of panic; it was blank, empty. She spoke like a robot. "I thought he was dead."

"He is not. And now you are shifting money from accounts you haven't touched in over a decade," Cyan explained.

"Sheer dumb luck and bad timing." Lucy gaped. She licked her dry lips. There was no moisture in her mouth. "Like everyone else, I thought he was dead. Trust me when I say I am not accessing my money to pass it along to that bastard. I'm sure your spies have told you my circumstances have changed. If it was just me, sure, I could go back to couch surfing until I got myself situated. But it's not just me now. I have kids that deserve a mom who is going to fight for them. If that means exposing myself to your open scrutiny, and maybe doing business with people I would rather have forgotten about, then that is what I will do. My soon-to-be ex is playing dirty. I'm willing to swallow my pride to protect my children."

Lucy relaxed the grip she had on the table. She eased back into her chair, unaware of when she began leaning forward so emphatically. She took a steadying breath.

"I would have thought Bentoncourt would have mentioned all of that. I need the money to buy my own house."

"So Lazarus has not been in contact?" The smooth accent rolled from Nando's tongue. Cyan spoke with the inflection of a slight accent. The results of diction training and no longer living in her native land. Nando's accent was similar but thick. As if he had not spent as much time away from speaking his native tongue.

Cyan shot him a glare.

What was their connection? He acted like some spoiled prince, yet Cyan was clearly the contact, the one in charge. He caught the expression and threw his hands up rather dramatically to accompany an eye roll and a head shake.

"What? I am allowed to ask her the questions. Why banter back and forth?" He turned his attention to his manicure. "She is not lying, and she smells of old blood. When was the last time you were fed properly?"

Lucy had forgotten what it was like to be around vampires. They sensed more than they could actually smell or see. It was what made normal humans think they had psychic powers. And when Lucy had a fresh transfusion, her senses were heightened as well. But for her it never lasted more than a day or two.

"It's only been a week or two since my last transfusion," Lucy defended herself.

Nando tossed up his hand. "Eh." He rolled his eyes again like a teenager, crossed his arms, and looked off to the side, clearly dismissing her.

Lucy shifted her glance to Cyan. Who was she supposed to focus on? Was Nando not the vampire in charge? Cyan exuded power, yet she was a daywalker. And they were never in charge when a vampire was around.

"Ignore my brother. He is here to learn. And it is hard to learn when one is already full of oneself." Cyan's words were sharp. Nando huffed and shifted so that he faced the other direction, dismissing Cyan.

"Your accounts are moving. You have three moving in a predictable and similar fashion, Cayman Islands, Swiss accounts. Yet a fourth is channeling through volatile markets in Russia. If all this money isn't for Lazarus, tell me exactly."

Lucy felt her breath stutter as she inhaled. She slowly exhaled and explained everything to Cyan. Bentoncourt was shifting her accounts to avoid a clear trail. But only three of them. And apparently it wasn't working. The other accounts they had yet to gain access to. Up until twenty-four hours ago they had been under the impression they were fairly well out of the reach and range of interest. She had been aware someone had tapped into that fourth account, but she was clueless as to who it was.

"And your plans for the money are to simply live your life out here?" Cyan lifted her hand, indicating the city outside the windows.

"Yes, it is." Lucy nodded. She felt defeated. She was never going to see her money.

Cyan quirked an eyebrow up, folded her arms, and leaned back.

"Tell me everything about Bentoncourt Roberts. Why did you call him?"

Lucy told Cyan their history, how he had been one of her keepers. How she had felt she could trust him, especially since he had slipped her a sizable amount of cash to help her run away. Contacting him again for the divorce had been a panicked move. But one she was glad she had made, since he had kept track of her accounts, was able to help her access her funds, and was even helping her to remain in hiding. "Not that it seems to actually matter." Lucy chuckled. "I mean apparently you knew about me all along, and have been keeping tabs on my money anyway."

"When were you planning on moving on the other accounts?" Cyan asked.

Lucy shook her head. "I don't know. I have to be able to prove inheritance. And if what you are saying is true, and Daddy isn't dead, then I won't be able to gain access."

"What will you do if you don't get that money?"

"Look, I don't live extravagantly. I don't need the money in those extra accounts if I can safely get access to my own trust funds."

"Hmm." Cyan lifted her head in a single chin-up nod. "Meet me again tomorrow. Lunch." It was not a question but a demand.

Lucy shot her glance at Nando before returning it to Cyan.

Cyan waved Lucy's obvious concern away. "He doesn't need to be there. We need to continue this conversation." Cyan stood. The assistant scrambled to pick up the tablet.

The guards formed in front of Cyan, ready to escort her out. Nando made a bit of a production, huffing and shifting in his chair. He wanted everyone to know he was ignoring Cyan.

Cyan paused as she was about the pass through the door and out into the night. "Tell Shane, he did well. I appreciate his information."

Lucy sat with a thud.

Nando stood, made a harrumphing sound, and smirked.

Oh, she now recognized that twitch of his lips from the poster in Stacey's room.

13

L ucy sat and looked out at the waves. The light caught
on the breakers that foamed and rolled in to shore.
There was too much to think about. She didn't want to think
about any of it. She hadn't felt this way in a very long time.
She wanted to run away from everyone and everything. But
she knew from experience that didn't magically fix a
damned thing.

Her phone buzzed with a text message. She ignored it
and continued to stare out into the darkness.

Her phone began to buzz incessantly.

"What the hell?" She grumbled as she fished it from
her bag.

She looked at the display. That lying bastard Shane.

She hurled her phone.

"Oh fuck! I need that." Lucy scrambled from her perch
and ran in the direction of her toss. She hadn't heard a wet
thwap, so maybe she didn't get it far enough out to make it
into the water.

She heard it buzz again. She spun around, not seeing
any illumination. "Text me again, text me again," she began

chanting as she creeped in the direction she thought she'd heard it.

More demanding buzzing. She turned again and this time caught a hint of light before the screen turned off.

She was on her knees and running her hands into the ice plant, trying to locate the phone. She couldn't see and hoped that she didn't shove her hand into a random cactus or dog poop.

"Buzz again." She growled through clenched teeth. She knew she was close, but in the dark she couldn't see a thing.

Hot tears of frustration ran down the side of her face. No one to help, no one she could count on, and no fucking phone. This was all Shane's fault.

She sat back on her heels. If she believed in anything, now would be the time to pray. To pray for guidance, for help, for another goddamned text message so she could find her phone.

She stared into the dark, willing her phone to make noise and light up.

A jingle of dog tags caught her attention. Next she heard the labored breathing and heavy footfalls of a jogger.

"Where do you think you're going," the breathless voice said. It was too low to be directed at her. They must be talking to the dog. "Come on." Pleading. The footfalls stopped.

A bark.

"Come on," the runner demanded.

Then lots of barking.

"What?" The voice grew louder. "Oh, hey, are you all right down there?"

Lucy looked up. She could make out a silhouette of a person and a sizable dog. It sounded like a woman, but she couldn't tell, and the person's shape divulged no information.

"I lost my phone and I can't see it in the dark," Lucy called back.

A bright light, and noises as the runner climbed down the embankment to where Lucy knelt.

"Here, does this help?" The light blinded Lucy.

"Yeah, I think it's over here somewhere." Lucy pointed into the area in front of her.

The cool nose of a golden retriever invaded Lucy's space and sniffed at her face. She laughed and scratched the dog between the ears.

"Candy, stop that." The dog was pulled back.

"She's fine. I appreciate your help." Lucy scanned the ice plant. Nothing.

"Hey what's that?" The runner moved the flashlight a little farther to Lucy's left.

Her phone.

"Ah, thank you!" She scrambled forward and picked it up. She dusted sand from her knees as she stood.

"Thank you so much." She squinted into the flashlight.

"Hey, no problem, glad Candy spotted you. Good night." The runner redirected the light and made their way back up to the path.

Lucy saw purple and green spots in her vision as she blinked the residue of the bright light from her eyes.

"Good night," she called after her running benefactor.

Lucy looked down at her phone. More messages from Shane and Stacey. Her mouth pursed together just reading his name. She wanted to throw the damned phone again.

She opened Stacey's most recent message and texted her back. *Sorry, ran late, be home soon.*

Lucy breathed heavily through her nose. She didn't feel as if this had calmed her or helped her to focus.

She was going to need to send this skirt to the cleaners, and she needed a shower to clean off the beach dirt and sand from her knees. She needed to talk to Shane. She drove home.

Traffic did nothing to improve her mood.

She followed the noise into the bonus room. His stupid bald head pissed her off.

"What the hell did you think you were doing, Shane?"

He stood and looked at Lucy with confusion. "Watching TV."

The kids scampered out of the bonus room and headed downstairs.

"You've been spying on me for the Del Fuegos. I thought you were my friend. I thought you were here because I needed you, and instead I find out you're here because you're at Cyan del Fuego's beck and call."

She jabbed her finger into his unyielding chest. It made her finger hurt. She wanted him to hurt; she wanted to hurt him the way he'd hurt her.

"Lucy... I..." Shane stammered.

"I thought you hated my kind. But you're working for one of us?" She stopped yelling at him and stared. She tried to bore a hole into his skull to read his thoughts. "You aren't even denying it?"

Shane reached up and rested his hands on her shoulders. She shrugged them off and pushed against him. He didn't budge. She stepped back.

"You can't even come up with a lie right now, can you? That's all you men are good for, lies, lies, lies. I honestly thought you were different."

"I am different, Lucy, if you would only let me explain." He kept his voice low.

"Why? So you can weave more lies for me?"

"Lucretia..." he pleaded. "Baby, I—"

She shook her head, her lip curled up in a sneer. "No, you don't get to 'baby' me. I don't want to hear anything you have to say right now. I tried to go out and think about things, you know, clear my head and figure this all out. And it all comes down to I can only trust me."

Shane attempted to bring his arms around her again.

"Stop it. You need to leave."

Shane turned in a circle.

"Lucy, don't do this. I love you."

"Don't say that to me now. You've had a whole lifetime to say that. Don't say it now. My God, have you been working for them the entire time? Like ever since you first found me after I ran away?"

"I don't work for Del Fuego."

"You're lying. Just go. You need to get out of my house and get out of my life."

He growled and then moved. Shane seemed larger as he stomped past her.

In a haze of red and blurred vision Lucy stormed into her bedroom. Shane was there pulling his bag from the second closet. She glared at him until he left. She slammed the door.

She wanted to shut her brain off. She fumbled in the bathroom cabinet and found the Xanax prescription. She downed two pills and crawled into bed. She no longer cared that her knees might have sand and dirt on them, or that she still had shoes on. Right now she needed to not be able to think.

～

Lucy rolled over. Her head pounded, and her mouth felt dry and gummy. Another fucking fantastic emotional hangover. She pulled her pillow in to hug it. If only it had arms. She snuggled against the smell. It made her feel protected and comforted. It was the smell of—Shane. She spit out fur.

Damn Shane, damn her for allowing him into her emotions. And double damn him for the wolf fur in her bed.

She slid out from the bed and pulled the sheets with her. They needed to be washed anyway.

A soft tapping sounded against her door before it was pushed open. "Mom?"

"Come on in."

She continued to pull pillowcases and the rest of the bedding.

Stacey pushed the door all the way open. "You okay?"

"I'm fine." Mentally beat to hell, but fine.

"Justin and I are about to head out. I wanted to make sure you were okay before we left. Shane said I should check on you. He's not coming back anytime soon, is he?" Stacey's voice was small.

"Probably not, so I guess we all have to get used to that." Lucy's words were clipped. "I'm fine. I will be fine. I have a meeting this afternoon, so I might not be home when you get off the bus."

"Another meeting with the lawyer? The one last night went late." She held on to the doorjamb, as if she needed it for protection.

Lucy sighed and dropped the laundry. "Oh, honey, I know I was out late. I got some bad news, and I had to process it. And I didn't do that very well. It just all made me madder about everything. Then I got home and I blew up at Shane." She played with a strand of Stacey's hair.

She began to talk but stopped herself. Stacey didn't need to know things were about to get worse before they got better. She didn't need to know there was a world out there of things that go bump in the night, and her mother used to belong in it. She didn't need to know that they were officially out of money, and Lucy had no clue if Geoff was going to make good with a support payment or not.

Stacey was sixteen. She had her own traumas to deal with regarding this divorce and now breakup. Was it a breakup? They had kissed a few times; they had snuggled. *Puppy* was something they had done as kids. It was comfort, companionship, protection. But was sleeping with your friend while they were in wolf form anything else? She'd let him into their lives, and now she didn't want anything to do with him. Yeah, it was a breakup.

None of that was a burden she needed to share with her daughter.

"You better get going."

"Love you, Mom." Stacey gave her a quick kiss on the cheek and ran down the front stairs, yelling for her brother to leave.

Lucy picked up the dirty sheets and walked down the hall to the laundry. She stuffed them in and began the wash cycle.

"Stupid." Now she would have to wait to take a shower. No, she pulled the knob, stopping the cycle. She just needed to remember to start this up again when she was done. She shuffled back down the hall to her room.

The hot water felt restorative. She was clean. Now if it only worked on her broken heart as well.

She didn't bother to dress up today. She was never going

to match Cyan's level of chic. And she had no clue who else would be there. Today Lucy needed to be gentle on her psyche, and that meant comfort clothes. She slid into a pair of yoga pants that could double as regular pants, and pulled out a hippy-style tunic with a string tie at the neck. For now she pulled a grungy T-shirt on over her head. She had enough time this morning to get a few hours in working on jewelry. That emerald bleeding-heart design wasn't going to make itself. And she was going to need the money from selling it sooner than later.

14

Shane stared up at the pattern on the ceiling. He had left Lucy's house and considered going right back as Dogstar. He knew she wouldn't let him in, so he got himself a hotel room. But he hadn't slept, just laid down on top of the blankets, fully dressed, and stared at the ceiling for hours.

The patterning in the paint reminded him of sunflowers for some reason. He should probably get up and do something. But why? What was he going to do? Was there any point to any of it?

Lucy had met with Cyan del Fuego last night, and no one seemed to think it might have been worthwhile to give him a heads-up.

How did they think that was going to go over with Lucy? She would just cheer right up and say, *Gee, thanks for keeping an eye on me and reporting my every move to the bloodsuckers I think I'm hiding from.*

He was pissed, and he didn't know who to be pissed at.

Well, he did. He was pissed at Cyan del Fuego. She had

used him. Tapped into his fears and turned his better judgment around and used it against him.

His phone rang.

He pulled the earpiece from his pocket and wiggled it into his ear.

"What do you want?" He didn't particularly care who was on the other end.

"Thought I'd check in, see how things were going. Cyan is headed down your way—"

Shane cut Morgan off. "I know. She's already in town. A little heads-up before she got here would have been good."

"Why? You got the information."

"I got the information last night *after*"—Shane growled the word—"Lucy met with her and had been told I was only here to spy on her."

"But—"

"No, damn it! I'm not here primarily to keep tabs on her for Cyan. I am here to make sure she is safe. To keep an eye on her in case Lazarus does decide to make contact. To be a barricade in case her ex decides to do more damage and try to get her out of the house sooner. Your little venture with Cyan was just a convenient way for me to be here on the company's dime.

"But Cyan just blew that right out of the water with some little comment to Lucy. Had either of you told me that Cyan was going to be here and meet directly with her, I could have let her know what's going on, so that it wasn't a surprise. And so that she wouldn't be pissed off at me."

"Shane, look—"

"No, Morgan, you look. How am I supposed to take care of Lucy if she won't let me near her?" he yelled. This was all that Del Fuego woman's fault.

"Shane."

"What?" he barked.

"I told you as soon as I found out. I know how important Lucy is to you. I want you to continue to keep tabs on her and that lawyer."

"I'll think about it." Shane reached up to hit the button on the earpiece, ending the call.

He swung his legs off the side of the bed and sat up. He ran his hands over his face and back over the top of his head. He needed to shave.

Shane shucked his clothes and stepped into the shower, He twisted the knobs to hot and let the simple mundane task of personal hygiene take over his brain.

He lathered his scalp and carefully ran the handheld razor, which looked like a toy car, up the back of his head. He took shaving in sections, feeling his way across the back, sides and top of his scalp. When he was finished, he let the shower wash any stray hairs down the drain.

He stepped from the shower, wrapped a thick hotel towel around his hips, wiped off the mirror, and repeated the process, with a different razor, on his face.

He finished by rubbing his skin down with cocoa butter until he gleamed. He pulled a fresh outfit from his bag and got dressed. In a light blue bowling shirt with white panels and tan slacks, he was prepared to face the world. Now, he was prepared to deal with his need to see Lucy, his need to know she was going to be all right. He perched his trilby on the back of his head and left the hotel.

Lucy was easy to find. She hadn't left the house yet. He parked along the street where she wouldn't notice him, and waited to see if she went anywhere. Her minivan passed him a few hours later, and he followed.

Balboa Park, interesting. This was out of the norm for Lucy, but he was glad of the opportunity to hide his car in among the hundreds of others parked there. She walked past several buildings and entered the visitor's center. Shane stopped when he caught sight of her lawyer and his assistant. Okay, so this was a lunch meeting. It still seemed out of the way for either of them. And it must be important if Roberts had brought along the blonde.

He followed at a distance. Tucked in against a wall, conveniently located behind a display banner, Shane watched as Cyan del Fuego and her entourage approached. Lucy was swept up in the flow around the other woman, and everyone entered the restaurant.

If her lawyer was involved, then maybe this had more to do with the funds she was trying to gain access to than anything else.

He wasn't equipped to listen in on their conversation, and he wasn't familiar enough with the lay of the land in the park to know how he could keep an eye on her through lunch without being spotted. He pushed off the wall, straightened his hat, and sauntered over to the neighboring museum building. Once inside he grabbed a sandwich from their snack bar and returned to his car, where he could watch for Lucy's return.

While he ate, he played cat and mouse. Who should he follow, and what would he find out if he did? By the time this lunch would be over—he estimated at least an hour and a half—Lucy would have to drive straight home. With traffic she probably wouldn't get there before the kids. Nothing new there; she had become predictable in her habits.

He didn't need to follow Cyan. She could take care of herself. Besides, he didn't particularly care at the moment what she got up to, and he wasn't being paid to follow her. The lawyer, on the other hand, might still have something hidden.

Shane pulled out of his parking spot and began slowly driving up and down the rows of cars until he spotted the lawyer's BMW. He found a nearby spot that would allow him to easily see when the lawyer left. As predicted, the lunch lasted closer to two hours. Bentoncourt Roberts lumbered back to his car. He exchanged what appeared to be terse words with his assistant, Celine, based on his expression and hand gestures. The assistant left with a hair toss and less of a bounce in her usual step.

Shane eased his car out and followed the BMW. Roberts did not return to his office. Instead he drove to his home in La Jolla. Shane watched as the big man entered his house, and forty-five minutes later, in a change of clothes, stepped outside with his two Pomeranians on leashes. Instead of turning left to walk around the block, he turned to the right. Shane jumped out of the car and followed as the lawyer walked toward the coast and the shopping area.

He was not surprised when the lawyer got himself a smoothie and water for his dogs before returning to his house. He seemed to like that smoothie shop when he came in this direction. Shane slid back into the car and shook his head. So the man mixed up his routine. It told Shane precisely nothing.

He pulled out of where he had parked and drove back to Lucy's neighborhood. With traffic he might make it within an hour, but he doubted it.

Over an hour later he eased his car along her street. He would cruise by first, make sure she made it home. Then he would drive the few blocks and park at the elementary school, shift, and see if Dogstar might not be welcome in her backyard.

A toss of blonde hair caught the corner of his eye as he

cruised past the house. Lucy was home, but what was Roberts's assistant doing sitting out front?

Shane continued around the long block before turning around. He parked along the curve of the street where he could see her, but she didn't see him. She was definitely watching the house. They sat like that for another hour; Shane watching the blonde, the blonde watching Lucy's house. When she eased in to traffic, Shane followed at a distance until they were on a main road. He let a few cars get between them. She drove into a mega apartment complex. Shane cruised through. And stopped when she pulled her car into a designated carport spot. He continued to watch as she removed a collection of bags from the car, slinging them over her shoulder. She moved like she was tired over to a bank of mailboxes, retrieved her mail, and then climbed a flight of stairs. Interesting. She didn't seem pleased with the end results of her day.

Shane risked leaving for a few minutes and navigated to a fast food restaurant. He used the restroom, ordered a meal to go, and returned to the assistance's apartment complex. Her car was still in its carport. He took one of the visitor parking spots and waited to see if anything else unexpected happened this evening.

Around three a.m., Shane took another chance and left to find some coffee from an all-night quick mart. When he returned to the apartment complex, nothing had changed, even his parking spot was still available.

It was another hour and a half before anything interesting happened.

A sleek, new model year car pulled into guest parking, at the end of the row where Shane sat. Shane slid down in his seat—not that he expected to be seen, but a black man sitting in a car in the middle of the night was always suspicious.

The man who exited the car was dressed in an expensive designer suit. Slim fitting, dark, probably Italian. Anyone who could afford to dress like that didn't live here. These were nice apartments, but not that high rent. Shane sat up as the man headed toward the assistant's cluster of apartments. He was probably going to walk right past; of course he didn't.

Shane's eyes went wide; he wasn't going to need another hit of caffeine now. There were four units up that flight of steps, including the first apartment on the left where Celine lived.

By the time the man closed the door to Celine's apartment, Shane was out of his car and sniffing around the black Lexus. If he thought he would be suspicious just sitting in the parking lot, breaking into the car without triggering the alarm should definitely qualify him as such now. Nothing in the glove box to give away details on ownership. Nothing. The interior was as clean as the day it was driven off the lot, which may have been today. It still had that new car smell. And that very distinct, gut-wrenching stench that only belonged to vampires.

Shane groaned. He did not want to have to deal with vampires. It was never good when they showed up. Never. And they were so freaking hard to kill, had to destroy their heart or their brain. Or at least the connection from the brain to the body. And biting back wasn't an option. Vampire blood was poison to wolves. Shane had learned that one the hard way.

Did Bentoncourt Roberts realize his assistant was a feeder? Shane huffed. He wondered where her marks were. He wondered what her human boyfriend thought of this situation. And what exactly was this situation? Was she a blood slave? Typically those particular pets were kept close in a coven house. So what was the deal here?

Shane slid back into his car. The vampire should be leaving soon; how soon depended on how far away his dark-room was. Sunrise was in less than an hour. This guy couldn't be set up too far away, or he was staying for the day. Daylight would be fatal to the guy. His skin would get all crispy, and his brain would boil away. Unless... did Celine have a hidey-hole in that apartment?

Shane needed to be able to clone himself to go in two different directions. He needed one of him to go upstairs and check on Celine, see what he could learn from her, and one so he could focus on tailing the black Lexus.

He followed the car along city streets, past the stadium, and onto Friars Road. They drove out past where the road merged with Mission Gorge; they drove into an area of new construction. Unassuming cookie-cutter houses.

Shane took note of the address and continued to cruise past the house. He noticed several cars that seemed to be a bit upmarket for this area in neighboring driveways.

He turned his car around and headed straight back to the assistant's. When he got there, the sun was up. She was in the shower when he broke into her apartment. Fortunately, water conservation didn't seem to be a concern of hers. The place was smaller than he had expected. Her furniture was old. A pet would have nicer things.

She was definitely a feeder. The smell of blood lingered in the air. So did the stench of her visitor. He picked up one of the throw pillows and sniffed at it. He could smell dog, pot from a while ago, but the scent of vampire had not permeated the fabric. The fan of hundred-dollar bills splayed out on her coffee table gave him part of an answer.

She was a blood whore. So that could very well mean this guy wasn't local, and they didn't have a "relationship." So who did she work for? Was Roberts a blood pimp? Oh, Lucy would not be happy if that were the case.

Shane took a few pictures of the apartment and was out her front door before the water to her shower turned off.

Shane wanted to go straight to Lucy's and check on her. He could lurk around the backyard as Dogstar. He shuddered. The name those kids had given his canine self made his gums want to bleed.

If she saw him, she'd throw a shoe at him or call animal control. Best to give her time to cool down.

He hadn't lied, but he hadn't told her everything. How could he when she was so fragile?

She would be fine for another day. Besides he needed to have a chat with Cyan. He wanted a closer look at those houses. And he needed to get some sleep.

He drove on automatic and found himself back at the vampire's subdivision. Interesting place for a lair. He needed to get closer to those houses than cruising through in his car. He turned around and returned to a big-box store he had passed on the way. He couldn't just pull in and begin poking around. Someone would see him. There would be daywalkers about keeping an eye on their masters. The stench was stronger around the three houses where his guy from this morning had pulled in, and the two nearest neighbors. And of course, those were the houses with the matching high-end cars.

Armed with a few work shirts, a ball cap, some patches from the craft section, and an aluminum storage clipboard, he had a plan. A little arts and crafts with a glue stick and permanent markers, and Shane had a passable uniform.

He approached the first house. Cap pulled low over his

brow, and a large cardboard box in his hands. The stench of vampire was strong. He rang the bell and knocked on the door. A whirring sound behind him caught his attention. He looked up and back. A small surveillance camera rotated. Shane made sure to position the cap to obscure a clear view of his face.

"Yeah, what do you want?" a voice from a hidden speaker asked.

"I have a delivery for one-one-eight Canyon Trail Court." Shane laid on a thick Southern accent. He held the box up to the camera.

The voice that responded was clear, and angry. "Wrong address."

"But this is one-one-eight. No"—he made a production of reading the name written on the box—"Lindsey Holt here?"

"This is one-eighteen Trail Head. Wrong address."

"Okay, sorry. That's a nifty security cam you got there. Y'all have a nice day."

That camera had been tucked in. He hadn't noticed it from the street. He returned to the car and placed the box in the back in case anyone was watching. Now that he knew what he was looking for, he spotted the cameras on the other two houses. He wouldn't be able to repeat this delivery ploy again.

Good thing he'd bought more than one shirt.

He pulled the car around to the next street over, changed, and started back toward the three houses that interested him the most. As he approached, he began walking around the side of other houses. He didn't know how far out those cameras were pointed into the street, and the houses were close. While pretending to check on utility meters, they may catch him nosing around as far away as two houses.

He made his way between houses, vampire house on one side, human on the other. While he appeared to be focused on the human's meter, he was noticing a lack of cameras down the side of the vampire house. He continued around back. Security seemed to only be at the front. Amateurs.

Windows were blacked out, boarded over from the inside. Shane approached the back sliding glass door. He tried the lock, it slid open, but it opened to nothing. Sloppy, it still should have been locked. The entire entrance had been sealed off with a sheet of black plywood. He carefully slid the door closed.

He needed Dante on this. He should be able to dig up some property info even from Atlanta. It was all computer shit. Shane took a few notes on the pad he carried around with the clipboard, and headed back to the car.

Shane ran his hand over the back of his head. He fought a big yawn and forced his eyes to open wide. Earpiece in place, he made a call and began driving.

"Dante! How do feel about doing a little digging on something for me?"

"Dude, I thought I was on leave. Why are you calling me to work?" The laughter in Dante's voice indicated that he wasn't too annoyed.

"I need some computer digging, and you know that's not my thing."

"I'll give you a couple of hours, but that's it. I need to be out of Geena's way today. This will give me something to do."

"The wife already getting sick of you?"

"Hardly, she has a Realtor coming to appraise the condo

and thinks I'll be distracting. Send over what you got. I'll see what I can do."

Shane gave him the addresses in question, the name of the builder on the sign at the front of the subdivision, and the plates on the cars. They all had temporary, new, paper tags.

He drove back to the hotel. He had to blink hard to fight tired eyes the last fifteen minutes of his drive.

His room was as he had left it, no maid service. That was fine.

He kicked off his shoes and removed his clothes, no need to wrinkle them excessively by sleeping in them. And he planned on sleeping this time.

15

Lucy perched on the edge of the office chair and held her breath. Bentoncourt, Ben, sat next to her with a satisfied grin. She signed by the *X*, initialed the next page, and signed again. She slid the paper over to Ben. He placed his signature where needed as witness.

She let out her breath. That was done.

She now had access to a substantial amount of money. It was hers. She and the lawyer had already made plans for the funds to be divided into accounts for the kids, an account to establish a living allowance fund, as well as a general access fund.

Money would be transferred into secure locations as soon as the banker did his computer magic and got the ball rolling. But the ball was now rolling around in her court.

She sat back and looked at the banker. Stress she had been carrying in her upper back melted away. She no longer needed to rely on Geoff for support funds. She was going to make him pay them, but she didn't need the money. She felt like she could take a full breath of air for the first time in weeks.

"So how long before the transfer can happen to pay off the mortgage?"

"Immediately. However it will take up to forty-eight hours to post."

"Why so long? You're just shuffling the money from one account to another. I mean, I have access now to this money, but..." Lucy shook her head and held up her hand, dismissing her thought.

"Let's hold off on the house just at the moment. We need to discuss that in more detail." Ben nodded at the banker.

"Never mind then." Lucy shrugged. "I guess we need to open a regular checking account, set up regular transfers, get cards. What else?" She looked over at Ben. "Right, transfer payment to you. Did you bring your account information?"

"Not today, Lucretia." He shook his head. "I can have the information sent over, or they can issue a check?" He directed his question to the man on the other side of the desk.

"Either is fine with us. The transfer will be deposited much faster once we have your numbers. But you can walk out with a check right now."

Ben nodded. "I'll get you those numbers."

The banker entered information on his computer, and Lucy had another stack of printouts to sign, setting up a day-to-day account that an allowance would be transferred into on a regular basis.

The banker excused himself. When he returned, Lucy and Ben stood.

He handed Lucy an envelope. "That should be enough to keep you until the cards show up. They will be FedEx-ed, and you should have them early next week. It will be another week for printed checks."

She resisted the urge to peek into the envelope until Ben nudged her. He raised his eyebrows and nodded at the envelope.

"Oh, right." She opened it and counted. It wasn't rude to count your money at the bank, she reminded herself. She gulped. It was the most cash she had seen in one place since she'd run away and finally understood the value of money. "Thank you, yes, this should take care of things for a week or so."

She pushed down the urge to shout and run out to the nearest shoe store and buy shoes, just because she could. She extended her hand and thanked the banker.

"I guess I'll be back in five or six weeks to do this all over again once I change my name."

The banker wished her well on the divorce, and she followed Ben down into the lobby and out to his BMW.

"I want to pay off the house and get Geoff his money ASAP. And be done with all of this. He and his lawyer can eat it." She felt great, euphoric, knowing the house was secure.

"I'd like to set up another meeting with Geoffrey and French," Ben announced.

"Why?" Lucy scrunched up her face and whined.

"I was thinking. Geoffrey wants you to buy him out of his share at current market value. But can he actually pay the house off in full? I doubt it. He would have to liquidate everything and then some. And let's be honest, Lucy, how much of a retirement does he really have? Not much. So here's my plan..."

Lucy cackled in delight as Ben described a counteroffensive. Essentially it was a put-up-or-shut-up maneuver. Geoff would never see it coming.

"What if he's been hiding money? I mean they were

pretty damned adamant about me not being able to touch anything from before the marriage."

"I still doubt he has the capital, but let's request those files and see what kind of trouble it stirs up. I think we'll get a little smarmy, smug reaction from them, thinking they have outmaneuvered us. Now that the emergency about your funding is taken care of, we can get back to the big-picture issues."

Lucy scratched her head and watched traffic. "What about those other accounts? How are the Del Fuegos really going to be able to help with that?"

Ben glanced at her and then back to his driving. "Cyan has more lawyers at her disposal. I'm just me and an assistant. Let her do the heavy lifting on those accounts. Besides..." He let out a sigh. Lucy knew that sigh was loaded with concern about what Cyan had told them. Her father was back and trying to regain his power. But he was also staying in hiding. "He faked his own death, and that's going to tricky to get past the banks."

He pulled his car into the alley and parked next to the trash cans behind the bungalow that served as his office building. Her minivan occupied the other parking spot behind the small house.

"Have you made a decision yet, regarding Cyan's offer?" he asked as they climbed out of the car.

"I have. I meet with her this evening to go over everything."

"And?"

She crossed in front of his car and stopped to face him. "And I want to know. I don't like being in the dark. The thought of being the hunter and not the hunted appeals to me. I don't want anyone I care about to be a victim of his ever again. If I don't do this, I will be constantly looking over my shoulder until I know for certain he is dead, and who knows how long that will take. Ben, my father has a pretty damned good track record with hide-and-seek. We've all thought he's been dead for almost twenty years now."

"Whatever you decide, be safe."

She nodded. "Whatever I decide, I'm going to need to appoint a guardian for the kids, and get my accounts listed into a will. Hey, you want another project?"

Bentoncourt chuckled. "I'll call you once I have an appointment set up with Geoffrey and French."

Shane made his calls, and although he was still pissed, he had a job to do, so now he sat in Cyan del Fuego's impromptu office at the library. This seemed to be her designated place to set up and hold court. He wasn't pleased that she had exposed his ulterior motive for hanging around Lucy and the kids. But in the end they were on the same side of this mess.

He shared everything he had discovered about Celine and the mini coven he suspected.

Cyan nodded. Her assistant took notes.

Her entourage's hotel of choice couldn't be too far away. Within thirty minutes of sunset they were joined by a vampire.

Shane's nostrils flared at the onslaught of the pungent order. How could they not smell their own kind? It was insidious and invaded everything—hair, fabric. It coiled around him like smoke. The muscles along his shoulders and neck tensed. His fingers bit into the arm of the chair he occupied. Bile burned his throat.

"Ignore my brother. He thinks every time he walks into a room he must make an entrance," Cyan purred at Shane.

"I am a star. That is what stars do." He spoke with a thick accent. Every time he tossed his long hair over his shoulder, Shane was assaulted with another wave of stench. It was as if the man bathed in it.

Cyan huffed. "You are not a star, Nando. You are an entertainer. And while you are here with me, you are to observe."

Shane shot Nando a glare and returned his gaze to Cyan, eyebrows raised in an unvoiced question.

She chose to answer. "Father would like Nando to have a better understanding of what it is exactly that I do. I know the covens. I know the region. And"—she lifted one perfectly sculpted brow at Shane—"I know when something is not right. Patterns are off."

"The group at the Mission Oaks subdivision." He nodded in agreement. He kept an eye on local activity as well, but his motives were completely different, always had been.

Cyan approached her need for knowledge as a basis for Del Fuego control. Shane, to keep Lucy safe. Always to keep her safe.

"So I'm gonna hand off the coven for you to explore further. Dante is digging up some information. I will pass that along when he gets back with me. I'm still not convinced that there isn't something more going on with Roberts, and there definitely is something with his assistant. I just don't know to what extent her services are."

"I think your assumptions on the girl are probably accurate. Is she selling more than just her blood? But Bentoncourt Roberts, he hasn't caused my people any concern until recently. And that specifically has to deal with the movement of Lucy Asher's money."

"And her inheritance, right?" Shane clarified.

Cyan nodded.

"It's no longer an inheritance if Lord Lazarus is indeed back. It's out-and-out theft." Nando didn't look up from polishing his nails.

"Don't ever call him Lord," Cyan spat. "Stupid pretentious titles. Only dictators give themselves titles."

"Please," Nando drawled. "Father is more dictator—"

With lightning speed Cyan was out of her chair. Long red claw-like nails bit into Nando's neck. "You are trying my patience, brother."

The air seemed to shimmer with tension so thick it was visible. Shane forgot that as far as daywalkers were concerned, Lucy was considered exceptionally weak. She did not possess the strength and speed that was so desired. But she also didn't exhibit the insanity that frequently accompanied the birthright.

Cyan let go of the vampire's neck and returned to her chair. She flicked a single strand of hair that had become out of place.

"If Lazarus insists on playing dead, I see no reason why we should not humor him and pretend he is. Thus Lucretia deserves to have access to her inheritance."

Shane huffed. Sure, give Lucy the millions. She had to put two kids through college.

"Bentoncourt Roberts is working with us to secure the funds for her. But I believe they already shared with you that someone else has tapped into one of the accounts in question. What I don't understand is why this unknown party doesn't simply transfer the funds. They made a sizable withdrawal at first, but recent account activity looks like they are using it like their personal checking account. A few hundred here, a thousand there. Unless they have no idea just how much they have accessed."

"Which would make no sense. If they can access the funds to transfer out, then they should be able to see the account balance." Shane finished the thought.

"Precisely."

~

Lucy ran up the last flight of stairs. She didn't have time to wait for the elevator. She was late.

She pulled open the door to the special collections room with a whoosh. And stopped in her tracks.

What was that stupid shiny bald head doing here? God, had Shane polished before this meeting? "What the hell are you doing here?" She spoke through clenched teeth.

Shane pivoted in his chair.

She glared at him.

He stood.

"Shane is informing me of some interesting activities he has been observing in the area," Cyan answered her.

"Oh, so telling her more about what I've been up to? So did you follow me to the bank? And then I bet you told her how I went and spent money like I have some and got a pedicure. And did you follow me to the grocery store where I bought a big cartful of food? Was that exciting for her to hear? Then did you tell her I drove home?" Lucy's word spit from her mouth.

Shane looked down and shook his head. Good, he looked like a kicked puppy.

"No, Lucy, I did not follow you today. I followed the people who were following you."

His words dropped like bricks from the sky. People were following her?

She sat in the closest chair. Speechless.

He turned to Cyan and said a few meaningless words. He stopped and looked at Lucy. Their eyes locked for a long, silent moment. Her heart thudded hard in her throat.

She watched as he strode from the collections room and out the door.

Slowly she turned to face Cyan. "People are following me?"

Cyan nodded. "But we will have it sorted out. This is why I asked for the favor yesterday. Do you have an answer for me?"

Lucy nodded. "I can do it. When do you want me to go? I'll have to make arrangements for my kids."

Cyan lifted a single eyebrow. "Perfect. Shane has uncovered a little situation we need to examine here in town first." She narrowed her eyes and cut Nando a side glare. He was already pouting, so either he was only seventeen, which Lucy doubted, or Cyan had already spoken sharply to him tonight.

"I think my brother is going to go make friends with some vampires who seem to be paying a long-term visit to the region."

"The hell I am." Nando rolled his eyes so hard Lucy heard it.

"Si, Nando, you are." Cyan turned her attention back to Lucy. "Your friend Shane has found a small coven of sorts outside of San Diego proper. We don't know how many there are, but he thinks it's three or four, no more than that. One of their associates was keeping an eye on you. But we don't know yet who they are. Are they associated with

Lazarus, or do they just happen to be here and mixing in the same circles as you?"

Lucy listened numbly as Cyan explained what other issues they were dealing with. Vampires were watching her.

"Cyan, why didn't Shane tell me why he was really in town?" Lucy figured Cyan knew everything.

"A misplaced sense of duty. He seemed to think that if you didn't know Lazarus was out there, it would somehow make your life a little less stressful."

Lucy nodded. "Then why did you throw him under the bus that way? He would have told me eventually."

"I wanted to see what you are made of."

Lucy was stunned silent. What was she made of?

Cyan stood, indicating their meeting was over. "I will forward some information I have to Bentoncourt. I'm advising you both to clear out those additional accounts as soon as you can."

Lucy nodded and began to follow Cyan out. She paused, then turned to face Nando. She fished a napkin and a pen from her purse. She needed to do this for Stacey. "I'm sorry, I know this is actually rude, but you're Fernando, that musician, right?"

He leveled a glare at her. The lifted eyebrow said, *Of course I am, peon.*

"Could I ask you a small favor. My daughter has your poster in her room."

"I will not come to meet your child," he sneered.

"I don't want you anywhere near her. However, I would like your autograph if that isn't too much." Lucy held up a scrap of paper and pen to him.

He rolled his eyes as if the thought of picking up the pen was exhausting.

"Nando, sign it for your fan. Remember it's her money that buys your music," Cyan chided him.

"My music is not for children," he muttered.

"Your music is for the world. You put it out there for everyone to hear. You really don't get to pick and choose who listens. But I do get to pick and choose who I let my daughter spend her money on. I don't have to tell her I met you, and I don't have to tell her you're an asshole. But"—Lucy nodded her head side to side—"if I did, she would then get online and tell everyone she knows, who will tell everyone they know, and then you can kiss your fan base goodbye. Because they will social network the hell out of you being a dickhead."

She returned his glare with a smirk.

Cyan let out a sharp laugh. "She's right, Nando. You might want to consider cultivating a better attitude."

He sneered. "She is nothing but a daywalker."

"And so am I!" Cyan snapped. Her eyes blazed with anger. Nando visibly shrank.

"Do not forget who you are, or who I am." She enunciated every word. "Lucretia Khalid could easily be in my place had her father's empire stood. And she survived on her own when it fell. Something I seriously doubt you could handle. Now sign the damned piece of paper."

Nando snatched the items from Lucy's hand and shoved them back at her when he finished.

"My daughter will love this, thank you." *But I'm still going to tell her you are a raging brat.*

16

"Hey, Mom!" Justin called out happily from the kitchen.

He had seemed so despondent the past few days, she hurried to see why his mood had changed.

"Dogstar came back."

Lucy stopped on the bottom step and glared at Shane. How dare he sit all furry and happy in the middle of her kitchen? Tail thumping the floor with her son hugging him and scratching his ears as if he were a real pet.

The animal whined and lay down, muzzle on paws.

"I think he slept on the patio last night. Didja boy? Didja?" Justin sat on the floor next to Dogstar.

She crossed her arms and wanted to yell and throw things and call him a flea-riddled mangy scumbag. But she looked at Justin and how much more improved his attitude was. Her boy was smiling.

Damn it, Shane.

"Whoa, the dog is back," Stacey announced as she entered the kitchen. "You know I almost wonder if he doesn't have another family. You know, he sleeps with them and hangs out here during the day, and some other days visa versa ."

"Don't say that," Justin whined. "He's ours."

"More like you're his. You know, Stacey, that's a very real probability. I mean, Justin, he hasn't eaten any of the dog food you've gotten him. So he's probably very well cared for." Stacey's suggestion was the perfect out for Shane. Lucy was going to push this one for all it was worth. She did not need Justin bonding any more with the fur bag. "I think I'll take him to a vet and see if he's chipped. Somebody somewhere is probably missing him."

She stared straight into Shane's eyes, hoping he would get the hint.

Stupid man wagged his tale.

Justin made a mewing noise, and his shoulders slumped. "But I really like him. And we already bought him dog bowls and stuff."

"How would you feel if your dog was out there, missing? Wouldn't you want some family who found him to try to get him home to you?"

"Okay. But do you think if he doesn't have another family, we could really keep him?"

"I'll think about it, J."

Justin's face lit up again. "Really? Thank you, thank you, thank you." He jumped up and wrapped his arms around her neck. When had he gotten so tall?

Lucy closed her eyes and held tight. She was going to break his little heart having to get rid of Dogstar. Maybe they should get a dog after all of this?

She inhaled, remembering his baby smell. Unfortunately his teenage stink wasn't as nice. "When was the last time you took a shower?"

"Mom!"

"Go take a shower and get dressed before your aunt gets here. And J, put on clean socks and clean shorts."

Stacey suppressed a giggle.

Lucy glared at her. "Oh, don't think you didn't stink at that age too. Are you packed?"

Stacey shook her head. "Not yet."

"Well, she said she would pick you up before eleven, so..." Lucy raised her eyebrows to mentally convey she needed Stacey to finish breakfast and get packed in time.

"Yeah, yeah, yeah."

"I'm going to get changed." Lucy rubbed her eyes, trying to get the extra sleep out.

Dogstar sat up expectantly.

She pointed at him. "You keep your furry ass downstairs, mister. Don't even think of coming upstairs."

She heard Stacey tell the dog, "Mom's weird."

Lucy had just finished getting dressed when the door-bell rang.

"I got it!" Stacey called out.

Lucy pulled her hair back into a ponytail, no time to deal with it any other way, and padded down the front stairs.

Jennifer stood just inside the door.

"You're early."

"Am I? I couldn't remember if we agreed on ten or eleven." Jennifer shrugged.

Lucy turned and headed back toward the kitchen. "Well, come on in. You want some tea while the kids finish getting ready?"

Justin was sitting at the table shoveling milk and cereal into his face. He had given Dogstar a large bowl of milk and cereal too. The wolf ate cleaner.

"When did you get a dog?"

"Awoot a weet." Justin tried to talk with a mouthful of food.

"He showed up a little over a week ago. While you guys are off gallivanting around, I'm going to find out if he's chipped, so he can get back to who he belongs to," Lucy said.

"I really hope he's not chipped. I want to keep him. He's awesome," Justin said without food in his mouth.

"I don't know about awesome, but he has better table manners than you do," Lucy said, reaching over and wiping a collection of soggy cereal pieces from the side of Justin's cheek. "What are your plans?"

"Well..." Jennifer took a seat across from Justin. "I'm going to buy a condo. I thought the kids could help me take a look at a few places."

"That's fabulous, Jen. You've been wanting to do that for a while."

"Yeah, I think I finally have enough saved up for a down payment. And I am so tired of rent constantly going up and up, and upstairs neighbors. I am so done with upstairs neighbors. I have scoped out some bungalow condos online, and we have an appointment with a Realtor to actually go in and look at a few today. And after that a movie and, you know, just hanging out together because we can."

"Sounds good to me."

The microwave dinged, and Lucy brought a cup of steaming tea over.

Justin put his bowl in the sink with much clattering and headed upstairs.

Jennifer watched him leave. Her gaze returned to Lucy. "Justin is going to be okay with me, but... how's Stacey? Is she still mad at me?"

"Stacey is mad at her father. I think... I want to think she knows you aren't the same person, even though you are his sister." Lucy sighed. This was all moving so fast. "Stacey still hasn't really come to terms with what he's doing. And frankly, I'm with her on this. What kind of a man unadopts his child, and turns around and gets his girlfriend pregnant before everything is finalized?"

Jennifer dropped her tea. Water splashed up and over the edge. She gasped. "Hot." She dashed over to the sink and plunged her hands under running water.

Lucy jumped and grabbed a towel from a drawer.

"You okay?" she asked as she mopped up the spilled liquid.

"Yeah, it was hot but not scalding, I don't think." She pulled one hand from the water and examined it more closely. "Just a little pink." She put her hand back.

Shane whined.

"What were you saying about Geoff? She's pregnant?" Jennifer let out a humorless laugh.

"Yeah. I don't think J knows that yet. I don't know. I'm sure he does. He and Stacey have banded together over this. I mean, I love that they have each other's backs, and for once they both know it. But I hate that this is what really brought them together. So yeah, Chrissie is pregnant." Lucy stopped talking. This hurt. She wanted to hate Geoff and be done with it. She wanted the divorce over, she wanted to know that her house was hers, and she wanted a reason Geoff had done all of this to her and her children. She needed more than he was being a selfish asshole. Why would he say the kids were her idea, try to disown them, but be perfectly accepting that his little simpering bitch was knocked up? She closed her eyes.

Shane pushed his muzzle into her hand. Instinctively she reached for the mane at his neck and dug her fingers in and held tight. Was Geoff doing all of this because Lucy wasn't capable of giving him kids with his own genetics? She clenched her lids tight and willed tears not to start.

Jennifer's arms snaked around her shoulders, and she felt the comforting press of a hug, and the hard lean against her hip from Shane.

∼

The door closed with a bang, and the house was suddenly silent. Lucy heard the clicking of Shane's claws against her floor as he trotted up to lean into her. She dug her hands into his fur and yanked.

He yelped.

"I'm still pissed at you, but I'm not going to yell at you like this. Go get changed so I can yell at your face."

Shane wiggled out of her grip, licked her fingers, and then charged up the stairs.

Lucy flopped onto the couch, crossed her arms, and glowered at nothing in particular.

Shane walked slowly down the stairs, fully dressed. He must have left an outfit in that extra closet.

Damn him. He had always been good-looking, even when he was young and skinny. But now. When had his shoulders filled out like that? At least sixteen years ago. Why hadn't she noticed? Or had she?

Shane pinched the fabric of his slacks on his thighs and hiked the front up slightly as he sat. She huffed. It was an old-man move to prevent saggy knees. He wore an old-man plaid shirt and an old-man short-sleeved cardigan. Nothing about him looked like an old man.

"I'm mad at you." She harrumphed.

"I know." He leaned forward, resting his arms on his knees. All his attention was on her.

Her toes wanted to curl up and wiggle.

"I don't want to talk to you."

"I know."

"What am I supposed to do, huh?" She threw her hands up. "My son is in love with you, and I kind of hate you right now."

Shane sat back, his eyebrows lifted.

"Dogstar." Lucy rolled her eyes and huffed. "He's in love with Dogstar. He's been moping around here for days, asking me every time I turn around if I've seen you." She stood up and gestured ineffectually, letting her arms fall to her sides. "This morning... I haven't seen that smile on his face for a while. Since before Geoff started this whole mess. And now what am I supposed to do about Dogstar? Huh?"

She didn't look at Shane. She just paced from one side of the couch to the other, thinking out loud. "I can't expect you to put on a damned collar and live as a wolf. I can't say you've run away. If I tell him you were hit by a car, he would be devastated. He needs the unconditional love I think he thinks he's getting from Dogstar. And I sure as hell am not going to keep buying you dog food. And what do we do when Stacey says you need to be fixed?"

She stopped and faced Shane. "What were you thinking? Showing up in my backyard in your wolf form. What the fuck, Shane?"

Shane cleared his throat. They stared at each other.

"Well?"

"Wanted to make sure it was my turn."

Lucy roared, threw her hands in the air, and flopped down onto the couch. She gestured at him to continue.

"I think your idea of taking Dogstar to the vet and having him checked for a chip is a good one."

She started to protest. Did he really want her to take him to a vet?

He held up his hand to stop her.

"And then, if you are serious about letting Justin have that kind of bond, you take him to the pound and find a dog."

Lucy looked away. She couldn't handle his earnest gaze.

Out of the corner of her eye she watched as Shane sat back and relaxed into the chair. "Luce, I do unconditionally love Justin, don't think that's an act. Some things are just easier to express, and get away with, in wolf form."

She felt the burning of tears in the back of her throat. She forcefully wiped at her face with the heel of her hand. She hated that she was a crier when she got mad.

"Justin gets unconditional love, and I get lies." She didn't realize she had said that out loud until Shane started speaking.

"I'm sorry. I did lie by omission. I was trying to protect you."

She glared at him. He ran his hand up and over his head. God, his head was shiny. Did he really have time after shifting to polish the pate?

"Why? From what?" she snapped.

"You've already met with Cyan del Fuego, so you know. I was trying to protect you from all of that. All the politics and all the rumors, everything you didn't want to know about."

"Why didn't you warn me?" Her voice was quiet.

"They were just rumors, Lucy. And why dredge up bad memories over something that wasn't confirmed? I wanted to be able to keep you happy in your bubble with your family. Not knowing. Not involved."

More tears welled up in her eyes. She blinked and let them spill down her cheeks. "So then why stay this time? Why not do your regular thing and pop in to say hi, then say bye before I'm used to you being around? Why now?"

The cushion dipped, and Shane's warmth was next to her. A strong arm wrapped around her shoulders and gently eased her to rest against him. His voice was a rumble through his chest.

"Because this time you're getting a divorce and you need me here. Because this time it's not just a rumor. Your father is back, and I don't want him anywhere near you."

His hand felt soothing as it stroked along her shoulders and back.

"Why didn't you tell me?"

She felt him shrug. The move shifted her around. She placed her hand against his chest for balance. She nestled into him. He felt good. She needed to feel good.

"At the time there didn't seem to be a reason to alarm you unnecessarily. You have a lot of other things on your mind. This was a burden that I didn't think you needed."

"And now?"

"Well, needed or not, you know. But yeah, things have changed. The Del Fuegos have concerns over some moneys that are shifting around, and I have some concerns about your lawyer."

Lucy pushed up out of Shane's embrace. "What about Bentoncourt?"

Shane shook his head. "I'm not sure yet. He says he's out of it. He doesn't associate with vamps anymore. And as far as I can tell, he doesn't directly. But that's not true about his assistant."

"Celine? She's normal, she's not involved, she's—"

"She's a blood whore. I watched a vampire go into her apartment. I saw the money."

"Did you see the bite marks?"

"No, but I smelled blood, and I smelled vampire. And I've certainly spent enough time around both to know what it meant."

"You sure she isn't a pet?"

"Her apartment isn't nice enough, neither is her car. If she's a pet, she has a poor keeper."

Lucy started to shift. She needed to get up. "I have to call Bentoncourt."

Shane tightened his hold on her, pulling her back to him. "No. I want to talk to him first. I want to see what else I can find out."

"I should at least tell Cyan." Shane's grip on her did not loosen.

"I already did."

"Figures." She creased her brow and looked at him. "Are you going to let me up?"

Shane shook his head and grinned slightly. "I don't think so. Look, Luce…"

He ran a knuckle over her brow to ease the tension there. "Justin isn't the only one I love unconditionally."

"You love Stacey too. I think it's great you accept them so completely."

"Lucy, Luce, shut up for a second." His lips were soft. Three tender kisses power packed with emotion that stole her breath. Her heart thudded in her throat.

"I love you." His voice was barely a whisper.

"I know; you always have. I love you too." She rested a hand against his cheek. They had always loved each other. That was never in question. But this new emotion did make her stomach flip.

"No, not like that. I mean, yes like that." He closed his eyes and started to laugh. "The English language needs better words. You are thinking of the deep affection we share. I know you have affection for me, and I know you consider me to be one of your best friends. But I have been in deep, amorous love with you for years. Lucretia"—Lucy felt her heart stop; the way her name rolled around on his tongue, it did things to her body—"you glow."

Lucy felt herself melt at his words, she—"What? When did that happen? Shane, I do not have the—Shit." She stopped talking. Lucy reached up and skimmed her fingers across his brow, over the top of his head, and around his ear. She couldn't be seeing what she was seeing.

Vampires don't see a mate glow.

17

S hane turned in a circle, nesting the blankets up. He lay down with his snout on his paws. This may not be the best idea. But if she was allowing him back into her life, he was going to take full advantage of being here.

Lucy stepped into her room and looked at him. "Do you really think *puppy* is such a good idea tonight?"

Shane thumped his tail against the bed.

"Fine. But remember I took you to the vet, and you've been picked up by your proper family. We can't do this any longer. So no more Dogstar after tonight."

She disappeared into her bathroom. When she returned, she was still dressed. He cocked his head to the side and stared at her, his tail beating against the bed slowly.

Lucy smirked and turned to face away from him.

Her ass lifted in his direction as she bent over to pick up her pajamas off the floor. If he didn't know any better, he would say she was doing it on purpose.

She stood, and placed her pajamas on the dresser. She pulled her shirt off over her head.

He breathed in heavily. He caught a glimpse of her functional panties as they bunched up over her pants' waistband. Her skin was smooth, with a small constellation of moles across her shoulder blade.

Her bra was a functional skin tone. The size and care instructions tag stuck out, and her hooks weren't lined up properly. It was the sexiest thing he had ever seen, better than red lace any day.

He barked when she reached behind her and unhooked the garment.

She covered herself with one arm and turned slightly to pick up her sleep shirt. His tongue rolled out of his mouth when he caught sight of the side of her breast.

She pulled the shirt on and dropped her pants.

Shane barked.

"Hey, no barking in the house." Lucy turned and glared at him. She pulled her jammie pants on and slid into the bed.

She reached up and ruffled the fur at his neck. "Good night." She rolled over and snicked off the light.

Shane shifted the fastest he'd ever shifted before. He put a hand on her shoulder and pulled her back to look up at him.

"What are you playing at, Lucretia? You know I can see everything as a wolf, and I remember."

She slid her hand over his chest and around his neck. She pulled him toward her. "That was the plan, idiot."

Her lips were fierce and seeking. He crushed her against his chest. He buried his hand in her hair. In Lucy's bed, pressed against her, this is where he belonged.

He growled low in his throat as his tongue reached out for hers. She tasted sweet, like perfection.

She moaned and writhed beneath him. Her legs kicked

at the blankets. Her hands felt like burning sparks of electricity wherever she touched.

Her teeth were sharp as they bit into his lip. She consumed his mouth, and he sucked her in.

He hissed when she ran her nails down his back. Her breast was pliant and soft. Her nipple tickled against his palm. His hand slid down her side. Her shape under her pajamas was perfect. Everything about kissing her was perfect.

She pushed at the elastic of her pants. He assisted and pulled her pants down past her hips. He knew she was exposed, but his mouth was too busy kissing her to let him look. Tonight, he would feel his way around, appreciating her beauty with his hands.

His hand trailed across her lower belly. Crisp, fine hair tickled his fingers as his hand caressed over her sex.

She gasped into his mouth as his fingers sought her nerve center. She was slick and wet.

He left her mouth and looked into her eyes. Their blue seemed to glow from within. She was perfection, but she really wasn't his. "I love you. I always have. I always will."

He moved his hand and wrapped it around her hip. She was married to another man.

He shouldn't be doing this. He pulled her pants back up and rolled away.

"Shane? What's wrong?"

He sat up, drawing his knees to his chest. He ran his hands up his face and over his head. "We shouldn't be doing this."

"What are you talking about?" She slid her hands up his back and across his shoulders.

Her hands on him felt so good. He twisted and laced his fingers with hers.

"You are married. And I don't want to do anything that Geoff could use against you."

Lucy let out a sharp laugh. "His girlfriend is pregnant. I don't think he is going to drag my good name as an adulteress into the mix."

"But he could."

It was hard to think with Lucy draped across his back.

"I don't care." Her hand trailed down his chest. He caught it as her fingertips started to tickle at his abs.

"I do." He kissed her. It wasn't full of passion. It was goodbye for the night. "I'm going to crash in J's room. After a long, cold shower."

He pulled a pillow with him as he climbed out of bed.

"You aren't even going to let me see you?"

He chuckled and gave her a good long view of his ass.

He stopped outside the bedroom door and leaned in. "I love you, woman, and when I do make love to you, it will be spectacular."

She called out after him, "It could be spectacular right now."

"No, Lucretia."

"I hate you!" she yelled.

"Love you too!"

"What are you doing here?" The door was barely open before the snide remark was out of Stacey's mouth.

"Well hello to you too," Shane quipped right back at her.

"Does Mom know you're in our house?" She stood with her hands on her hips, blocking the door. She jolted forward as Justin pushed on her back.

"Get your fat head out of the way. Jeez, you know, walk through the door, don't block it."

It sounded like he was throwing his sister's words right back at her. "Shane!"

"Hey, J-man, how are you?"

Justin shrugged and lugged his bag upstairs. "Hey, you wanna shoot things with me later?"

"You know it."

"Stop acting like you're his friend. You're not, you know."

"I am his friend. I thought I was your friend too." Shane wanted to reach out to her, but her barbs were up.

She turned and stormed off toward the kitchen. "Mom!"

As Stacey left, another woman followed in. She took one look at Shane and stopped. She slowly eyed him up and then down again. Slowly her hand came out and she approached for a shake. "I'm Jennifer. I think we've met."

Shane gave her a genuine grin. "We have. Shane. It's been a really long time. Nice to see you again." He pointed off after Stacey. "Did everything go all right this weekend?"

Jennifer shook her head. "Not exactly. Is Lucy around?"

"She should be right back, had to run a quick errand."

Stacey stormed back into the living room. "Where is my mother?" Tears streaked down her face.

"Hey, I'm right here." Lucy stood in the door, arms full of shopping bags.

Stacey ran to her and wrapped herself around Lucy. Lucy looked wide-eyed from Jennifer to Shane.

Shane stepped over and took the bags from Lucy. He unhooked her purse from her shoulder and carried everything to the kitchen table.

When he returned to the living room, Lucy was on the couch. Stacey was in her lap, sobs racking her back. And Jennifer stood over them stroking the girl's hair.

Whatever, whoever had caused this, Shane was ready to inflict pain. He turned and ran up the stairs, two at a time.

Justin was already shooting things up on a video game. Shane slid down into the beanbag next to him. "So what did you do this weekend?"

"Why not just ask why Stacey is being a drama queen?" The kid did not take his focus from the game. He twisted his arms and grunted, as if the controller responded to his full range of motion and not just the movements of his thumbs and fingers on buttons.

"I give. Why is your sister being—"

"'Cause our dad is an asshole, that's why."

"What happened?"

"He showed up."

Getting this kid to provide more than a few words at a time was going to be a challenge.

"I didn't think your aunt was going to facilitate visits. So this was a surprise?"

"It was a fucking ambush." Justin growled and emptied the video game's gun into a twitching zombie. "Look, are you going to keep talking? I need to focus here."

Shane understood—Justin needed to be angry and blow shit up. He didn't need to talk about things right now. It would come, and Shane would do his best to be here to listen when it happened.

He headed downstairs by way of the kitchen. Lucy had picked up some last minute items, including ice cream for tonight. He put the groceries away before joining everyone else in the living room.

Stacey was curled up with her arms around Lucy's neck. She sniffed. The shattering sobs had eased off.

Jennifer sat in the overstuffed chair across the coffee table from the couch.

Shane sat next to Lucy. He tried to pet Stacey's back. She shrugged him off.

Lucy's attention was on her daughter. He looked to Jennifer for an explanation.

"Their father stopped by unexpectedly, and uninvited, as we were getting in the car to come back." She frowned and shook her head, looking at Stacey with deep concern. "He wouldn't talk to them. Treated them like strangers."

"Why doesn't he want us anymore?" Stacey sniffed. Her tone broke Shane's heart. She sounded like she was dying inside.

"Your father is being stupid," Lucy started.

"He's getting married, and we're not invited," Stacey wailed and started sobbing again.

Shane saw red. He was ready to storm over to Geoff's girlfriend's apartment and start breaking things, like Geoff.

Lucy froze, her eyes went wide, and she shot Jennifer a terrified look.

"I'm not going either," Jennifer announced. "He showed up to hand deliver an invitation. And he made certain to point out that uninvited extras were not welcome." She glanced nervously from Shane to Lucy. "I tore it up and threw it at him. He did all of that on purpose. Putting on some kind of shit show."

"They're gonna have a baby. He's replacing us." Stacey's voice quavered.

"He's an idiot," Shane grumbled. Geoff had everything Shane, literally, wanted. The perfect woman, fantastic children, and he was throwing it all away for what? To be able to prove he was a man by getting some girl pregnant? That's not how Shane would define being a real man. But that was the example Geoff was providing to his children.

"He doesn't love us. Did he ever want me? Nobody ever wanted me."

Shane wrapped an arm around Lucy. It was the best way he could hold on to both of them. Stacey leaned her head against his shoulder. He closed his eyes and breathed in. There was no way he could take away the pain Stacey felt.

Unloved, unwanted, uncertain of who you were and what your place was in the world was a feeling too familiar to Shane. How could he tell Stacey it would get better, when it had taken years for him? And even now he still had anxiety and nightmares about it. His mother had loved him, he was certain about that. But they'd had so little time together. Stacey had Lucy. She had more love than she realized. What did it matter that she was surrounded by love right now? When that empty feeling took over, almost no quantity of love could fill the void. She didn't have the love she craved or needed.

"The day we brought you home, your father couldn't keep his eyes from you. I had to drive while he sat in the back seat and watched you in your car seat. You slept most of the way, but he was back there the entire ride home. He thought you were the most perfect little girl he had ever seen."

"Yeah?"

Lucy nodded. "Yeah. Whatever he says now, that's not how he's always thought. He loves you still. He just doesn't know how to do what he's doing without cutting all of us off. Just you wait, after Chrissie has the baby and they need a babysitter, he'll be calling you."

"I won't do it. I won't."

"No one is saying you have to. No one is saying you even have to like him anymore. What relationship you decide to have, or not, with him is fully up to you." Lucy stroked Stacey's hair back from her face.

Stacey pushed up and looked from her mother to Shane and back. "So you two made up?"

Shane nodded.

She turned back to her mother. "Did you even try to make up with Daddy?"

Lucy looked stunned.

Stacey pushed out of her mother's embrace and ran upstairs.

Lucy started after her. Shane stopped her with a grip on her arm. "Let her go cry it out of her system. You know she didn't mean that."

Lucy withered him with a glare.

"She hurts right now."

"And I don't?"

The tears he saw in her eyes broke him. He pulled her down and wrapped her into his embrace, not unlike how she had been holding Stacey.

"I didn't know he was going to show up. I swear. They had a good time right up until then. Um, Justin has been sort of obsessing over that dog. I don't see it around. So you might need to break it to him easy. He's had a pretty tough morning. They both have."

Shane nodded as Jennifer stood.

"I'm really sorry. Geoff is a total asshole." Jennifer rested a hand on Lucy's shoulder.

"He's gonna hurt. My lawyer is going to make him pay," Lucy answered through clenched teeth.

"Good. You do that. I'll see you later. Call me if you need anything."

Lucy buried her face into Shane's shoulder.

He could hold her like this forever. He did until she began adjusting her position, and her breathing evened out.

"Hey, Luce." He stroked her back. She nodded. "Why don't I take Justin for a ride? And take care of getting him a dog."

Lucy pushed back and looked at him. "Do you really think that's a good idea? I thought waiting would give him time."

"Those kids need something they can hold on to, something Geoff can't rob from them. I feel bad enough letting them latch on to Dogstar. That was really stupid of me."

Lucy's lips twitched into a smile. "It was, wasn't it? But you're gonna make good."

She rested her hand against his cheek. He leaned into the caress. He would make good the best he could.

Shane bumped Justin's arm with his knee, causing the kid to lose control of his game character.

"Hey, what gives?" Justin complained.

"Let's go for a ride. C'mon." Shane nodded his head, indicating they needed to leave. "We need to talk."

Justin whined, "You're not gonna talk to me about my dick, are you?"

Shane laughed. "The only dick we're gonna talk about is your dad. Let's go."

Justin shrugged and powered off his game.

Shane drove for about twenty minutes in silence before Justin started talking.

"So I thought you and Mom broke up."

"We just had an argument, man. It happens." Shane suppressed a smile. It was good that Justin had started talking. All his informal therapy sessions with Melinda had taught him that much.

182 | LULU M SYLVIAN

"But you didn't come back. I didn't think you were gonna."

"J-man, me and your mom go way back. And I always come back around. Always. You're my family. You, Stacey, your mom, a little argument isn't going to drive me away for very long."

"Then why is Dad divorcing us? We're his family, and he's just walking away from us. He's being mean about it too."

Justin turned and stared out the window. He shrugged and adjusted in his seat. Shane figured he was wiping at tears. This was all too much for the kid to handle. He didn't need to hear what Shane thought of the man. He didn't deserve to be their father. He didn't deserve their tears.

"Dogstar wasn't there when we got back. Mom took him to the vet, huh?"

"Yeah, J-man. She got him back home where he belongs." Shane felt that was about right. He was with them where he belonged.

They pulled into a parking lot in front of a stucco building with a low tile roof. Shane cut the engine off.

"What are we doing here?" Justin looked eagerly from the building to Shane.

"Well, your mom thought that maybe..." Shane shrugged.

"I can get a dog?"

Shane nodded.

"Really?"

"Really."

Justin ran inside the Humane Society office, leaving Shane to follow him.

The house smelled like garlic and onions when they got home.

"Stacey, get down here!" Justin yelled as soon as they walked in the door.

Lucy came in to the living room first. She looked around, and her eyes fell on a carrier case. "I thought you were going to bring home a dog, not a cat."

"Cats," Shane corrected.

"You got cats?" Stacey asked as she walked down the stairs.

She went straight to the carrier and peeked inside. She lifted one black-and-white cat out. The animal shivered as she sat and cooed at it, stroking its fur. Justin lifted out a second cat, this one whiter with black markings. The kids sat and held their new charges.

Lucy pulled Shane aside. "What have you done?"

"We got a beautiful little girl," Shane practically purred. "She looks like an Australian shepherd. It was love at first sight. They let Justin meet a few dogs, but she crawled right in his lap. She's getting fixed in the morning, and we'll pick her up after school. The cats were Justin's idea. He thought Stacey would like the cats."

Lucy slid into his arms. She felt so right.

"Justin was right, she's gonna love those cats."

18

L ucy and the kids thought Shane was returning to his hotel room for the night. He hated it at the hotel. He knew he couldn't sleep with Lucy; but he felt that she was safer with him under the same roof.

He let the car cruise through Roberts's neighborhood. As expected, the lawyer could be seen through the window watching TV, one of his fluffy dogs curled up on his lap.

He contemplated cruising past the coven he'd located, but Cyan had told him she would focus on that little problem, if he could focus on what their involvement with Bentoncourt's assistant was.

Celine's car wasn't in her carport when he pulled into her apartment complex.

He backed his car into the same spot in guest parking. He had a perfect vantage point for when she returned.

He didn't pay any attention to the bright red SUV until it slid into her spot. Celine got out, followed by the man from the food cart and his golden retriever.

Shane's phone rang.

"Whatcha got for me?" he asked.

"I have all kinds of fun information you aren't going to like," Dante announced.

Shane listened to what Dante had to tell him. He ran a hand over his face and back over his scalp. This wasn't the best news that Dante could be giving him.

Shane was smart and could do basic math. He could easily put two and two together.

Those houses were owned by an agency out of Vegas.

Vegas. He really did not want to go back there.

"And you've already told all of this to Cyan?"

"And Morgan. Conference call. Thought you might appreciate being kept in the loop. Cyan apparently has someone in Vegas already. So yeah."

"Thanks, man, I appreciate the intel."

He ended the call. Vegas. That didn't necessarily provide a damning connection, but it was too close for his personal comfort.

He waited several hours. Shane was about to give up on learning anything informative by watching Celine's apartment. Then the sleek Lexis pulled in and out got the slick-suited vampire.

Shane sat up. This was going to be interesting. He ventured out of his car after the door to Celine's apartment closed. He didn't need to be closer than the landing below to hear there was a serious shouting match going on inside.

The door slammed and out came the human boyfriend and the dog. When he reached the ground floor, he began cussing. "Shit, shit, shit, fucking shit!"

"Hey, buddy, you okay there?" Shane asked

"Stupid bitch has been fucking some other guy, and she kicked me out."

"Yeah, we all heard," Shane said. He reached down and ruffled the dog's ears. He watched as the guy angrily fussed with his phone. "Damn it!" He started to throw his phone but stopped short of actually hurling it to the ground.

"You need help?" Shane lounged against the stairs as if he lived in one of the ground floor apartments.

"I can't get a stupid ride because I have Candy with me. None of the drivers out tonight are willing to allow a dog in their cars."

"Don't you have a car here?"

He blew air out of his mouth. "No, she was supposed to take me to work in the morning, home after that."

Shane wanted to stay and see what he could find out here, but on the other hand, this young man needed a ride, and he was plenty chatty. It was as if a wealth of information had been dropped into his lap. He just needed to listen.

"Hey, I'm headed out. Can I give you a lift?"

"Really? Let me take Candy for a quick walk. I'll be right back." He whistled for his dog to follow and headed out toward an area with trees and ground cover.

Shane pulled the car around, and his new source of information climbed in with his dog.

"So where to?"

"Chula Vista if that's okay."

"That's a bit of a hike," Shane commented.

"Well rent is a helluva lot cheaper. Celine used to live there too, but she got a big raise at work, and now thinks she has all kinds of money."

"Oh yeah?" Shane hoped this guy would continue to talk without too much prompting. "You've been together long?"

"About two years maybe. And in the past few months, she's kind of been turning into a real bitch. You know how they say money changes a person?"

Shane made noises of confirmation.

"She moved over here four months ago, and is paying

almost five hundred more for the same sized apartment. That's not an improvement. And she just got a new car, and was complaining about Candy getting fur all over the back seat. If the dog in the car was going to be a problem, why insist on driving? I could have followed her over just as easily. And now"—he threw his hands up—"she's seeing some other guy. And instead of breaking up like normal people, she just let's him come over and expects me to think it's no big deal. Fuck that noise. I'm dumping all her shit that's left in my apartment on her boss's doorstep."

"You know where she works?"

"Yeah, she works for some old gay guy with fussy little dogs. Hey, turn here. It's over this way."

Shane followed his directions.

By the time he pulled into the apartment complex where the boyfriend and Candy lived, he knew that Celine's newfound wealth seemed to coincide with when she started seeing the new guy, and was not in fact a raise. This timetable put the vampires in the area mid- to late summer.

He eased his car into late-night traffic and headed toward his hotel. He would be able to get a few hours of sleep in before he reintroduced himself to Bentoncourt Roberts in the morning.

"I wouldn't have recognized you had we met on the street," Roberts announced as he sat across his desk from Shane. "I understand you have been keeping an eye on Lucy."

Shane shifted in his seat. He grunted a positive response.

"Well, she doesn't need your assistance anymore. She now has friends in some very high places. I'm certain you are more than aware of who I am referring to."

Shane let out a sharp laugh. "Who do you think sent me down here to begin with? Look, Roberts, we're both here because we care for Lucy. It's not some competition. You don't need to strong-arm me. I will do whatever is in Lucy's best interests. So you can have your assistant stop following her.

"I've even been keeping my eye out on you, and something is not adding up. That's what I hope you can answer." Shane leveled his gaze on the lawyer. He shifted his gaze to the office door. He stood and closed it.

"Celine? I don't have her following Lucy. What an absurd thing to suggest." Roberts huffed.

"How well do you know your assistant?"

"She's worked for me for several years. Why?"

"When was the last time you gave her a raise?"

"I pay her very well. How is this any of your business? What do you mean, she is following Lucretia?"

"I mean, I spotted her sitting in a car outside of Lucy's house, so I followed her. Are you aware that your assistant is a blood whore?" Shane removed an envelope from his back pocket. He tossed the printouts he had made from his phone camera. The money, the car, the man in the suit.

Roberts moved slowly, picking up one photo at a time. He shook his head as he looked over the images of the vampire.

"Are you certain?" He looked up at Shane.

"I couldn't capture the smell on my phone, not that daywalkers can smell it. Do you know him?"

"This is speculative, inadmissible." Roberts dropped the images.

"I'm not planning on taking it to court. I want to know who she's feeding. I want to know how she was introduced into their circle. I want to know what they have to do with Lucy, and what they have to do with Lazarus.

"Celine broke up with her boyfriend last night. According to him, she's had a bit of a personality change, and a change in finances starting about four months ago."

"I don't see how…" The lawyer trailed off.

"We only started being aware that Lazarus was trying to make some kind of a comeback this past year. At first it was rumors. Next it was sightings. He dropped completely off the radar over the summer. We figured he was regrouping. This would indicate that maybe he has put some people in place to monitor some old friends of his," Shane explained.

"Celine has worked for me longer than that. She's not a spy they put here to keep an eye on me. No one could have predicted that Lucretia would call me about a divorce. That's ridiculous."

"I agree. I don't think she worked for them before she started working for you. But after, if she was financially motivated, they could have tempted her. Look, you aren't exactly in hiding. You just aren't part of that life anymore. Maybe they have been monitoring your activities for longer. Maybe they have nothing to do with Lazarus, and it's a coincidence they're from Las Vegas. But we know they have nothing to do with the Del Fuegos either, and that's concerning.

"I understand that movement on Lazarus's accounts didn't start happening until you began digging around for Lucy. Seeing what kind of money she had access to. And that's a red flag in my book."

Roberts shuffled in his chair. He opened his laptop and began typing. The printer next to his desk whirred to life. He studied the printout before sliding it across his desk to Shane.

"You're right. Here is an overview of the account histories over the past year. You can see only interest deposits until a few weeks ago, I don't think we need to go back further than that."

Shane looked at the spreadsheet.

The numbers meant nothing to him, only that it was a lot of money. A lot of it.

"This one account seems to be getting used," he pointed out as he handed the page back.

"Yes, that's the one they have managed to gain access to. Cyan and her team are doing the groundwork to help us get into the other accounts on behalf of Lucretia."

Shane nodded. The accounts were locked up pretty tight from what Lucy had told him.

"But the timing doesn't match up for them to have Celine spy on me. You say they have been paying her for months. Lucy has only been a client for a few weeks. That makes no sense."

"Sure it does. That's a lot of money. You had access to the account information when you worked for Lazarus. Did Lazarus know that kind of information? Would he have bothered?"

Roberts chuckled. "That man had people to know for him. Social Security numbers, birthdates, he did not track records. He would not have known his own account numbers. That's why he kept minions. What he had was a very strong ability to get into people's heads and convince them to do what he wanted. And when he could no longer control those around him, he lost control completely."

"Is that when Marat swept in?"

"I would think you of all people would have taken an active interest in Lazarus's downfall. Yes, that's when Marat seized control."

"Look," Shane practically growled. This was the part of his past he wanted dead and gone. The sheer fact that it wasn't dead gave him night sweats and panic attacks. "By the time all of that went down, I was as far away from anything or anyone that resembled a vampire as I could get. Was I pleased when I found out Lazarus was gone? Yes. Did I care that Marat came in and was ten times worse? No. I was gone. I was out of there. Lucy was out of there. We were safe and living like normal people. I didn't care."

"But you care now."

"I care now because this is a threat against Lucy. Be clear on that. I have no love for the Del Fuegos. My boss works with them, and that is why I work for them. No other reason. I am here for Lucy, and Lucy only. As long as there is any potential threat against her or those kids, I will stand between them and anyone who wants to cause them harm."

Shane had stood at some point and leaned heavily on his fists, bringing his face closer to Roberts's.

"So this divorce must be driving you crazy?"

"I'm just waiting for an excuse to beat Geoffrey into the ground."

"Hi, baby," Shane called out as he walked into the house. It felt like coming home.

He approached Lucy, who worked in front of her large wood jewelry-making table. She called it her bench. He stood behind her and watched as she used a small jigsaw tool to cut a sheet of copper.

She tilted back until her head rested on his stomach and she looked up at him.

"I missed you last night." Lucy sighed at him.

"Well, I can't very well play puppy anymore. You got rid of Dogstar, remember." He ran his hands up and down her arms. If he leaned down, he could kiss her. The problem with that was he wouldn't want to stop.

"I wasn't thinking puppy. I was thinking making us a little more official. You know, have you move in here. Live with us. With me." Her eyebrows lifted, conveying more than one meaning.

Shane sighed. He wanted nothing more than to live with Lucy, and everything that came with that.

"What are the kids going to say with you having a live-in boyfriend, while their dad is off with a new live-in girlfriend?"

Lucy righted her neck and returned to sawing, following a black outline she had made. "You can ask them. They'll be home in a minute." She stopped moving and tilted her head to the side. "Bus."

She put her work down and spun to face Shane. "I'll go get something started for dinner, and you can have a little chat with my kids. How does that sound?"

Shane sat awkwardly across from Justin and Stacey. He'd faced tougher adversaries before, yet this confrontation made him want to throw up. If they said no, his future would be bleak—very very bleak.

"I thought you were already dating Mom?" Stacey asked, a little confused. "But aren't you like her brother?"

"That's like me wanting to date Stace. That's gross, ew," Justin added.

"Not exactly. We aren't related. Your mom and I were not raised together as brother and sister, just together. We have been friends for a very long time. I've only ever wanted to protect her. I want to protect this family. And that includes dating your mother."

"Isn't she older than you?"

"Age is irrelevant. Besides, you'll find that as you get older, age isn't nearly as big of a deal as it is now," Shane explained.

"Does this mean you're going to beat up Dad?"

Shane chuckled. He wanted nothing more than to land a bone-crunching punch to the middle of Geoff's face. "Not unless he jumps me first. I've already promised your mom that I won't beat him up."

"But you want to," Justin stated.

Shane did not hide his nod.

"I thought you were friends with our dad," Stacey added.

"I liked your dad just fine as long as he treated you and your mother well. I am fully taking sides in this divorce, and I am on your side," Shane explained.

"So will you be mad at me if I still like my dad?"

Stacey looked with horror at her brother. "How can you? Traitor!"

"I was just asking a question," Justin whined. Shane felt certain the boy would want a relationship with his father if the man ever came back around and stopped being evil toward them.

Shane looked at Justin thoughtfully. Children were always the unwilling victims when their adults went to battle. "I'm still going to be your friend, no matter who your other friends are. That includes your dad. But if you start in on your mom, we will have words."

"So what if Mom says no?" Justin asked.

"We are already sort of dating, nothing official yet. She's not going to say no, but if she did, I go back to being family friend and unofficial uncle."

"And what if we say no?" Stacey asked.

"Then we keep this between us, and your mom and I

stay at the sort-of-dating phase and nothing gets serious until you're over eighteen and out of the house. Me dating your mom affects all of us in this room. And I respect you enough to include you in this decision. If it's not something you can handle, then I won't pursue the issue." Shane looked from Justin to Stacey. "Discuss this amongst yourselves for a few minutes; then you let me know." He stood, leaving them in the living room.

Lucy leaned on the kitchen counter, her eyebrows raised. "How did it go?"

Shane slid his arms around her hips and pressed against her. "Our fate is in their hands."

Lucy rested her head against his broad chest. "They like you. I'm sure they won't object. Besides, if they think you'll make me happy, I'm sure they'll say yes."

"Do I make you happy, Lucretia?" Shane looked down into her face. She glowed. Shane blinked. He would never get used to the thrill of seeing that radiance coming from her skin. He didn't want to; he wanted to always be thrilled by looking at her.

Lucy rested her cheek next to her hand on his chest.

"You have always made me happy, Shane. I just never realized how happy before."

A cough from the doorway called their attention.

They turned to see the two kids smirking.

"Mom?" Justin asked tentatively.

Stacey stifled a giggle.

"You look like you're gonna say yes to what Shane asked you. But I think you should know I'm going to date him no matter what you decided. I deserve to be happy," Lucy said.

"We want you to be happy," Stacey said.

"And we like Shane. It would be cool to know he's gonna be around," Justin added.

Lucy backed up and opened her arms toward her children, inviting them in for a group hug.

Shane hadn't realized how much he had been clenching all his muscles. As Justin's arm came around him, Shane felt his entire body relax and fill with love. The woman he loved was in his arms. Her children, whom he'd always loved, were embracing him. This was what having a family was supposed to feel like. He loved them all so much, and this was just the beginning of their relationship. He couldn't imagine loving the three of them more than he did right now.

Justin sniffed and squirmed. "Can we go get my dog now?"

19

S hane had officially lived in her house for less than twenty-four hours, and he was already pissing her off. They had actually argued over whether or not he would sleep in her bed before the divorce was finalized. His sense of duty to not compromise her honor was going to be the end of their relationship before they even got it off the ground.

They compromised with a locked bedroom door and her curling up against a large wolf. A night of puppy when she wanted man was one night too many.

She didn't care if Geoff knew she was sleeping with Shane. She actually kind of wanted him to know that she was. She wanted him to squirm with the thought that she'd recovered from his betrayal and had moved on to someone she knew she could always count on. Someone younger, taller, with broader shoulders and more muscles than Geoff would ever have.

She wanted revenge sex with Shane. But she also wanted him to touch her because she was about to burst with love, lust, and raw need.

She stood outside the bathroom door until the shower stopped.

"Get out, Lucy," Shane barked.

"No. My house, my bathroom," Lucy all but purred. She took in Shane with her eyes. She had hoped to catch him completely nude, fresh from the shower, covered in drops of water. Instead she opened the door as Shane finished wrapping the white towel around his hips. The contrast in color from the light towel emphasized his dark coloring and his muscular form. The contouring in the muscles around his hips and lower abdomen seemed artistically unreal. Lucy licked her lower lip. She could imagine licking the droplets of water from him.

Shane turned, exposing his muscular back to her. She closed her eyes and silently groaned. She wanted him, but his resistance was strong. Stubborn man.

Shane sighed heavily, leaning into the counter as if it held him up. Opening her eyes, Lucy saw his knuckles turn dark, then almost white as he gripped the countertop.

"Don't break my bathroom, baby."

"Lucy, Luce. You can't be in here." Shane's voice sounded shaky.

"Why not, baby?" She leaned into his back.

Shane arched away from her.

"You aren't divorced yet, and I'm not going to do anything to jeopardize your case."

"Shane." Lucy ran her hands up his back. The water let her fingers glide across his skin.

Shane sucked in a breath.

"Lucretia. You know I can't touch you."

"Can't or won't?" She pressed against his back, wrapping her hands around him to hold him in place. "Are you rejecting me?"

Shane twisted in her grasp. Deliberately placed his hands back on the counter behind him. "I'm postponing you, Lucy. I won't touch you until you can be mine free and clear. Geoff can pull you into court during the waiting period. He can extend this whole mess. And I'm not going to give him any ammunition to use against you. They aren't going to be able to call me in for a disposition and ask me if I'm your lover, and get a positive answer. And…"

"And I'm not asking you to perjure yourself. I doubt Geoff will play the cheating wife card, not when he's already gotten that girl pregnant. So…" Lucy ran her fingertips up and down Shane's chest, tracing circles around a nipple. His skin felt smooth and perfect. She smiled wickedly as it pearled up under her touch.

"You're not going to touch me. You will be able to honestly say that you did not touch me in a sexual manner." Lucy pulled the towel from Shane's hips.

His cock sprang out at her as if it wanted to touch her and also thought Shane was being stupid. She blatantly stared at his engorged manhood. "That's just lovely. No wonder you were hiding it." She let out a low growl-like laugh.

"This one"—she pulled out an anatomically correct vibrator she had tucked into her waistband at her back— "isn't nearly as nice, especially now that I know what you've been packing. And it was my favorite one too." Lucy licked her lips and eyed Shane with a desire to consume him. She wanted him to touch her, could feel the need in her core. Hopefully her plan to touch him, and have him watch while she pleasured herself would take the edge off her need. She twisted the base of the vibrator. A low hum filled the bathroom.

"Lucy, what are you doing?" Shane's voice was rough with withheld passion.

She ran the vibrator up the base of his shaft.

"Ahh, Lucretia." His head fell back, and his breathing increased.

"I'm touching you. You have the willpower of the most stubborn bull I've ever encountered. You won't touch me. I get it. Suddenly it's something that I find very sexy. Very sexy."

She ran the vibrator over his shaft again. "I won't cause any part of you to penetrate any part of me. They won't be able to get you to confess to anything more than heavy making out. However, I intend on touching you in a very sexual manner, and I intend on touching myself in one as well, while you watch."

Lucy watched the Adam's apple in Shane's throat jump as he swallowed hard. "You're a cruel woman, Lucretia."

She laughed as she ran the phallus-shaped vibrator between her breasts.

"I think it's a toss-up as to whom is the cruel one. Me for teasing you, or you for not touching me."

"This is torture, Luce."

"But you aren't saying no. Are you? 'Cause I'll walk away, taking my toy with me, leaving you to yourself if you tell me to." *Please don't say no, Shane, I need to touch you even if you can't.* Lucy closed her eyes, took a deep breath, and then faced Shane again. "Are you saying no?"

Shane shook his head. "I know I should, but God help me, I'm not. Rules first."

Lucy nodded in agreement.

"No penetration of either party by either party, toys included."

"Amendment, I will not penetrate you with my toy, and I

will not cause you to penetrate me. I fully retain the right of penetration by toy at my own hand." Lucy continued to nod.

"You've been hanging out with a lawyer too much. Okay, my hands do not touch you."

"Keep them right where they are, on the counter," Lucy added.

"No kissing," Shane included.

"Why no kissing?"

"Because if I kiss you, and you're right here, and we're both naked, I will lose control."

"Fine, I won't kiss you on the mouth."

"Do I need to amend that rule to no mouths? I think I will. No mouths."

"I can accept no mouths since you are willing to play." Lucy turned the vibrator off and set it on the counter next to Shane. She let her breasts brush against his arm. "I had better get prepared."

She stepped back from him so he could watch as she peeled her clothes off. The bra and panties she had changed into while planning on seducing him were thin nude tone with panels of black lace.

Shane growled low in his throat in appreciation.

Lucy ran her breasts across his arm again as she reached for the vibrator.

She twisted it on. She ran the device down the center of Shane's chest and over his nipples.

"See, I'm not even touching you," she whispered.

She then ran the vibrator over her chest, letting it toy with her nipples through the thin fabric of her bra.

"Does that feel as good as it looks?" Shane asked.

Lucy nodded. "Where else should I put it?" she asked.

"Will you put it on your naked flesh? I want to see you, Lucy." He sounded hoarse and out of breath.

Lucy leaned forward, lowering one cup of her bra, bringing her breast out. "Like this?"

"That will work for now."

Lucy ran the vibrator directly over her exposed nipple. She hissed as it tickled. She kept her eyes on Shane. His hungry gaze made this game well worthwhile.

She eased closer to him, pressing her leg against his before guiding her exposed breast across his skin.

"That works even better." He groaned.

Lucy stepped back and ran the vibrator over the skin on Shane's torso where her breast had just caressed.

She turned and brushed her ass against his erection. "Hmmm, that feels nice." She rubbed, lifting so his shaft grazed the fabric of her panties by her core. "Hmmm, that feels even better." Lucy began pulsing her ass against Shane's cock. He hissed at the contact. She reached down and ran the vibrator over her core from the front, brushing it against Shane. His skin felt so good, slick and warm. He was rock-hard, prodding against her underwear. It would be so easy to slip the panties aside and let him ease in. But no penetration, she had agreed. At least no penetration by Shane.

She straddled Shane's leg, then began pulsing up and down along his hard, muscular thigh. As she thrust her hips, she ran the vibrator over Shane's nipples.

She delighted as she watched his thick erection jump and throb with need. Lucy changed her position again. "I think I liked this angle the best." She placed her ass against his cock again and began her gyrations. Having Shane so close to her entrance felt so good. She leaned back against him and let her body throb and hum. She wanted him to reach up and cup her breast. She wanted him to roll her nipples between his fingers and lips. But he wouldn't. So she would have him the only way she could right now.

She reached down and slid her panties to the side. The vibrator followed. She guided it in a circular motion around her clit. She pretended it was Shane. She had his body against her back, and his smell in her nose. She slid the vibrator in and began pulsing against it. Heavy breaths caressed her neck as Shane rocked against her backside. Matching her strokes with the motion of his hips. It was Shane making love to her, his voice, his sounds were in her ear, his breathing on her skin.

Lucy bit back a loud cry as her muscles began to quake and an orgasm took over control.

"Did that work for you, baby?" His voice was soothing and gentle, as if he was the one to have physically given her that pleasure.

Lucy relaxed against him. "It worked. Now it's your turn."

She pushed away from Shane, the vibrator still in her hand, wet with her passion. She ran it over Shane's shaft.

"This looks almost painful with need," she purred.

"It could use some assistance. Hands-on assistance," Shane teased.

Lucy twisted the vibrator off and tossed it to the counter.

Pressing her breasts against his arm again, Lucy leaned across Shane for a bottle of lotion. She picked up his container of cocoa butter. She sniffed at it as she twirled the top off. "No wonder you smell so good." Rubbing her hands together, she warmed the lotion before caressing him.

He was hot and hard. She glided her hands from base to tip, cupping his balls—ball, singular. She had never realized they had fully removed one. She hadn't exactly examined him when they were younger. She probably had noticed when he was in wolf form, but the connection to what damage had been done to him and how he would feel under her touch had never occurred to her. It was pulled tight against his body. She ran her hand lightly down the scarring on his inner thigh. She had done that to him, yet he was here now, letting her do this.

She ran her hand up the base of his shaft. It throbbed. "Oh," she said as she realized Shane was ready for her.

"This won't take long. You're touching me. That's more than enough to get me going."

"Shane." Lucy paused in the rhythmic stroking.

"Don't stop," he groaned. "Not yet." He thrust his hips against her hands as she worked his cock. Shane growled as he released across Lucy's breasts.

She stepped back, laughing. "I guess that worked for you too." She trailed her fingers through the come on her breasts and licked her fingertips.

"That is the sexiest thing ever." Shane gasped for breath between sentences. "Me on your breasts. Damn, woman. Can I not touch you again?" His hands still held on to the counter with a firm grip.

"I love you, baby. You thought that was good, just wait until you touch me back." Lucy dropped her panties and stepped into the shower.

"I think about it every day, Lucy. Forty-nine days to go, just so you know I am counting down." Shane made noises that sounded like he was cleaning himself and pulling on pants.

"Lucy, I've been thinking about this. And I've waited for you this long. Let's not do it until we're married."

The shower door swung open with a bang. "What?"

"I don't want to have proper sex with you until we're married," Shane repeated.

"You're going to make me wait for what?" Lucy wasn't sure what she was hearing, what was the man asking her?

"I'm saying I want to marry you, baby. The day after the divorce is cleared. You, me, justice of the peace."

"Nope, we're having a big wedding. I did the judge one once. You want to marry me. I get a big, obnoxious white wedding." Lucy pulled the door shut and ducked her head back under the water. She waited.

The door flew open again. Shane stepped in with her. His arms wrapped around her, and his lips claimed hers in a scorching kiss. He had been right. If they had both been naked with a kiss like that, penetration would have happened. They were safe to kiss now, both satiated and clothing between them.

20

Shane leaned on the doorjamb and looked at Lucy. She smiled at him, and with the added mate aura, she was dazzling. Even folding laundry, she was the most beautiful woman. This living-together thing might not be the best idea, now that he actually thought about it. Especially since he, for some dumb-ass reason, decided that not having sex with her before the divorce was final was the thing to do.

She was trying him at every turn. And he was sore put to withstand her much longer.

She moved one of the cats and picked up the folded stack of laundry and placed it into a case he hadn't noticed, blocked from his view by blankets on the unmade bed.

"It's only been two days, Luce. Are you leaving me already?" he teased.

She sighed heavily. "I'll be back. It should only be for a day or two tops."

He stepped into the bedroom and spun her around to face him. "What?" His grip was probably harder than he intended.

She shrugged her arm away from his grip.

"Chill. I'm going to Las Vegas for a couple of days."

Shane's heart fell to the floor. His head was full of cotton; sound wasn't getting through. Vegas. She had escaped. Hell, her finally getting out of that place had been significantly more important to him than his own successful attempt at running away. He sat, jostling the bed and knocking over a stack of towels waiting to be put in the hall closet.

"Why?" The cat head butted against his arm. He wanted to be mad, but the visceral pain in his chest left him more stunned than anything. He picked the cat up and put it on the floor.

"Cyan wants me there. I know the area. I know some of the places he could hide on the old property."

"Would Lazarus really go back to the compound? I thought the mansion had been destroyed?" Shane stared at her. "Cyan has people there. You don't need to do this."

"The property hasn't been touched. It's a ruin, but it's still there. I know that place better than most. There was an entire labyrinth of structures underground that may still be in use. I'm going to help her people navigate."

He stood, crossed the room in a few long strides and pulled his own bag from the closet. "Then I'm going with you."

"No, baby, I need you here to take care of the kids."

"They can go to Jen's."

Lucy shook her head. Her touch was light as it ran up his arm and caught on his shoulder. She pulled him away from his case, and then she moved into the space. Instinctively Shane wrapped his arms around her.

"Shane, I need you here to take care of my children and

their pets. We can't haul all of them over to Jen's apartment. Look, I agreed to do a job for Cyan. I can't back out. I already said I would go."

Shane stepped back and dropped his arms. "Why? What were you thinking? That's not smart, Lucy. You don't owe her anything. Once she gets her claws into you, then she'll ask another favor, and another. I thought you wanted to stay out from under the rule of a coven?" Frustrated, he gestured at her before running his hand over his face and up and back over his scalp.

"I know, I know. But this is something I need to do. I just up and left. And now I find out my father isn't dead."

"He should have been dead to you all those years ago," he growled.

"Yes, but he isn't, is he? And he's my father. Was my father once. I owe it—"

"Don't you dare say you owe it to him to go find out," Shane snarled. He could feel the wolf surge through his brow.

"I owe it to me. I need some closure, some reassurance that part of my life is over. Cyan thinks that anyone lingering around might talk to me if I can convince them I'm there to offer support. Tell me where he is. Hell, maybe he is even there."

"And if he is? Lucy you don't have it in you to kill him, do you? You aren't strong enough to fend off an attack."

She shook her head. "No. But I will hand him over." She sighed. "I can hand him over. Shane, he hurt so many people. He literally tortured you. That kind of person doesn't need to be out there in the world. I can hand him over."

She was convincing herself.

"I'm coming with you." He would at least be able protect her.

"No. you can't." Her eyes blazed. He had never seen that flash of passion before, almost like she had wolf eyes. "It will destroy you."

"My psyche isn't so damaged that I can't go back there to keep you safe."

"But I need you to stay with the kids. I need you to be here taking care of them if anything happens to me." Her tone pleaded.

"The kids will be fine with Jennifer. I'm coming with you. Like it or not."

Lucy huffed. Shane crossed his arms. He should be glaring at her, but a smile pulled at his lips. She was a fighter. She hated it, she avoided it, but when it was time to take action, she did with a ferocity that made him proud.

"I know she loves the kids, but if anything happens to me, I want you..." She blinked a few times. A shimmer of tears reflected back at him. "I need to change my will, and I wanted to ask if you would be interested in..." She paused again. "I don't want Stacey to become an emancipated youth. I need to know someone is willing to fight for her. Would you be willing to be their guardian, or split custody with Jen if something happens?"

Lucy stared at him. There was so much she was having to deal with, and she felt she needed to ask if he would do this.

Shane grinned. Hell yes, he would take care of the kids. "Of course. Put my name down next to Jen's. For now."

"What do you mean for now?"

"I mean for now. Like how you are married, *for now*. And at some point you won't be married. At some point Geoffrey is going to relinquish custody—"

"Not if I can help it."

"Lucy, let him. I want the kids. I'm marrying into this family."

"You've already been part of this family the entire time."

Shane sighed heavily. "You want them to know someone is willing to fight for them. I don't want to be some guy who married their mom. I want to be the guy who also fought for them."

Lucy wiped a tear as it traced down her cheek. "Your timing sucks. You know that. Now is not the time to be all romantic and mushy." She slid her arms around his waist and rested her face against his chest.

His heart thudded. His tail would be wagging if he were in his other form.

"Who's being mushy? You're the one crying." Shane scooped a finger under her chin and lifted her face so he could look into her eyes.

"Wanting to adopt the kids is probably the most romantic thing I've ever heard."

"Hardly. It's selfish as hell. This way Stacey can never pull a"—he pitched his voice to mimic the teen—"'you can't tell me what to do, you aren't my father.'" He let his voice return to normal and chuckled. "I would work that angle so damn hard, and you know it."

"And Justin?"

"I don't need to be his father to teach him how to be a man, but it would sure be great to pull out the whole 'I'm your father; let's talk about your dick' conversations. His head would explode."

"You just want to adopt my kids to mess with them." She smiled and thumped him on the chest. "You're messing with me, aren't you?"

He shrugged. "I don't have to be Justin's father to have

those 'how to be responsible with your dick' talks. And Stacey will fight me whether I'm her father on a piece of paper or not. But I do want them to know they are loved, they are wanted."

"See, that's why you are going to stay and take care of them."

"No, that's why I'm coming with, so that they have you returning to them."

A car beeped out front. Luna, Justin's new dog, barked.

"That's my car. No, Shane, you stay. I'll call you as soon as I get there." She slammed her case closed and hauled it off the bed.

Shane took the case easily from her.

"I don't like this." He followed her downstairs and out the front door.

The breath Lucy took lifted her shoulders. She shuddered letting it out. "I love you. I have to go, Shane. I have to."

She kissed him lightly and took the case from him. She shoved it into the back seat before she sat in the car. She began to close the door and then stopped.

"Shane. I need to find out who I really am. I need to know why you glow."

Shane stood in stunned silence as she closed the door and the car took off.

Had Lucy just said he glowed? Vampires don't have a mate glow. Hell, vampires don't have mates. That was a wolf trait, and as far as he was aware, limited to his kind.

He ran back upstairs and finished packing his own bag.

He straightened the bedroom and put the folded towels away.

The kids would be home soon. He needed to make arrangements.

"What do you mean, Mom took off without telling us?" Stacey glared at Shane as if he had done more than deliver the news.

"She had an opportunity, and she thought it would be good to get away. She's been really stressed by this whole divorce. So a few days seemed like a good idea."

"And you don't think it is?" She gave him a side-eye, waiting for him to say anything she could start yelling about.

"I was as surprised as you are. And no, I don't exactly think it is."

"If you just want to go off and have a weekend together, why don't you just say so? Why all this"—she waved her finger around in a circle—"pretending it's something else?"

Shane breathed slowly through his nose. His nostrils flared. This kid should grow up to be a lawyer.

"You're mother sprang this on me as well. Your aunt is going to come stay with you guys, and I'm going to drive out and find her."

Stacey rolled her eyes at him. "Have you ever been to Vegas?" Her tone was trying his patience.

"I grew up in Las Vegas. I am more than familiar with it, Stacey. I also have a pretty good idea where to go look for your mom. I'm not taking a blind shot in the dark."

Stacey shrank under his return glare. "She's not in trouble, is she?"

He shook his head. "No, she's not in any kind of trouble. And she's not running away from you or your brother. But I do think that her being alone isn't such a good idea. I'm not lying to you. I'm not going to pretend this is something other than it is. If that were the case, I'd tell you this was a jewelry show or something, and that I was suddenly called back to Sonoma for something with my boss."

Shane crossed his arms and continued to lean on the kitchen counter. Stacey moved back and forth, filling food and water bowls for their new pets. She grabbed a bag of cat treats and crinkled it. The two cats scurried into the kitchen. They twined around her legs in front of their food bowls, mewing until she gave them each a head scratch.

"So you expect me to tell Justin why you left, after Mom left you in charge of us? That kind of makes you a crappy babysitter." She sneered at him.

"Stacey." Shane pinched the bridge of his nose. "I am neither your babysitter, nor am I saddling this on you. I'm just telling you first, since your Aunt Jen is going to be here any second. As soon as Justin learns you're going to LEGOLAND in the middle of the school week, he won't hear anything else I have to say. This way when he asks you, you know what's going on."

She sat on the floor and stroked the white and black cat's back. The other cat, the one that was mostly black, butted at her hand. She stroked it once and then it ran out of the room. The other cat followed. Stacey watched the animals forlornly. "You want to ditch us. Just like Mom. Just like Dad."

Shane launched from the counter. He was on the floor sitting next to Stacey, a hand on her back. He wanted to pull her into his lap like a little kid, but she was too big, and she would think he was being a creep.

"Hey, no. No one here is ditching you. Not your mom, and not me. Ya know, kid, we were actually talking about making me your official guardian if anything happens to your mom."

"And what did you say? No?"

"Exactly."

Stacey tried to shove Shane away from her, and she started to stand up.

He held her in place with a hand on her upper arm. "I said no because I want to adopt you. You and your brother."

Shane let her go, and she stood over him. "Why?"

They hadn't told the kids yet, and Lucy would probably be mad at him but he needed to get Stacey on his side.

He let out a breath. "Your mom is gonna kill me for telling you first, but I'm gonna need your help planning everything anyway."

Stacey's brow furrowed and she tilted her head to the side.

Shane grinned. "We're going to get married as soon as the divorce is finalized."

Stacey jumped and squealed. She squeezed Shane in a fierce hug. "No way, oh my God, no way."

He laughed. Well, that was a mood changer.

He stood. "Yes way. And I need your help getting a few things set up. You think you can handle it?"

"Yes. I can totally do this. How big? When's the divorce over? You're going to need invitations. I'm going to need a dress. Mom is going to need a dress." Stacey's eyes were wide with excitement. "Can I tell Justin?"

Shane shook his head. "Let me talk to him real quick first."

Luna came trotting back into the kitchen from the front of the house, her leash trailing behind. She plunged her face into her water bowl.

Stacey began vibrating in place. "You have to tell him

now," she whispered as Justin followed his dog into the kitchen.

"Tell me what?"

"They're getting married!" Stacey squealed.

"So much for letting me talk to him first." Shane smirked.

21

T he kids were buzzing with excitement when he left. Stacey over the wedding. Justin over LEGOLAND. Jennifer said they would be fine for a few days.

He navigated the car through traffic. Shane had promised Stacey he would find out a range of dates for her for the wedding. He called Roberts. The lawyer would have an idea on the specific dates everything would be final.

"Ben Roberts, can I help you?"

"This is Shane. I was hoping you could help me out with some specifics regarding Lucy's divorce."

"Mr. Vincent." The lawyer's voice sounded shaky. "I think you might be able to help me. I'm glad you called. But first, I can't give you details about Lucy's case."

"I realize that, but can you tell me when everything will be finalized? I have tasked Stacey with booking a dinner party at Del Coronado, and it's important that Lucy no longer be legally married."

"Just a moment."

Shane heard what sounded like the phone being set down on a desk and papers being shuffled through.

"Lucretia should have this information." He provided a date five weeks in the future. Shane grinned. It was closer than he expected.

"Yeah, well, she's taken off to do a little project for Cyan del Fuego. Were you aware of that?"

"Yes, I was."

"Why didn't you tell her not to go?" Shane yelled.

"Mr. Vincent, Lucretia doesn't listen to me regarding anything other than her divorce. She is a very stubborn woman."

"I've noticed," he huffed.

"I'm afraid she's heading into something quite nasty," Roberts commented.

"Me too, that's why I'm driving up there right now. You said I might be able to help you out with something?"

"Yes, my assistant, Celine. She hasn't shown up for work for two days. The young man she recently broke up with dropped off her belongings here, and then this morning showed up to see if she had come in. Apparently he hasn't been able to get in touch with her. And with the news you shared with me regarding her additional employment activities... Could you go check on her? See if she's home and just blocking her gentleman friend's calls..."

"Or see if she has fallen afoul of her nefarious vampire masters?"

"You certainly have a flair for the dramatic. But yes, that precisely," Roberts confirmed.

"I'll call you back." Shane ended to call.

He wasn't too far from the apartment complex where Celine lived. He made a U-turn and headed back to check on the woman.

He was beginning to think this spot in guest parking was reserved for him. Not seeing her new red SUV in her spot, he parked and sauntered up to her apartment. He knocked on the door.

"You're awfully early. Aren't you? She ain't here."

Shane turned at the craggy old voice. He expected to see a withered old crone. Instead he caught an overly tan middle-aged woman with a cigarette hanging from her mouth.

"Pardon?" he asked.

"Her men typically come around late at night. It's too early; she won't be home until later."

Shane stepped over to her neighbor. "Her men?"

"Oh, she has different men here all the time. You didn't think you were special, did you?" The woman coughed.

"I'm not her date. I'm here to do a wellness check on her. You haven't seen her around lately?"

"She left the other night. Hasn't been back since. Left her stupid alarm clock on. I had to go in and turn it off yesterday morning."

Shane couldn't stop the grin forming on his face. "You have a key? You wouldn't mind letting me in?"

As she began to hem and haw, Shane pulled out his wallet and removed several twenties.

"I suppose, hold on." She disappeared back into her apartment and came back carrying a set of jingling keys. "You're dressed too nice to be some kind of thug. Mind you, I'm gonna stand right there and watch to make sure you don't take anything."

She twisted the key, and Shane followed her in. How she didn't flinch at the stench, he didn't understand. Then again, daywalkers couldn't smell it either.

He poked around her living room. Celine wasn't a tidy person. Shoes under the paper-covered coffee table. In the small kitchen, dishes sat in the sink. The coffeepot was half-full. Shane pulled a handkerchief from his pocket and opened the refrigerator. The coffee creamer was still good, so if Celine had taken off, it was recently, as her neighbor described.

He thumbed at the bedroom. "You need to come monitor me in here too?"

"Eh, just don't go sniffing her panties." The neighbor had sat and was flipping through one of the fashion magazines scattered around.

Shane had no interest in smelling panties. But he did smell the bedding. His stomach lurched; the smell was strong. Vampire and blood. He used his handkerchief again as he pulled the covers back. A large stain covered at least a third of the bedding. That wasn't good. Vampires are supposed to know how to not damage their food sources. That much blood indicated damage.

He flipped the covers back into place.

He pushed the door to the bathroom open. There was a lot of blood in the shower.

He walked back out into the living room. "Well, thanks, I've seen enough here. You're not going to want to come back in here, okay?"

"What's the matter?" She put the magazine down and stood.

Shane leaned over and reached for the magazine. He stopped. "Go ahead and take that with you." He nodded at the magazine.

He followed the woman back onto the landing.

"Is she in trouble? Wouldn't surprise me one bit." She pulled the money Shane had given her earlier from her pocket. She eyed it knowingly. "I could easily forget you were ever here." She cut her gaze back to Shane. "If you know what I mean?"

He knew exactly what she meant. He paid her enough to forget and headed back down the stairs.

Back in his car he called Roberts.

"It doesn't look good. I think you need to call the Del Fuegos in for a cleanup job. The neighbor has a key and a very expensive case of amnesia."

The arts-and-crafts work shirts were still in the back of his car, as was the empty delivery box. He changed before navigating out of the city limits and into the Mission Oaks subdivision. Of the three houses, only the middle one had a car. And the garage door was up.

Celine's red SUV was parked in the garage. Shane approached the house. He glanced at the car. He needed to take a closer look. For now he paused and nodded at it. Giving anyone who might be nosey in the neighborhood a chance to see him admiring the vehicle.

He stepped up onto the stoop with a skip. The camera didn't whirr or buzz. It didn't move. There should have been a guard on duty at this time of afternoon. He rang the bell. No annoyed voice demanding to know why he was there crackled through the intercom. He knocked again. He set the box down as he continued his delivery charade.

He returned to the car. Ducking into the garage, the smell of too much blood caught his attention as he moved in closer. He looked in the front, placing his face close to the glass—wasn't tinting this dark on front windows illegal in this state? He walked around to see if he could see anything from the windshield. He caught a glimpse of a shape that looked like an arm flung over some lumpy forms in the far back of the car. He moved around to the opposite side and put his face close to the back window.

"Fuck."

He looked around. No one from any of the houses had

come out. He knew from his last visit there was at least one daywalker guard around here. Or there should have been. Unless they all jumped ship recently. He tried the door into the house. Unlocked.

The smell of vampire assaulted his senses. Even with the wolf sense shut down, the stink of vampire was impossible to miss. Shane quickly checked the downstairs. No one was here. Extra paneling over the window and luxury furnishings identified the larger bedroom as the designated dark-room. Of the other two bedrooms, only one of them had a bed. It was made with military neatness. The guard's room.

Shane skipped back downstairs and out through the garage. None of the other cars were around. He walked across the small ground-cover excuse of a lawn and sidled up to the garage of the first house and tugged on the door. The other day he had thought their security endeavors were sloppy. The garage door lifted, confirming that assessment. No car.

He opened the garage door all the way and entered the house. This time the smell announced dead body. Dead vampire. If they truly were the undead, this would make him double dead.

Shane leaped up the stairs, and because the houses were mirror-image floor plans, he located the master bedroom and en suite bathroom immediately. Those really large Jacuzzi tubs were great for containing messes. There was no recovering from the hole in the middle of that guy's chest. Shane didn't look too closely, but he figured the heart was missing.

He let out a string of cuss words as he closed the garage door behind him.

He crossed back to the middle house, grabbed the box from the porch, slid back into his car, and made a call.

"I need you to connect me to Cyan del Fuego," Shane announced.

"What's up, man?" Morgan asked.

"I think that coven I found outside of San Diego has fled town. And I just found the exsanguinated body of Benton-court Roberts's assistant. And one heartless vampire."

"Ouch. You sure?"

"Yep, hole in his chest the size of a football. And Celine is very much dead, and I'm fairly certain she bled out in her car. It reeks of blood, vampire, and more blood. Dante told me these houses were owned by a group in Vegas. I have gone vampires, a dead body, and Lucy is on her way to Vegas right now!"

"Shit. How soon will you be in Vegas?"

"If I don't get pulled over, four hours. How did you know I was headed out there?"

"Seriously? Your mate is diving into the viper's nest, and you're gonna stand by and watch? I know you like a brother. Besides, if it were my mate, I'd be headed to Vegas. I'll meet you there."

Shane let several phone calls during his long drive occupy his mind. The most enjoyable was giving Stacey a set of dates to see if she could secure the wedding location. She announced that she had already decided on an overall style that she was pretty sure her mom would love. As long as it was formal enough for Lucy, and he didn't have to wear a tie, he'd be good.

No, they weren't going to need invitations, there wasn't enough time to get them printed. Everyone would be phoned directly and then sent an e-vite. Screw proper etiquette. He wanted to marry Lucy as soon as legally possible.

The call with the bad news about Celine to Roberts had been necessary.

The call to Cyan had just pissed him off. He didn't like the way she played with him and Lucy. She was too vampire, even if she was only half of one.

Starting several hours past the time he had wanted to chase after Lucy had him pulling into the parking lot for the hotel where Morgan said he would meet him well after sunset. And well after the time Lucy would have arrived in Vegas.

This entire town made his gut twist in on itself. He had managed to not return here since Lucy left to attend classes at UCLA, and he had followed her like some lovesick puppy.

He had lived on the compound since before he could remember clearly. Vague memories of his mother in a small set of rooms. He figured it must have been an apartment. Then excitement as they suddenly lived in a much larger space. And then that dank hole. His mother didn't cry as much. From time to time Shane wondered what had been really going on.

The kitchen was his first clear memory of the compound. The kitchen and Lucy. The experiences had been polar opposites. He had not been welcome in the kitchen, and a swift kick to his legs drove that point home. Too bad he hadn't learned. The kitchen was large and shiny and smelled of good food. It was a lure to a toddler seeking a cookie. And then a beacon to a hungry little boy, and a challenge as he got older. Could he sneak in and steal food without being caught? The food had been worth it. A treat to his tongue when he got away with it. And sometimes the beatings really weren't that bad.

Lucy had hugged him immediately and claimed him as her own. Her very own baby brother. At least until he wasn't allowed to play with her. By then the rules of the adults didn't stop him from seeing her. Even the beatings hadn't stopped him. She became more of a steady presence in his life than his own mother had.

His mother. Had she been beautiful? She had been stressed, overly thin, and she cried a lot. She had long flowing hair, he remembered that, always pulled back into a ponytail. She had been paler than him, but not Anglo, at least not fully. He had loved her. He was fairly certain he had. She never hit him. Then again, she hadn't done anything to stop the others. In his last memory of her she had given him a wary smile. The discoloration around her eye suggested a fading bruise. He was entirely too familiar with those colors on his own skin. She had been round with pregnancy. She hadn't said anything to him about having a baby or giving him a little brother. But she had constantly run her hands over and around the distended belly.

It wasn't until he was much older that he had figured out why that had been the last time he had seen her. She'd carried a daywalker. Those pregnancies were always dangerous to the birth mother. Looking back, there hadn't been any babies or children around other than himself and Lucy. That baby probably hadn't survived either. How many pregnancies had there been that he hadn't noticed?

Shane stepped out into the cool night air. He shook his arms and rolled his shoulders. He reached up, crossed his arm flat in front of his chest, and repeated the move with the other arm. He stretched his limbs back to where he felt almost human after hours behind the wheel and the last thirty minutes of tension growing in his neck and shoulders from being back.

He strode into the hotel lobby and found Morgan at the bar, where they had agreed to meet. Shane wasn't in the mood to settle into a room and see what could be done in the morning. Lucy was out there now. The bloodsuckers were out there now. He needed to be out there now.

Running blindly into the compound was all kinds of stupid. At least he was aware of that.

"What do you know?"

"Hello to you too." Morgan gave him a once-over.

"Is Del Fuego in town, or did she send Lucy in on her own?" The stress of being back was channeling into nervous energy. He needed to take action soon or he would go crazy.

"I told Cyan I would let her know as soon as you got here. They are over at the compound. I guess that mini coven you found in San Diego definitely originated here." Morgan signaled for the bartender, and he closed his tab. He led Shane from the building and back out to the parking lot. "I'll fill you in on the way over."

The unlock bleeped on a large black sedan. "Are you going to be okay doing this?"

Shane looked into his friend's and alpha's eyes. "Lucy is there; it doesn't matter if I'm okay or not. I'm not going to fall apart on you. I always manage to hold it together while I'm in the middle of the nightmare. It's only after I wake up that there are problems, and I'm already awake."

Shane slid into the passenger seat and let Morgan navigate the rental car into an area west of the airport. Christ, it looked like a neighborhood. It had been fairly built up when he had lived on the streets, but now there were monster houses every half a block.

They turned down a familiar road. One that Shane knew ended in a gate and a wall. And behind the gate…

Three large black Cadillac SUVs, parked as if they were

ready to chase off down the street at a second's notice, lined the street in front of the gate.

"Wait here." Morgan stepped out of the car and met with one of the obvious guards in front of the gate. The guard nodded to one of the cars, and Morgan approached the vehicle. The door opened. Morgan disappeared inside.

Shane glowered at the activity outside of the car. Lucy was on the other side of that wall. Morgan had said to wait; he didn't specify it had to be in the car. Shane knew he was losing his cool. He paced back and forth, waiting. He texted Lucy to let her know he was here for her. She would be pissed at him. Fine, let her, but let her be pissed from the comfort of a hotel room.

Morgan stepped out of the SUV. He waved Shane over. They both slid into the back.

Cyan sat cool and comfortable. She looked as if she could have been relaxing in a living room and not the back of a big car.

"You came to rescue your woman? I doubt she needs rescuing."

"Let me judge for myself. Where is she, Cyan?"

Cyan tilted her head, indicating the compound on the other side of the gated entrance. "She went in with a small team several hours ago."

"And you're just sitting out here waiting around? Has your team checked in?" Shane was not pleased with this report. Anything could be going on, and those of them out here would be completely clueless to any danger. The drive wasn't the only way on or off the property,. It was just the official one. He knew that from years of sneaking in and out to see Lucy after he managed to escape.

Morgan's phone buzzed. He looked at the screen. "Excuse me, I have to take this." He stepped from the car.

"They've already killed that girl in San Diego. We don't know what kind of actual danger Lucy is in, and you expect me to wait around with you?"

"Of course not. As soon as Morgan returns, we will go over what I have. But I do expect they will be walking out those gates at any moment."

The door opened. Morgan looked ashen.

Shane jumped out and grabbed him under the elbow for support. "What's wrong, man?"

"Honey." Morgan gulped. "She's hemorrhaging. I need to go." He spoke slowly, as if he weren't quite processing everything. "I need to go now. Jinx has taken her to the hospital, and Caro is with her. But I need to go."

"What's wrong? Did they say why?" The muscles in his forehead tightened in concern.

"Miscarriage. I guess she is pregnant, or was. I need to leave."

Cyan was next to him,. She gestured toward one of her guards. "Of course, you need to go home to your wife. Franco will drive you to the airport."

Morgan moved like a man in shock as he climbed into the passenger seat of one of the other SUVs.

"Take care, Morgan, and give Honey a hug when you get home for me. Okay?" Shane clapped him on the shoulder.

"Yeah, yeah. Will do."

Shane watched the SUV drive down the private road before it turned onto city streets.

He turned on Cyan. "Tell me everything you know." He growled.

Cyan smirked.

22

Lucy had been in here since before sunset. They were hoping to locate any darkrooms currently in use. It was eerie, familiar, and completely foreign all at once. Half of the main house had been destroyed in a fire. The other part sat in ruins. The pool looked like a swamp.

Graffiti covered the front of the long garage. Someone had squatted in the upstairs apartments for a while, but they no longer lived there.

It was surreal to see such a ruin in the middle of Las Vegas. Had no one noticed after all these years? Then again, the property was hidden behind a tall wall.

She had gone in with two of Cyan's guards. Large daywalkers who sneered at her. They knew who she was, what she was. Both of Cyan's guards still had their fangs. Lucy's had been filed down years ago as punishment. A reminder of how much of a disappointment she had turned out to be.

They started their search with the garage. Nothing. They circled around, checking the outlier buildings first. Tool sheds and random workshops. Lucy was having a hard time remembering where access to the underground portions of the property lay. She had thought the pool house was one. But it had collapsed, blocking anything that was underneath.

The main house had proven to hold more promise. The structure was fairly sound, even with a good portion of it destroyed. Lucy found her old bedroom. The dry desert had saved items from moldering, yet much of it had dried out and crumbled into dust.

She searched her old closet and let out a gasp of surprise when she located a stack of old diaries. They had lost their shine, but she could still tell they had been sparkly and bright at one point in time. The keys to the latches had to be long gone. She couldn't remember where she had even hidden them. She tugged on the latch of one; it sprang open.

Flipping through the pages showed off her loopy, bubbly letter forms from when she first learned script. She read a passage and cringed. She had been spoiled. She flipped to another page, but before she could start reading, the guards called for her. It wasn't what she had been sent in here to look for, and she had forgotten about them completely. Finding the books felt like she'd found hidden treasure. She tucked the books into the waistband at her back and said goodbye to her childhood room.

The Lexuses in the front drive when they arrived indicated someone was here. From what she had learned from Cyan, they were definitely part of the small San Diego coven. Apparently, when Nando had gone in to learn what he could, he made a mess of things instead. Gave away too much information. And now because of his careless banter, Celine, Bentoncourt's assistant, was dead. They had killed her.

Somewhere in this collection of buildings were possibly

three or four vampires. Their daywalker guards were nowhere to be found. Apparently one of the cars Shane had reported was also missing.

She went back downstairs and into the kitchen. "Hey," she called out. "Wouldn't the big walk-in refrigerators work for a darkroom?"

"No oxygen." This one looked like that actor who was always the bad guy in those action movies—the actor's name was something like Billy Manchester, so she mentally called this guard Billy. The other one had flaming orange hair, so he was Red.

"They could punch holes to let in air," Red mentioned.

Vampires could go prolonged periods of time without oxygen, but they would not awake with out it. Eventually the body would decay and rot away. They could die; they just tended not to.

She stayed back as they approached the stainless steel doors of the two large units. It was almost like watching a cop show in 3D, except the guns were real and she was in the same room. She decided to step back into the hall where she could watch but also run away if needed.

Billy kicked open the door, and Red swooped forward, gun ready to fire.

Lucy covered her head and cringed, ready to drop to the floor. There was no noise. No gunfire. No one in the refrigeration units.

They hadn't turned up anyone or anything, and the sun had set. Vampires should be up and about by now.

"Should we leave, or call for more of you guys?" There were no functional lights in this ruin of a mansion. Lucy wasn't afraid of the dark, just what, or who, went bump in the dark. And right now they were in the ruins of vampire central.

Why had she agreed to this again? Right, closure. *Hey look, Lucretia, your childhood house was the scene of a power struggle in the underworld, and you have some old diaries. I think you can call this closure.* She wanted to go home and wrap up around her kids and Shane and watch TV. She wanted to go home and pretend she was normal again.

Red grunted, and Billy indicated they needed to head into a dark passage on the other side of the kitchen.

Lucy's gut clenched. At the end of that hall was a spiral stair case that led down.

"Hey, guys, that's the entrance we were looking for." She pointed.

"Why didn't you say so earlier?" Billy asked.

"I kind of forgot. I wasn't really allowed down there as a kid, and it's been a while since I've been back, ya know?"

Red sighed heavily and strode into the dark. Just as he was about to disappear from view, he clicked on a flashlight and continued down the passage.

Billy nodded for Lucy to follow, and he took up the rear.

She had her own flashlight, but it didn't chase away everything, and who knows what was lurking just along the dark edges. The stairs ended and opened onto a hallway. The hall was functional and white, and covered in thick dust and sand. Doors lined both sides, so that this looked more like an old hotel or a school even.

Could she even remember what had been down here? Hadn't Shane said he had a room down here? Maybe it was household staff quarters, and nothing as nefarious as she was currently thinking.

Red kicked in the first door. He and Billy seemed to have this whole enter-and-search routine down to a science: one kicks; the other steps in, gun at the ready; the kicker follows.

Once they left a room, having determined that there was

nothing of interest inside, Lucy would poke her head in and look around. The first room looked like someone's office with a desk in the center and large white board calendars on the walls. The next few rooms were austere bedrooms. So she had been right, staff housing. There had even been a large, multi-person bathroom at the end of the hall, like a dormitory.

This first hallway intersected another at a T junction. Billy and Red continued their kick-guns up-search-clear routine. Lucy followed behind, more slowly. Spending more and more time in the rooms. They became bleaker, more cell-like. Suddenly they were no longer living spaces but examination rooms, rooms with lab equipment. Rooms with shackles mounted in the wall. Lucy's jaw was slack as she entered each new space.

The conditions grew worse. She entered another stable. That's what it was; it was a stable. Chains, no paint on the walls, straw on the floor. A bucket in one corner. A sob broke from her throat. She walked slowly to the corner, shining her flashlight on a pile of rags. That was the old stuffed bunny she had given Shane as a gift for Christmas one year. God, how old had they been? She must have been eight or nine. And on the wall, childlike drawings of a girl with braids—well, she assumed the triangle was supposed to be a dress, but the bangs and the braids were obviously meant to be her. She was holding the hand of a little boy with a headful of curls. She smiled, remembering Shane's hair before it was shaved away. He had the biggest, softest fluff ball of hair on his head. That was all trimmed by the time he was six or so. He must have drawn that when he was really little. And it stayed there all this time. Bile rose in her throat. Had this been where he slept? There wasn't even a bed.

She pressed her hand to her mouth and fought tears. Had Shane been living like this while she was upstairs whining about the designer label on her nightgowns?

She walked back out into the hallway. She could no longer see the flashlights from the two guards. She cocked her head to the side and listened. There was some muffled noise coming from her right. She couldn't remember if that was back the original way they had come in or not. Another hall intersected this one. She followed down the new hall, thinking it was where she heard Billy and Red making their search.

It was dark, and this place held too many bad memories. Maybe not hers, but it felt like those memories were seeking her out, needing to be felt again. Needing to be remembered. She pointed her flashlight into a few open doors. Some of the rooms looked like an old-fashioned hospital ward. But the equipment that was left out on the tray tables... They were less like examination rooms and more like torture chambers.

Lucy swallowed down panic. She could no longer hear the guards. This place was creeping her out. They weren't going to find any vampires hiding out down here. No one had been in these spaces for a very long time. The thick dust on the floor bore witness to that.

She turned down the hallway and followed the markings her own feet had left in the dust. She had been walking for too long. The hallways kept twisting into other halls. Was she just following her own tracks in circles?

"Hey!" she called out. She felt bad she couldn't call out Billy or Red's names because she didn't know them. She just had the nicknames she'd made up for them in her head. Okay, the redheaded guy would probably respond to Red, but the other guy was no way going to know she was calling for him if she yelled out Billy.

Great, she was lost. Thirty feet above her was the building she had grown up in, but she hadn't a clue where she was down here

Shane stormed up the drive. Shoulders rolled forward, fists clenched.

His intention was to barge in, swing Lucy up over his shoulder, and leave. And punch anyone who got in his way. Cyan had sent Lucy in here knowing the vampires from San Diego were here, knowing they had drained Celine. Knowing they were acting irrational. It didn't help that everyone expected that the Celine debacle had been unintentional.

The look on Morgan's face, that sucker punch that something was wrong with his mate; Shane knew that feeling entirely too well. He had felt it when Lucy first ran away and joined up with the coven in LA. She should have talked to him; he would have helped her then. He felt it again when she announced she was getting married and he met Geoff and had to be nice to Geoff. He felt it when he met her children and they weren't his. And he felt it now. Only now he was too pissed off to be afraid.

He punched one of the Lexuses as he passed the cars. It didn't do anything beyond making the car chirrup its lock system, but Shane felt a modicum of satisfaction.

Damn, the old place was really shot to hell. It had been pretty grand once, multiple wings, red stucco walls, tile roofing, grounds that were somehow green and indicated a lushness the natural desert did not provide. Now, in the dark, it all looked gray and dead. The entryway was open, windows broken and missing. The entire wing to his right was nothing more than a collection of burned-out rubble and sticks.

He opened his senses and scanned for Lucy. Nothing. He walked into the ruin. There she was. A faint hint of her scent. She had been here. The problem was, she had been everywhere. He couldn't track her. Her scent was all over the house. Strongest in her old bedroom. This one room where he had felt safe. She had stayed in here for a bit. He could tell less by her smell and more by the footprints and mess of tracks she'd left in the dust covering the floor.

He followed her scent to the kitchen. He saw the dark hallway that led to the underground rooms, and he knew where she was. Damn. He really didn't want to have to go down there. But screw that. If that's where Lucy was, then... he didn't hesitate in his actions as his head warred with his gut instinct to turn the other direction.

At the bottom of the stairs he opened his senses further. There was no light down here, and he didn't have a flashlight. *Stupid move.* He closed his eyes since they weren't helping him anyway. His nose caught dust, daywalker, vampire, Lucy. Damn his brain, it told him he should secure that vampire. He checked again; yes, only one bloodsucker. Shouldn't there have been more?

There were multiple daywalkers. They were harder to distinguish, but they were there. Funny, he knew Morgan couldn't scent them at all. Then again, he hadn't been raised around them. They smelled like people, only different. Logic told him one thing; his heart told him something else.

He followed his heart.

The scent of daywalker grew sharper. And blood, he smelled fresh blood. He could hear labored breathing. He opened his eyes and strained to see. Even with wolf eyes, he needed some light. It was black as tar down here. He picked up the glow of a watch dial. The closer he got, the stronger the smell; then he could sense a body. Someone was down. Was it one of Cyan's guys, or did this one belong to the vamp?

Kneeling down, Shane placed his hand on the watch to identify the arm, he followed it up past the shoulder and to the neck. No pulse. This guy wasn't breathing. He didn't smell like blood either. He patted down the rest of the body. He found an extra gun clip on the form's belt. He pocketed it. Down one leg. A knife. Shane added that to his belt. He felt around just past the hands, maybe this guy had dropped a flashlight or his gun. His hand hit something that rolled away. Bingo, flashlight. He found it again and clicked it on.

He shone the light on the figure to identify the man. He was dressed like special ops, Kevlar vest and cargo pants. But his head was at an unnatural angle. He had to be one of Cyan's. Shining the flashlight around, Shane found that the daywalker had fallen onto his gun. Shane checked the chamber; it was loaded. He tucked the gun into the back of his waistband.

Shane patted down the guy one more time, with the help of the flashlight, to find out if he had any other weapons. Another clip. Good.

Shane stood and shone the light around. The ground was practically swept clean by the fight that had happened here. From the smell, two daywalkers, and the other one was bleeding nearby.

About twenty feet down the hall he found the source of the bleeding. Leaning against the wall, the other daywalker. Shane guessed by the black suit and the smell that lingered around him like stale cigarette smoke, that this one belonged to the vampires.

He sat propped against the wall, a fine sheen of sweat glistening over his pallid skin. His eyes were glossy and unfocused. A dark stain pooled around him on the floor. Shane swept the light over him. He was bleeding badly from his abdomen. Had been for a bit too, by the amount of blood. Shane checked his pulse. It pounded away like a hummingbird's wings. Yeah, this guy wasn't too long for the world.

Shane shook his shoulder. "What's your name?"

The eyes didn't even shift to look at him. Shane shoved the body over. He was already dead; the body just hadn't caught up yet.

The two dead guys meant Lucy was down here with one guard and an unknown number of other daywalkers. And at least one vampire.

Shane continued down the hall, his pace was much faster now that he could see.

He heard her before his nose told him Lucy was here. He shown his light into the room and up to the ceiling, to provide more light and not blind her.

"Hey, baby," he crooned as he stepped into the room.

She stood in the middle of some kind of laboratory setup. It looked like a mad scientist's lab from the movies. She clutched an old faded blue bunny. His heart caught in his throat. He saw the tears just before she blinded him with her flashlight.

"Oh God, Shane! What were they doing here?"

He was by her side and wrapping his arms around her before the purple and green spots cleared from his vision.

"You found Blueboy." He pulled the mangy old stuffed

animal from her grasp. She had given that to him. It was the first present he could remember ever getting.

"Shane, they were monsters. Look, I found notes." She rotated in his embrace and flashed her light onto the stacks of notebooks in front of her on the table. She sniffed. "I'm so sorry. I think this was your mother." Her finger traced a dated line.

Shane focused on what she was pointing to. His eyes went wide. These read like breeding records. He flipped the page back. There was no name, instead there was a descriptor and a number: *Lupine 23, grn, brn.* Was twenty-three her age, or how many came before her? Lucy was right, that was his mother. He felt it in his gut. She had green eyes and brown hair, that had to be what *grn* and *brn* referred to. *One live birth, full lupine.* The date was close to when he thought his birthday was. But no father was indicated. Damn, that must be him. Date of acquisition, then *one breeding quality bitch.* She had been acquired like an asset to be purchased. She was referred to like a puppy-mill breeding dog.

Dates and names, a list of pregnancies followed. He felt sick to his stomach. Lazarus was on that list more than once. No wonder he hadn't seen her much. Most pregnancies did not make it to term. The ones that did either reported a still-birth, or the baby didn't survive more than a few hours.

The last entry indicated she had died along with the baby during birth. He nodded his head, just a few weeks from the last time he had seen her.

He flipped through the book. There were other breeders listed like livestock. He knew others had been kept down here; sometimes they cried. Mostly he was just aware of them in their silence.

"Shane." Her voice was so little and tentative. "I think this is me."

She pushed an open notebook into the circle of her flashlight. Her finger rested on a single line. *Lupine 16, blu, blk.*

"That's my birthday. And my mother died while giving birth to me. Father once said I had eyes like hers. This has to mean blue eyes and black hair, like me. I wonder if I look like her..." Lucy's voice trailed off. "The dates are the same. And look, no end date for the offspring. Shane, I'm an experiment." She gulped hard, and a sob escaped her lips.

She turned and clenched on to him like he was the only thing that could save her.

He stroked her hair and pulled her in tight. Her frame shook as she cried.

"How can you love me even though you know what I came from? What horrible crimes my father committed. They were conducting breeding experiments. What does it mean, Lupine? Why did they list my mother as Lupine? I'm not a wolf. Am I? I can't shift. Oh God, what am I, Shane? What am I?" She looked up at him. Her big blue eyes glowed, illuminated from within.

"If you are lupine, you are something unique and amazing. You are the woman I love." He lowered his face to hers, his intention to kiss her tenderly, lovingly.

Her response was hungry and fierce. She pressed against his mouth, sucking in his tongue. Her hands pulled at his shirt until they found purchase against his skin. Her fingers felt like fire as she grabbed at his flesh.

His body roared, and he needed her touching more of him; he needed to be touching her. They struggled with each other's clothes until they broke the kiss long enough for Lucy's T-shirt to be pulled over her head. She undid Shane's shirt buttons, and he worked on her jeans.

He stopped and looked at her. He didn't need a flashlight to see her. She was illuminated from within.

"Don't say no," she whispered. "I need you."

He pulled her pants and panties from her in a single tug. "I'm never gonna say no to you again." He lifted her onto the table. She removed her bra as he kicked free of his slacks.

Shane growled low in his throat before she pulled his head to her breast. She let out a moan as he sucked one nipple into his mouth. His touch was not gentle as he palmed her other breast. She pulled on his shoulders and wrapped her legs around his hips, bringing him closer.

Lifting his face back to hers, he consumed her mouth. He no longer thought; he was all nerve endings and need. He scooped her ass to him and sank his length into her, pressing his hips to hers. She cried out against his mouth. Her noise only drove him to action.

He pushed into her, and she counter thrust. Nails bit into his back. It was the second sweetest feeling he had ever experienced, only after this feeling of being surrounded by her heat, held by her, in her. He could feel the pulling of her muscles on him as he continued to thrust. He seized as she screamed. They came together in a crash of muscles and cries.

He gasped for air and held her close. He did not want to let her go, ever.

Lucy laughed. "I couldn't have waited another minute longer."

Her face nuzzled against his chest, her warm breath caressing his skin. He sank his hand into the hair at the back of her head and tilted her so he could look into her eyes. "I love you, baby. I have since forever. And I should say the wait was well worth it, but," he breathed heavily, catching his breath, "why did you make me wait so long?"

"You're the fool that said another five weeks." She reached up and stroked the side of his face. "You know I wanted to marry you when we were little. But you didn't like girls that way."

"I've always loved you."

"No, you didn't. Look." She twisted and pulled a worn, glittery purple diary from the stack of notebooks, and picked up her flashlight.

The latch had been popped off. Lucy flipped to a page somewhere in the middle. She began reading. "'Shane is being a turd.'" She looked up and smiled at him. "I really must have thought I was cussing." She dropped her gaze back and continued reading. "'He said he won't marry me because girls are gross.'"

Shane pulled the diary from her hands and looked at it. "Apparently I was being stupid for that conversation, because all I've ever wanted was you. And by the time you were sixteen and I actually understood what wanting you meant... Well, you had moved on to flirting with security guards, and I was discovering the joys of jacking off."

She pushed against his chest. "Oh, stop it."

He bundled her in closer. "Never. I'll pull one off thinking about you any day, but I'd much rather touch you than think about touching you."

He stopped moving.

"You heard that too?" she whispered.

Shane stepped back and handed her jeans over. "Get dressed. There's a gun in my pocket."

He pulled the wolf forward. He felt it in his brow first, then in his limbs. In a few breaths he shook, settling his new skin and fur into place.

He could hear the noise better now. He stood at the door, head lowered, ready to pounce as Lucy finished getting dressed.

"I should take the notebooks."

Shane snapped his teeth at her.

"Right, I can come back for them." She shoved one flashlight into her back pocket and picked up the other one. She fished the gun out of his pants' pocket and tied his pants around her hips. "Fuck, this thing is heavy. Don't look at me like that. You're going to need pants later."

She ran her hand up his back and dug into the fur at his neck in that familiar grasp of hers that told him she needed him to be strong for both of them.

He nodded, and she pushed the door open, shining the flashlight down one direction of the hall and then the other.

Shane led the way, turning left out of the room.

He could smell the vampire now; it was close. He picked up his pace, pulling Lucy along.

She ducked and cursed. "Sorry, thought I felt something in my hair."

They continued down the hall and turned onto another one. Shane backtracking to get Lucy out of this labyrinth.

Her flashlight landed on a pair of boots. He didn't remember passing another body. She trailed the light up until the light illuminated a head of bright orange hair.

"Red," she gasped. She let go of Shane and ran over to the figure. She dropped the gun and placed her fingers against his neck, and then leaned down, listening to his chest. "He's alive, but out cold."

Shane wrapped his mouth over her wrist and pulled.

"No, we can't leave him."

He tugged at her again.

Shane heard a roar and dropped Lucy. With a growl he

faced the opposite direction and braced for impact. Someone was rushing them. A dark form leaped over his back and tackled Lucy.

Shane was on the figure, teeth sinking into skin. Daywalker. The man screamed and launched himself backward. Shane let go and placed himself between their attacker and Lucy. He looked at Lucy, gave the gun a brief glance and a quick growl.

If he only had vocal cords. She needed to pick the gun up and shoot the man.

The loud blast of a gunshot rang out behind him. Good, she got the hint. The shot thunked into the wall behind the daywalker. A second shot and the man screamed. Shane was on him again, teeth at throat.

"Wait, we need answers. Don't kill him."

Shane growled low in his throat. Lucy crawled over to where the two figures lay. The eyes of the daywalker were wide with fear. Lucy hit him in the temple with the handle of the gun. The daywalker groaned but did not pass out. She changed her grip on the gun and hit him again. He went limp under Shane's bite.

"What? That's how they do it on TV. Don't shake your head at me."

Shane heard her fumbling around the guard she called Red. She returned with handcuffs. "Help me."

She pushed the form over and pulled his hands together until she could click the cuffs into place.

"We can send Cyan's other guards back in to get these two."

Shane yipped in agreement. He wouldn't have been able to change and carry both men out. His priority was to get Lucy out of here.

They passed the other daywalkers. Both were now dead.

Lucy gasped, "Billy."

Shane pressed Lucy to keep going and not stop.

She looked back at the one she called Billy. "Are you sure he's dead?"

Shane yipped and head butted her in the ass.

The smell of vampire was thick. He should have expected something.

Lucy's scream was cut short. Shane spun, and there was the sharp-dressed man from Celine's apartment with an old knife to Lucy's throat. It was not gleaming and well-polished. The blade was long and rusty. It would not leave a clean and almost painless cut. It would cause so much damage that even if he didn't manage to slice through her jugular, the hack job would kill her.

Shane froze.

Lucy's eyes were large and filled with panic. Her hands hung, shaking at her sides.

"So you're Lazarus's daughter." It wasn't a question. He said the word *daughter* like it left a bad taste in his mouth.

"He wanted us to find the money. But then you practically sat right in our laps. It was like a Christmas surprise. You should have never hired that lawyer. We had no idea where you were before that."

Shane watched as Lucy gulped for air. Her lips open and closed several times.

"You... you work for my father?"

The vampire huffed. "We believe he could be a valuable asset. I think right now it's more that he works for us."

Shane knew that was a bluff. Lazarus, no matter how weak, would never work as an underling for anyone.

"So you're with Marat?"

A pause. "Marat is nothing."

The look in the vampire's eyes and the delay in his

response was Shane's clue. This guy didn't know anything. Didn't know their history, didn't know about Marat or how he was the vampire that supposedly killed Lazarus. This guy was all bluster and bluff. A lowly minion sent to spy on a lawyer, who lucked out and found his Lord's actual daughter. Shane shuddered.

"I don't think you will find my father to be very cooperative if anything were to happen to me."

"I got the man his money. He'll be very grateful to me. Do you think he even cares about you? How would he ever know if something happened to you? I could leave your body to rot down here, and who would tell him?"

"So he's not here?"

Good girl, Lucy, keep asking questions, keep him talking.

The vampire let out a sharp laugh. "He refuses to come back here. We have permission to burn it to the ground once we have made use of it."

"You keep saying we. Who is we? There were two cars out front."

He tightened his grip and jostled Lucy. She gasped for a breath.

Shane let out an involuntary growl.

The vampire loosened his grip. Lucy loudly sucked in air.

"Randolph didn't make it. He accidentally killed the lovely Celine. She was an excellent fuck and quite tasty. I told him to pick her up, not bleed her out."

That must be the body back at the Mission Oaks subdivision. That was one vampire; where were the rest?

"So it's just you?"

"Well, my little flock seems to have been led astray. Draven and his driver"—the vampire sighed—"seemed to have gotten lost." He seemed to get wistful and gazed off into the distance. "Poor Christof."

Lucy moved with a swiftness Shane didn't know she possessed. While the vampire was distracted waxing mournfully about his coven, she had changed her grip on the gun. She swung her arm up and smashed the handle of the weapon into the man's mouth.

He dropped her and cupped his face with his hands. Lucy rolled, and as the vampire collapsed, she stood, emptying the clip into his body.

Shane shifted. He placed a gentle hand against her arm as she continued to click the empty gun at the body.

"You got him, baby, you got him." He stepped over to the limp vampire and, with a concentrated effort, twisted the head until there was an audible tearing of tissues and popping of broken bones.

Shane pulled Lucy against him. He took the gun from her hand and dropped it on the floor.

She shivered and sweat glistened on her brow.

He unwrapped his pants from around her midsection. Smart woman. He pulled on his clothes before picking her up and climbing the stairs. She was in shock. He needed to get her out and into the fresh air, and wrapped in a blanket. This place smelled too much of death.

23

S hane set Lucy down once they were back in the
kitchen. His eyes hurt from straining in the dark below.
The ambient light aboveground felt ridiculously bright,
even though it was night and there were no lights on the
property. He looked her over, made sure she wasn't hurt. He
skimmed his hands over her shoulders, down her arms.

"I shot him, Shane. I shot him."

"I know you did, baby. It's okay, it was him or you. You
made the right choice." He crushed Lucy to his chest. Her
breath tickled his skin. It was the best feeling in the world.

"Come on, let's get you back to the hotel. I'm taking you
home tomorrow."

She lay a hand against his chest. "No, we have to finish
here. I need to know what else is in those notebooks. Shane,
I read that correctly, didn't I? It said my mother was a wolf,
like you. I need to find out more about my mother. Who was
she? I'll never know my background, will I?"

"We don't even know if that was you, Lucy." He shook his
head. He didn't understand it either. Something in wolf and
vampire biology was not compatible. They had known that

for years. Vampires could not feed from wolves, and they couldn't turn wolves into vampires. The process always—always—poisoned the wolf.

But Lucy had found something that looked important. That would explain why wolves stayed away from vampires. Why the Nevada wolves stayed in hiding even from others of their kind. She was right; those notebooks were important.

"Okay, I'll go back for them, but I want you safe first." He scooped her back into his arms.

"I can walk, you know," she announced, but she didn't fight him. She snaked her arms around his neck and rested her head against his shoulder. He didn't put her back down until they were at the front gate and Cyan's guard outpost.

He set Lucy into the back of the large SUV with Cyan. They found a blanket for her, and someone handed her a cup of coffee. Confident that Lucy was safe and going nowhere, Shane found one of Cyan's guards. He looked for the oldest one with the least guns.

"You the one in charge?" Shane asked the guard with the buzz cut.

"Ms. Del Fuego is the one in charge," was the man's gruff response. This was the guy Shane needed to talk to.

"But you're the one heading up the muscle, right? Look I need to go back in there. And you need to get your guys out."

The other man nodded. "What have you got?"

Shane started ticking items off on his fingers. "Red is down. He's alive but unconscious. We cuffed their daywalker to him. He's knocked out, but I don't know how long he'll be down. Your other guy, Billy..."

Buzz Cut scrunched his brow. "Who?"

Shane huffed and shook his head. "She called him Billy,

I don't know. Ponytail, one eyebrow?" Shane pointed at his own face, indicating eyebrows.

The guard nodded. "Mason, yeah."

"Sorry, Mason didn't make it. But he took out another one of their daywalkers. So that makes two of their vamps down, one here she just took out—"

The guard lifted his eyebrows at Shane's words.

Shane smirked. "She's good. And one of their own that they dismembered back in San Diego. A missing Lexus, there were three in San Diego, and there are two here. We have one dead daywalker on their side, and one that will hopefully talk."

The guard nodded, his mouth pulled into a tight frown. He brushed his hand over the top if his bristled hair.

"Ms. Del Fuego told us there should be two vampires back in there. I don't know how much muscle they have with them. That's an unknown."

"Well, your guys were the only ones armed from what I saw."

"What about you?" He shifted his gaze past Shane. "Hey, someone get this guy a shirt."

Shane shook his head. "I'm going back in. There is a room with some notebooks. It looks like there is valuable information we're going to want." Shane crouched down and drew an impromptu map in the dirt. "Room's about here. Get the notebooks, my clothes, and there should be a blue bunny stuffed animal."

The guard lifted his eyebrows at Shane again. "Why don't you bring all that out?"

"I'm not going to have opposable thumbs, man. And remember the bunny, okay?"

Shane strode over to the SUV and Lucy.

She looked frail and scared. Her world had just been rocked, by more than just their lovemaking.

"You doin' okay?" Shane slid his hand around her neck and cupped the back of her head.

She nodded slightly and blinked.

"I want you to stay out here."

"I've had enough excitement for tonight," she agreed. Her voice was shaky.

He leaned in and kissed her forehead. "I should be right back."

"You better. You're still going to marry me even though I gave away the cow?"

Shane laughed. "What is that supposed to even mean?"

"It's something they say to girls so they don't have sex before they get married. Why buy the cow when you give away the milk for free? And you wanted to wait, and..."

"You tell your daughter shit like that? I have some serious damage control to do with this family when we get home. I love you."

He kissed her again, walked behind the SUV, and shifted. He shook, readjusting back into this skin again tonight. He didn't look behind him to see if any of Cyan's men were following. He had to find another vampire.

Shane sniffed all around the outside of the perimeter. No one had been able to tell him if the second vampire had made it out of the compound or not. At least no one had seen anything. That meant little to him. He would smell if the bastard had left over the wall. Shane pressed close to the wall as he made his way around. Vegas had grown so much since he left. They were no longer hidden in the middle of a deserted area. What was once a lone walled-off mansion now had neighbors with their own walls and fences and motion detector lights. He made it all the way around the outside without picking up the stench he identified as vampire.

Shane repeated the same patrol along the inner perimeter of the wall. If he had to spiral in on his quarry, he would. But first he needed to eliminate the obvious and hone in on the specific identifying stink.

It didn't take long before Cyan's guards returned from their retrieval foray back into the underground labyrinth.

Lucy was glad to see Red walking on his own two feet. He held his head and didn't exactly appear to be stable, but he was moving under his own power. That was good. She did not see them haul out the body of Billy. But by the grim expression on everyone's face and the shaking of heads, they had pulled him out.

The daywalker she had knocked out had also made it out on his own feet. But apparently he wasn't talking. Cyan left her to sit in the back of the luxury vehicle. Lucy watched as she slinked her way across the pavement, approaching the man. Lucy shook her head; he had no idea what he was up against.

Cyan was a surprising woman. Once Lucy got past her suspicions and distrust, she found herself liking her immensely. Maybe it was because she didn't tolerate fools, and that included her vampire brother, or because she took no shit from anyone. Lucy leaned back into the soft upholstery. Could she have really been like Cyan had her father continued? Lucy shivered. No, she would not have been able to oversee whatever crimes that monster was conducting. Those hallways had been filled with slaves. Female shifters that he had systematically raped as part of a breeding program. The thought made her stomach clench. And she had lived above it and never knew?

She had never questioned why Shane was there, why he was allowed to play with her. Why had she thought they had given him to her? Hadn't the words been that he was 'for her'?

With a grunt a large stack of the notebooks she had been looking at were placed on the floor by the open car door. A second guard deposited a second stack. This one had Shane's folded clothing and shoes on top.

"Here," the guard huffed and shoved Blueboy into her face. "He said bring you this."

Her heart thumped at the sight of the bedraggled toy. She wondered if it would survive a cleaning. It really was dusty and neglected, but the memories attached were too precious to just toss it.

"Thank you."

She knelt down and began flipping through to see if she could locate any more information. She sorted the stacks into what she thought looked like breeding records and 'other.' 'Other' required deciphering someone's chicken scratch. She did not have the wherewithal tonight to fight bad lighting and bad handwriting.

She relocated the records that she thought were Shane's mother. She ran her fingers over the woman's history. Her whole life reduced to a list of dates. Lucy could only imagine the pain these lines bespoke of. Had his mother loved Shane, or had he been just one in a long line of pregnancies? His birthdate was listed, and then the next date listed was about four years later next to "acquired." It made her stomach clench.

She flipped the page and found another Lupine female, more heartache and disappointment reduced to a series of dates that hid rapes, miscarriages, and deaths. So many deaths. Lucy ignored the tears as they trailed down her face. What good did her grief do these women now?

They weren't all wolves, at least if she was interpreting the notations correctly.

Daywalkers were sterile, yet here it was indicated they were trying to impregnate them. The names along the side were all the same. Her nose flared in distaste. Then she noticed they weren't names at all; it said *Lupine M*. Lupine male. They were forcing male shifters to penetrate female daywalkers. Her stomach clenched again. No one had been safe. These pages showed her the future that could have been. Was she just potential breeding stock for her father?

Lucy sat back on her heels. She covered her mouth, fighting back the nausea.

She pulled the stack of 'other' toward her. She didn't know exactly what she was looking for, but she scanned frantically.

Cyan returned to the car. She stopped outside the door and looked at Lucy. Lucy stared back in shock.

"He was trying to breed a hybrid. And he succeeded, with me."

24

L ucy's head swam from reading about the atrocities that were conducted under her very feet when she was a child. Her father was trying to create a stronger daywalker, one who would be able to change into a fierce beast. He wanted an army of wolf shifters that he could control. Their wolf would give them strength; their daywalker would give them the need for blood. And if he controlled their supply, he could create raging monsters that would hunt and destroy to get to the blood they needed. His plot was the evil of fairy tales. Lucy couldn't believe what she was reading. He wasn't sane, and people let him get away with this. They assisted and enabled him to be able to carry out his lunatic plan.

The notebooks documented case after case of forced impregnation of female wolf shifters being raped by either Lazarus or one of his chosen. Marat featured prominently in these notes. He had a high impregnation success rate. It turned Lucy's stomach. The results were recorded with clinical apathy. Observation notes so detached you had to know that the bitch or the stud they referred to were humans and not animals. The dates indicated these attempts at cross breeding had been going on for over a decade before she was born.

The results were disappointing, always disappointing. She was the only result to survive infancy. She was a result, not a daughter. Half wolf, half vampire. She was a failed result. She didn't even display typical daywalker characteristics. Based on the notes she read, Shane's mother had been acquired to provide guidance for her as a young wolf. But clearly something had gotten all messed up along the way. His mother had been around for only a brief time that Lucy could remember.

She let out a sharp laugh when she found a passage where the observer—the note books were dated, but none had a name identifying who they belonged to; she could only assume it was her father's handwriting she was reading —was frustrated that she was not shifting. They hadn't known that wolves shifted only after they hit puberty. Ignorance always seems to feed evil.

Apparently that was why Shane was allowed out to be with her. He was supposed to trigger something in her, to make her want to change. She hadn't found the notebooks that dated from her teen years, but she guessed that's when Lazarus started hitting her. Maybe he had finally learned that the wolves shifted with puberty, if they were able to shift at all. She hit puberty and turned into a royal brat, but not a wolf.

She wasn't going to find all the answers tonight. The contents of the notebooks left her heart sick, and wanting to throw up.

"Here." Cyan placed the notebook she had been reading on top of the one in Lucy's lap. "You are going to want to read this one."

Lucy let her gaze trail over the words. It was about Shane. It had to be. Male, youth, lupine. They knew he was sleeping with her. Lucy placed her hand on her stomach as it clenched. Marat ordered that the boy be neutered before he could start having sex with her. She hadn't even known that Marat was in her father's ranks at that time. Had she even paid attention? No, of course not. She had been a child, consumed with childish considerations like who, what, and when anything was for her. She could hardly bring herself to touch Shane when he was wounded. The thought of sex at that age made her skin crawl even more than it already was reading the notebooks..

They knew he was hiding in her room. She let out a sardonic laugh. Why had she even thought she had managed to hide him successfully? Because no one came and got him, no one said anything to her. Because they let her, and she believed it.

She slowly turned the page. The notes in this section were more scribbled, as if written in haste or anger. The male was now "damaged," but a bond had been made with the female result. She read the next line, looked up quizzically at Cyan, then returned to the line in the notes.

"Couple pairing between male youth and female result to occur naturally now highly probable. I may not kill Marat for harming male youth if he is still capable of successfully mating."

Did that mean what she thought it meant? Was Shane there to... was she expected... She tossed the notebook away from her. Staring at it as if it physically hurt her. She covered her mouth with both hands and began to maniacally cackle.

"What is the matter?" Cyan asked, reaching for the notebook.

Lucy had naturally gotten together with the male her father had intended to attempt to breed her with. "My father

had intended for me to be in his breeding program with"—
she cleared her throat—"Shane."

Cyan looked at her like she was nuts.

"I guess Daddy got what he wanted after all."

"Are you sure that's what he meant?" Cyan pulled the
notebook to her.

"Shane was the only male youth I can ever remember.
And I remember this incident clearly. So that pretty much
confirms I'm 'female result.' I was never a daughter; I was
the next generation breeding program."

"But you're daywalker. You should be incapable of
reproducing."

Lucy nodded. "I'm sterile, like all other daywalkers. I had
fangs, and I need the blood. I had no idea about my mother
being a wolf shifter. I was always led to believe I was just a
flawed daywalker, but because of who my father was I was
the princess."

"Did Lazarus have other offspring?"

"Not that was around, not that I knew of. I'm the only
name on the inheritance, so either I really am the only one,
or I'm the only one he thought he had control of." She
shook her head and breathed deeply. "If I had known any of
this was going on, I would have run away with Shane years
earlier." She looked off, gazing at nothing, processing it all.

She felt Cyan's eyes on her. "I don't think any of us had any
idea how extreme Lazarus's experiments were. Or how badly
the shifters were treated. How badly Shane was treated."

Cyan's eyes were wide. Lucy felt her own eyes had to be
as big as saucers. "And Shane voluntarily went back in," she
managed a whisper.

"He is a very brave man."

Lucy nodded. "He always has been." She extended her

gaze past Cyan and scanned the guard post that had been set up around the front gates.

"I don't see him." The rest of the guards had returned with their fallen comrades and the notebooks. But that had been a while ago. "How long has he been gone?"

Cyan set the notebook in her lap aside, climbed out of the car, and gestured to the man with the buzz cut. He approached and they exchanged a few words, and she stepped back to the car.

Leaning against the open door, Cyan said, "He's been inside with another guard for over two hours now."

Lucy shrugged the blanket from her shoulders. She reached down and began pulling the shoes she had kicked off back on. "He's been gone too long. I'm going in after him."

Lucy was safe with Cyan, and Shane was back in the dungeons. He could never think of them as anything else. Darkrooms, torture chambers, and kennel-like stalls. The problem was, the only reason he came back down here was to locate the other bloodsucker. It had to be down here, but it wasn't. The smell was off.

He had already scoured every inch of the compound aboveground, including the darkrooms in the basement level of the main house. Nothing.

Cyan had confirmed that her brother encountered four vampires in San Diego. One was left behind without a heart, Lucy had filled one with enough led the EPA should be concerned, and one car was missing, meaning that blood-sucker never made it here. The daywalker he had led the

Del Fuego guards to hadn't divulged anything before Shane had taken off again.

He marked intersections so he knew which direction he had turned last time. He remembered these halls better than he cared to admit. He was running in circles, going down the same halls he had checked earlier. He was fairly certain he had now peed on every wall down here.

There had to be another place to hide. But where?

Shane reviewed all the aboveground buildings. The pool house was leveled. He had checked the gardener's sheds, surprised they were still upright. He had nosed around in the ruins of the main house, but... No, there just wasn't anything he could come up with.

A map would be helpful. He closed his eyes and called to memory the layout of the property. Where were the secret places he had found? He had crawled all over this compound as a kid. Where were the secret tunnels? He sighed. There hadn't been any, just hiding in the shadows, and slipping in between the times anyone would catch him.

He was missing something, and it felt like it was something obvious, something he would feel stupid about for days once he realized what it was.

He yipped at the guard trailing him, and tilted his snout upward.

"Headed up?" The guard shone his flashlight on Shane

Shane nodded again. Maybe fresh air would jog his memory.

He loped up the stairs.

The fresh air carried the scent of vampire. There was another one here. But where?

He could leave it and just head back to the gate, pick up Lucy, and go back to that hotel. They could leave this mess at Cyan's feet. After all it was Nando's big mouth that sent those vampires running.

He trotted down to where the cars were parked. The smell was thick here, but then the scent scattered, and Shane could not pinpoint where else there was a concentration thick enough to announce vampire.

What had that asshole said while he had his hand wrapped around Lucy's neck? He had said that they considered Lazarus to be working for them. But they were young bloodsuckers, barely enough swagger to have kept Celine properly as a pet. Something they had not succeeded in doing.

He had admitted to being a connection to Lazarus. There was that. But what was it worth?

At this point, nothing. That meant Lazarus was still out there. Lucy would not be completely free or feel safe knowing her father was at large. Shane didn't want to think what that meant for him and his psychological issues.

He growled low in his throat. He would keep Lucy safe, and she would keep his traumas at bay.

The color of the night sky shifted, and he sensed more than saw that dawn would start soon. They had been out here all night and had very few answers.

He almost hated how his wolf had no chill when it came to Lucy. Her scent tickled his nose, and his damned tail began thudding the ground. He smiled as she walked up the drive to him. His paws tapped the ground, and he pranced in a circle at her approach.

He jumped and put his paws on her shoulder. She grabbed into the thick scruff around his neck and ruffled his fur.

"I missed you. Got worried." She shoved against his chest. "Down." Funny how she changed her patterns of speech when it came to dealing with him as a wolf. She spoke to him like he was a big dog. Her puppy, not her lover.

He sat and whined at her. Then again, he acted more like her puppy in this form.

"Any luck?" She leaned against the car. Shane pressed into her and whined again.

"You searched the house?"

He made yawning whining sounds, expecting that she would fully understand him.

"Basement too?" Lucy slid down the side of the car so that she sat, mostly crouched down, butt on heels, back against car. She kept her fingers laced into the fur around his neck.

Shane bumped his snout into her face and licked her.

"I'm not kissing you as a wolf, that's just... No, stop it."

They sat side by side in silence, thinking. Every now and again Lucy would name a different building or location on the property. Shane would nod or whine in response.

"Has anyone searched the cars for any clues?"

Shane looked at her, he hadn't thought about that. The cars smelled of old stale stench, and it was the strongest concentration of vampire smell he had encountered. Even though it really wasn't that strong. They knew they were here on the compound, so why would anyone search the vehicles?

He stood, his tail wagging. He barked a few times.

Guards from both directions approached, the one who had been combing the buildings with Shane and a few up from the gate.

"You find something?" Buzz Cut asked.

"Has anyone searched the cars, you know, opened them up and looked inside?"

The men looked at each other, brows furrowed, mouths

frowning, heads shaking. Buzz Cut put out his hand and swept it back, getting Lucy to move.

She stepped out of the way.

One of the men lifted his rifle and smashed the window.

Shane growled. The two men closest to the car covered their noses. "Ugh, what is that smell?"

It was potent, and the car had kept it sealed in. It smelled like manure and a hint of bloodsucker.

Another rifle butt to the trunk was followed by the loud *pop pop pop* of gunfire as Buzz Cut shot into the lock. The trunk lifted.

Shane put his paws up on the trunk and looked in. The smell was stronger. But the trunk was filled with potting soil, a combination of dirt and stinky manure.

"That makes no sense. It's not like they need to sleep on the soil of their fathers. So why dirt?"

Shane jumped into the trunk and began digging.

Lucy screamed before he realized what was going on. An arm shot out of the dirt, and then there was a body wrapped around him and a face burying into the fur on his neck.

Shane flung himself side to side, but he could not dislodge the body. He felt the scrape of fangs along his shoulder and froze. He knew his blood wouldn't play well with the vampire's. He had been told time and time again. Usually right before the evil bloodsucker would penetrate his skin and force their teeth into him.

They had loved to torture him and take his blood anyway. They would lure him into trusting them, offering him sweets and comfort and warmth. Soothing words, a tender touch, and an invasion of his veins. This time there had been no attempt to seduce him into compliance. This time everything was dark and all Shane could sense were those teeth. Sounds were muffled. This time it wasn't good. He forgot how to fight.

"Shane!" Lucy's voice cut through all the other sounds. Sounds he could now hear. Men were yelling.

"I can't shoot. I'll hit the wolf."

"Where the hell did he come from?"

"Get her out of here!"

And again, Lucy's voice filled with fear, "Shane!"

Shane twisted his body with a sudden fury of motion. He wrenched from the grip the vampire had on him. He was blind with rage, lashing out at the nearest body. His fangs clamped down on a wrist he found. Someone screamed in pain. He turned and clamped his jaws down on the throat nearest the scream. Warm blood splashed into his mouth. It stung, but he didn't let go. Shane shook his victim until there were no more noises, no more struggles.

"Shane!"

He turned and growled before he could see anything. Lucy filled his nose, and his vision cleared.

Her hand was in his ruff, and she was pouring water over his jaws. "Don't swallow, you big idiot. That much vampire blood... Someone get me some hydrogen peroxide. There's got to be a drugstore nearby. I need more water." She was crying.

She massaged his neck. "Don't shift, and try not to swallow." She poured more water on his face.

She ran her hands over his sides. "Did he bite you? Are you okay?"

Shane whined and tried to nuzzle into her lap.

"Where is the fucking hydrogen peroxide? I could have walked to the store and been back by now." She dug her fingers into his fur.

She rinsed his mouth out with another bottle of water.

"Here, we had some in the first-aid kit in the car," a voice somewhere behind him said.

Lucy stroked his side. "Okay, baby, you need to drink this. Wait, how much do I give him?"

"He's big, but it won't take much."

She poured the liquid into his mouth. It tasted like cold spit, but he swallowed as instructed.

He rested his head in her lap and let her stroke his neck.

"Get him up and walking."

"Okay, come on, baby, let's go for a walk."

He pressed into her legs as they walked farther up the drive. She was shaking. "What were you thinking? You know that vampire blood is poison to wolves."

Shane felt a roiling in his stomach. He left Lucy's side. He didn't want to vomit in front of her.

She kept her distance as his insides convulsed and he threw up the contents of his stomach.

After he walked around on his own for a few minutes to make sure he was done, he nudged his snout into Lucy's hand.

"Come on, let's get you some clothes so you can change. I am so ready to leave this place." She sounded beyond exhausted.

Lucy stroked the skin behind his ear with her thumb. He leaned against her, letting her hold him. Someone had given him charcoal tablets; they were supposed to help pull out any toxins he may have ingested if he hadn't vomited up all the blood he had swallowed.

He was quiet, he didn't feel well, and he was bone-tired. But he was alive, and here with her. The bad guys were dead. Well, most of them were, at least.

"I think we are done here," Cyan said.

Shane didn't feel like talking; he grunted.

"Too bad that little daywalker wouldn't talk. All the other possible informants are dead or missing. I don't think we are going to find out anything else from this place."

She nodded toward the stack of notebooks. "Do you want to take those and see what else you can learn from them?"

Lucy moaned. "I don't ever want to see those notebooks again. I don't need the details to know what Lazarus was doing was wrong."

"Do you mind if I keep them? Maybe there is a clue in there regarding where he's hiding or what he's planning."

Lucy made an uh-huh noise.

Cyan confirmed that the one account they had been concerned with had been completely drained. One vampire was missing. And no one knew anything about him. Had he taken the money to Lazarus wherever he might be at the moment? What had his role been in the little coven that was now destroyed? Had the well-dressed vampire been the boss? He had certainly acted like it. But half of what he had said sounded like lies and false bravado.

They were still left with questions. Questions that were not going to be answered today.

Shane just wanted to take Lucy and curl up in a comfortable bed and go to sleep.

25

Shane groaned and rolled over. His arm wrapped around a warm Lucy, and he pulled her into his embrace. Light filtered into their room. He did not feel like getting out of bed to fix the curtains they had left open when they finally settled in.

They had both been so worn out that even though he had her alone and they had a large, comfortable bed, Shane had simply pulled her against his chest and fallen asleep.

Lucy patted him on the arm that was wrapped around her middle, keeping her secure. "I need up, baby."

He nuzzled against the back of her head. "I want to keep you here forever."

"And I want to pee; let me up."

Shane released his hold on her and rolled onto his back.

He watched her pad into the alcove that hid the sink and the bathroom. He rolled over and leaned out of bed, flicking the curtains closed, and lay back down. They would need to get up soon enough, but there was no hurry.

They didn't need to rush back home to the kids. They could take a day or two for themselves. Besides today was a school day, and tomorrow he knew the kids and their aunt would be at LEGOLAND all day.

Shane wondered if this hotel had room service. He really didn't want to go anywhere, and he had no desire to go sightseeing.

Lucy slid back into bed and pressed herself against his torso. "Are you still planning on heading back to Sonoma after this?"

Shane nodded. He traced the smooth skin on her arm. "Yeah, I need to pack up. Get my things. I'll only be gone a couple, maybe three days."

"I have a meeting with Geoff and the lawyers next week."

"Do you need me to be there for you?"

"Of course I do. But I can handle them. You go get your things. How much furniture are we talking about?" she asked.

"No furniture, I live at my boss's compound. But I do have a couple of motorcycles."

Lucy pushed up and looked at him, her brow crinkled.

"I should probably tell you that I'm not a smuggler, and I haven't transported anything illicit for at least ten years, probably more. The Palatines have been good to me, a family. And they have never asked me to do anything more nefarious than sneak around behind the boss's wife's back to get her a show-quality baby alpaca from Peru."

Lucy laughed. "You were in Peru for an alpaca? What about the emeralds?"

"I bought them for you, fair and square."

"And all this time I thought you were a gem smuggler."

"I am. I didn't claim them on my customs forms. My past isn't the best, you know that. And yes, there was a time I was smuggling more than just baubles into the country. I did what I needed to, to survive. I was out there on my own for a long time. You have always trusted me, and I just wanted you to know that you can keep on trusting me."

Lucy snuggled closer. "I love you, baby. I know you're one of the good ones. Do you honestly think I would have allowed you around my children if I didn't think you were safe?"

Shane huffed. She was right. Lucy knew him, the real him, all the ugly, all the scars, all the fear. And she was still here.

"You are comfortable. Can we stay in bed all day?" She sounded sleepy.

"I don't have a problem with that." His eyes were heavy. He could stay like this all week.

"Good." She nestled her face into the crook of his neck. "Does this hotel have room service?"

"If they don't, we can get delivery." Shane stroked her hair. She felt so perfect leaning on him. He dozed back off.

He woke to the heavy *click* of the room door closing. He bolted upright, a moment of panic washing over his not quite awake brain. It was dark, and he was alone in bed. "Lucy?"

"It's okay, Shane, I'm right here. I just went down the hall to get some drinks from the machine. I ordered some pizza too. I was getting hungry. I figured you would be too when you woke up."

She crawled into the bed next to him, sitting with her legs folded in front of her.

"We need to talk."

Never in his history had those words meant anything good. His stomach sank.

"You've changed your mind, and you aren't going to marry me." He sighed. Last night had been difficult. He could understand her not wanting anything to do with any of that world again. Living with a wolf would be a constant reminder that the monsters were out there.

She smacked at him. "Don't be stupid, Shane." Her tone was light and playful. "Nothing like that. In those notebooks I left with Cyan, I read that you were..." She sighed. "We were... intended to be the next generation breeding pair. Us together in bed was Lazarus's intention all along. He didn't know if I could or couldn't bear children."

Shane's eyebrows lifted. "And?"

"I'm a daywalker. I'm sterile. I think." She looked back at him as if she could read his thoughts. "I'm forty, and I've never had a scare, and I've never used protection."

"Never?"

"Well, you know what I mean. Yes, I used protection, but not because of getting pregnant. I was with Geoff for sixteen years, and we didn't use anything. Didn't need to."

A low growl rumbled in his throat. "Why are we discussing this?"

"What if you can get me pregnant? I'm part wolf. Does that change anything in my baby factory settings?" Lucy motioned at her lower abdomen.

Shane curled around her leg and wrapped an arm around her hips. He placed a kiss on the exposed flesh of her ankle.

"How do you feel about your factory settings? Do we need to keep them protected, or are you willing to risk it?"

Lucy shrugged.

"Have you ever been tested, Lucy? Do you have confirmation that you inherited that particular trait? After all you don't have other typical daywalker talents, and you certainly have a few wolf traits." Shane chuckled. "It makes sense now that I know. Why didn't I ever suspect before?"

"What do you mean, like what?"

The door banged with a sharp knock. Lucy jumped from the bed and collected a stack of pizza boxes from the delivery service. She slid the boxes onto the low table under the TV.

She climbed back into the bed and pinned Shane with a glare. "What do you mean? What makes sense?"

Shane grabbed her by the hips and dragged her over the blankets to straddle his lap. He caressed over her ear. "You have exceptional hearing, and when you get angry, your eyes flair like a wolf's. They are little things, but they are not daywalker things. I'm sure there are other quirks that don't seem to fit. But with this missing piece of information, they will all start falling into place."

Lucy stared at him. "You mean like how I'm super hairy and am constantly shaving?"

Shane laughed. He shook his head. "No, not your body hair. But there is something. You'll think of it. But for now —" He dumped her off his lap. "Pizza."

Lucy scrambled up and pulled one of the boxes onto the bed with her.

Shane picked up the other box and slouched into the side chair. He propped his feet against the bed and crossed his ankles, placing the pizza over his nudity.

"When the divorce is final, you're changing your name, right? Going back to Khalid?" Shane took a bite of his pizza.

"I don't know. I'm tired of the names I've had; they have all meant death."

"What do you mean? Lucretia doesn't mean death."

"No, but I was named for Lucretia Borgia with the expectation that I would live up to her legacy as a master poisoner. And Asher, it's all ashes and death. Hell, my father's own name is some affectation on the theme. Lazarus Khalid, cheater of death." She sighed and took a bite of her food. "Who knows what his real name was, but it wasn't Khalid. And I don't think I'm Middle Eastern. I want something new, something that—"

Shane cut her off. "How about Vincent?"

She smiled weakly at him. "I love your name, baby, but I need something that means light and joy."

She crawled across the bed and reached for her purse. She pulled out her phone and began poking at it. She held the screen up to Shane. "See, even Vincent means conqueror. That's kind of oppressive.

"I want something like..."

"How about Dawn, or Ray?" Shane suggested.

She laughed. "Lucretia Dawn, sounds like a country singer. I don't think so."

"This one's nice, Anwar or Asad. That might work. Oh, or Zain."

"Stacey Zain sounds like a rock star, but baby, Shane Zain isn't going to work."

"I'm not asking you to change your name." She looked up at him. Those big blue eyes of hers made his heart skip.

"No, but I asked you to marry me. And if you aren't going to take my last name, then I'm taking yours. And if the kids get your new last name, then I want in on the deal too. I want us to be a family, Luce, and a name seems like the way we can tell the world that we belong together."

She smiled at him, and Shane no longer wanted any pizza. He was hungry, but not for food.

He tossed the box that had been on his lap onto the table. He leaned forward and grabbed the box from the bed and put it in a stack with the other one.

He was on the bed and pulling Lucy to him. She still held her phone. "If you don't like Anwar, what about Hubert?"

Shane pulled the phone from her hands. "Give me that." He tossed it off to the side and pulled her face to his.

He had her in a big, soft bed, and he had every intention of keeping her here for another day.

Her lips were soft and pliant.

"I like Lux," she said against his mouth.

His hand skimmed down her back and found the waistband of the yoga pants she wore. He pulled down, exposing her hips.

Lucy shimmied the pants down her legs and off. The T-shirt she wore was gone, and her skin pressed against his.

"You can have any name you want, baby, as long as I can have you." His teeth scraped against her chin, and then he was kissing her again. "I don't have any condoms. You think the baby factory will be safe?"

"I guess this is one way to find out." She hooked a leg around his hip.

He slid into her warmth. They groaned in satisfaction as they moved together. Her skin against his was perfection. A breeding pair, new last names, he didn't care about any of it as long as she loved him.

26

F or the first time since Geoff had started this ordeal, Lucy was not nervous. She knew the ball—and it was a big one—was firmly in her court. The smug smirks on her ex-husband's face and that of his lawyer's didn't piss her off. Today they made her want to laugh.

These men had no idea what was about to come crashing down on them. It helped her self-confidence that she no longer felt like a victim. She knew what she could— no, would do to survive. She had faced down threats more terrifying that either of these two flaccid-egoed assholes would ever be to her again.

She hated that her backbone was made from dollar bills, but all those zeros in her accounts were stronger than steel rods in her spine.

The new dress didn't hurt either. Lucy had taken a page out of Cyan del Fuego's style book. Well, what she imagined her style book would look like if she had one. She was the daughter of a vampire. Vamp was in her blood, power was in her blood. And a lot of money was in her bank account, so she decided to spend some of it. The dress was sleek and black and expensive. The neckline a little too low to be considered professional. But Lucy didn't care. She wasn't here to be professional. She was here to destroy Geoff's preconceived notions of being able to kick her around.

She was the one about to do some kicking.

To think, it had barely been six weeks since all of this had started. She smirked and took a seat at the large conference table. Bentoncourt sat next to her and pulled a sheaf of documents from his briefcase.

French spoke first. "Is your client prepared to write a check today?"

"Yes, of course," Ben responded.

Geoff huffed an almost laugh and squirmed in his chair. It was as if he actually thought he had won.

Ben handed over one pack of papers. "Per our request, Mr. Geoffrey Asher provided his financial records. Thank you for that. It was noted that all savings and retirement accounts established prior to the marriage were not included. We had agreed that all prior accounts of both parties were to remain out of consideration. However, at this time Mr. Asher does not have the resources to finalize the purchase of the property in question. Were my client to pay him fifty percent of his investment, he would still not be able to complete the purchase of said property. Even taking into consideration Mr. Asher's personal accounts that are not to be a part of these proceedings, he does not have the recourses to buy out the property." Bentoncourt was smooth. Lucy dared not blink lest she miss something.

Geoff's skin was already starting to look a little flush, and French's smile was leveling.

"We had countered by giving you and your client up to six weeks to demonstrate that Mr. Asher had access to the moneys for this purchase, and..." Bentoncourt flipped through the papers in front of him, stopping when he found what he was looking for. "You will see on page three, paragraph six, this extension was declined. At that time this led to one of two conclusions: Mr. Asher has the funds, or he does not and he accepts our counterproposal."

"This is ridiculous. The property value has increased almost fifty percent since we bought the place. Lucy doesn't have that kind of money either," Geoff blustered.

His lawyer held a hand up in front of him.

"So does this mean your client accepts the counteroffer? Since there was no stipulation that she cannot access money from her personal account for the purchase of the property in question, she is prepared to pay off the mortgage in full. Is Mr. Asher?"

French leaned over and whispered something to Geoff. His face was beet red. Lucy imagined his blood pressure pushing on the veins inside his brain. She suppressed an evil giggle.

Bentoncourt continued. "Let's face it, gentlemen, if you are not prepared to write a check right now to cover the mortgage of the Asher family home, my client is, and is capable of doing so."

"Then we take this to court," Geoff grumbled.

"No, Geoffrey, we won't. You want to get married, you have a child on the way, you served me illegally, you cannot afford a long-drawn-out court battle where you are the adulterer and are abandoning your children." Lucy sneered.

"Oh and you can?" He sneered right back.

"Actually, if proceedings are found in my client's favor, then you would be responsible for all court and legal fees, Mr. Asher. Are you prepared to pay both me and your own lawyer?"

"Mrs. Asher was not in a financial position to undertake these fees before. Why is she now?" French asked.

"My—"

Bentoncourt cut her off with a glance. He returned his gaze to one of the documents in front of him. He slid a copy across the big table to French. "My client was cut off from her family, and at great personal loss—" He took a deep breath. Lucy knew he was thinking about poor Celine, who had gotten herself entangled in the wrong world of vampires. She had probably been looking for sexy, lavish, and fun. Instead she was used and murdered. "Reestablished those connections in order to have access to her funds. Now, she is prepared—"

Geoff sat up and leaned forward on the table. "You mean you had money all along? Why didn't you ever access it while we were married? That could have made a difference, you know?"

"Oh, it does make a difference to know you would have stayed with me for my money. Geoff, that's almost worse than knowing you have had a long-term affair with a girl practically half your age, that you are willing to just give up the family we made. I never would have touched the money if you hadn't put me in a position where my children's lives were on the line."

"The kids were never in any danger."

Lucy breathed in deeply. She closed her eyes and counted to ten. It didn't help. She still wanted to eviscerate him. He had no idea how much danger. Truthfully, she still didn't really know. Were the only people who knew about her location really dead now? "Disowning your children and making them homeless is putting them in danger. You crossed the line."

"And you could have changed our quality of life with that money." Geoff huffed back into his chair.

"That is why my client is willing to buy you out of your half of what has already been invested in the property. Cash, today. The property will be paid in full by the end of the business week. And that resolves the issue regarding the property."

Geoff glowered. Lucy could tell he was thinking, trying to figure out how to access her money. But everyone had signed on the dotted line; premarital accounts were off-limits.

Bentoncourt slid another document across the table. "My client has decided to not countersue regarding Mr. Asher relinquishing custody of his children. The petition to emancipate the youth known as Stacey Yolanda Asher is to be withdrawn. Mr. Asher will sign over any and all custody rights. My client will not seek support payments."

Geoff smirked as French slid the custody form over for his signature. Of course Geoff was smirking; he thought he had won. He was getting almost everything he wanted, out of the marriage and out of child support.

"And here is the restraining order preventing Mr. Asher from coming within one hundred yards of the minors known as Stacey Yolanda and Justin Patrick."

Geoff glowered as he signed more and more documents. Lucy had signed everything earlier in front of the witness, who now took the documents from Geoff and witnessed his signatures. Lucy enjoyed his pained expression. This wasn't the outcome she had originally thought she was fighting for; this one was so much better. She had won. She had the house, she had the kids, and she didn't need him for anything.

Bentoncourt collected the signed documents from the

witness that French and French and Associates had provided. She was so quiet Lucy practically forgot she was there. Even the soft clicking sound of her official stamp faded into the background.

"My client has contracted with a private judge for the final signing of these forms. That way no one has to wait a minute longer for this divorce to be over. One last piece before we are done here." Bentoncourt shuffled to the bottom of the stack of documents.

Lucy found it difficult to suppress her grin.

"This is a premarital agreement between Mr. Asher and Christine Strnad. My client reached out to Miss Strnad in hopes that she could prevent any of these actions from hurting her or her unborn child."

The door to the conference room opened, and the receptionist escorted Chrissie inside.

"What?" Geoff was out of his chair. "How dare you interfere in my relationship with Chrissie!"

Bentoncourt stood when Chrissie entered the room. He pulled out a chair for her. Geoff was now in a position where he had to look at his wife and his lover, sitting next to each other across the table from him. Lucy batted her eyelashes at Geoff.

"Geoffrey, what's the matter? Don't you love me? The prenup won't really mean anything, you're not going to leave me and the baby, so don't worry about it." Chrissie was all smiles.

Lucy tried hard not to roll her eyes. Chrissie really was clueless. Geoffrey Asher would just as quickly ditch her as he had dumped Lucy.

"It really is a simple document, Geoffrey. You can see Chrissie already signed it, and was witnessed by an associate here at French and French," Lucy purred. She was tempted to lick her claws, except she didn't have any. Ah, maybe that's why Cyan kept her nails long and pointed? "It establishes a custody support structure for the child should anything happen to your relationship with Chrissie. I know how important your child with her is to you. After all, that is your DNA she is incubating. I can understand how this child replaces the children you raised in your heart." *Your cold, dead little heart.*

"Oh, that makes him sound like the bad guy. Geoffrey, tell her they aren't being replaced."

Lucy rested a hand on Chrissie's forearm. "It's okay. He's already relinquished custody. But that's why we included it in the prenup. Because we all know he will love your child forever. Geoffrey, sign the document, or Chrissie here will think that you don't really love her or your baby. You will see it's quite fair. We really did have her and the baby's interest at heart."

She had his balls in a vise. If he loved the girl, this shouldn't have been a big deal, but he was busted in his own game.

Geoff flipped through the brief document. It really wasn't requiring much of him, but it did require he accept full financial responsibility for the child if he and the mother were to separate. Lucy really didn't give a crap if Chrissie was taken care of, but she wasn't going to let him ditch out on another kid.

Geoff aggressively scrawled his name across the bottom of the document. Chrissie beamed.

"Are we done?" Lucy asked her lawyer. She was ready to get out of here and never see Geoffrey Asher again. Sitting next to, and pretending to be nice to, Chrissie was making her stomach turn.

"My check," Geoff growled.

Bentoncourt picked up his briefcase, opened it, and removed yet another document. He slid it in front of Lucy. She signed it with glee and handed it across to Geoff with a flourish.

Chrissie gasped as she caught sight of the amount the check was made out for.

"Now we are done." Bentoncourt stood. He held out his hand to help Lucy from her chair.

"I would like to thank you on behalf of my client for expediting this entire process. I am sure Miss Strnad is also grateful to not have to wait for her impending nuptials."

Lucy turned and left. She didn't need to say goodbye.

She was remarkably calm considering sixteen years of her life had just ended with a few signatures.

The meeting with Geoff and French and French and Associates was over. Lucy could breathe. Her chest felt as if she hadn't taken a breath the entire meeting.

It was nice to be in the sunshine again. Everything about Las Vegas had been so dark, from the night to the memories. And French's offices had felt so constricting. Maybe that had to do with Geoff's presence. She had ridden back to Bentoncourt's office with him in his BMW convertible with the top down, and now they strolled down the street. He had suggested they get a smoothie, and since he no longer had an assistant, they would have to pick them up themselves.

Lucy felt bad for him. He had liked Celine. Apparently she had been a competent relief after a string of questionable hires.

"I'll go through the agency where I found her. But how do you interview for someone who isn't going to be lured into doing something like that again?"

"Do you even know what she was promised?" Lucy asked.

Ben shook his head. "No idea, but it had to have been very seductive."

Lucy laughed. "Have you met the people of our fathers? By definition their very nature is seductive. Next time hire someone who isn't into all the vampire movies. Get an assistant who reads nonfiction instead."

"I guess that's one way to approach it. Now, how do you want to dispose of this piece of property in Vegas?" Ben pulled the door to the shop open and stepped back for Lucy to enter. "Or are you thinking of keeping it?"

The man behind the counter had arm muscles that could rival Shane's. But where Shane was ripped and narrow, this guy was thick and broad with a full beard. He smiled at her when she entered, but he beamed when he saw Bentoncourt. "Benny, you haven't been in for ages."

Was Smoothie Guy pouting?

Was Ben blushing?

Oh, this was good. No wonder Ben liked this smoothie shop.

Ben nodded and looked a little forlorn. "My assistant died suddenly. and I was rather taken aback by it all."

Smoothie Guy was out from behind the counter and wrapping an arm around Bentoncourt's shoulders. "You should have come in. I would have given you an immunity boost. Some extra D3, vitamin C, and St. John's Wort for a little mood stabilization. I'm going to make you a banana cacao smoothie with an extra boost to it." He helped Bentoncourt to a seat and looked up at Lucy. "And what can I get you, honey?"

Lucy bit her lip and scanned the menu again. She wanted to ask for his number so she could set him up with her lawyer. Instead she asked for a blueberry banana with a ginger shot.

She took the little iron chair across from Ben and watched him as he watched the Smoothie Guy work. "You should ask him for his number, or skip all that and just ask him out for coffee when he gets off work."

Ben sighed. "Am I that obvious?"

"You both are. So do you think I should keep the place? I mean, how can I sell it knowing it has to be haunted from all those poor people he kept enslaved there?"

"If you decide to sell, I can't recommend strongly enough that you have a cleanup crew go in and scour the rooms. No one needs to find what was going on down there."

"You knew, and you did nothing about it."

"I didn't know to what extent. I was an upstairs guy. I didn't venture down into the catacombs much at all. I didn't want to know."

Lucy thought about it, she had been an upstairs guy too. She could have done something. She knew Shane had lived in the underground. She shook her head. It was all in the past. Maybe she would seek forgiveness for not having done anything. Maybe she would take Cyan up on her offer to help out when they needed someone to get close to Lazarus when they did finally locate him, and not just his disposable minions.

A wide plastic cup was placed in front of her, filled with a soft pink concoction. She smiled up at the man who didn't have a spare glance for her. But he did have a soft look about his eyes for Bentoncourt. She smiled and took a sip of her smoothie. It was perfect and fruity.

"Thank you, Jets," Ben said as he stood. Lucy picked up her drink and followed Ben back out onto the street.

"His name is Jets?"

Ben shook his head. "No, it's Jerry on the name tag, but he told me to call him Jets."

Lucy stopped walking. "Oh my God, Bentoncourt. Are you completely blind?"

He stared at her, a puzzled look crossed his face.

"Are you not even mildly interested in him?"

"Well, but, he's not..." Ben sighed.

"He calls you Benny, and he wants you to call him Jets. You think he's cute." Lucy put her hand out with a flourish. "Give me your business card." She leveled him with one of her better mom stares.

Ben fished a card out from his wallet and handed it to her.

She turned and headed back into the smoothie shop. Jets looked a little disappointed that she was alone. She leaned over the counter, handing him the card. "Here's his card. You don't need an excuse to stop by at any time. The office is just up the street."

Jets gave her a knowing smile.

Bentoncourt stood waiting for her.

"That's done." She slid her arm into his and continued walking up the street. "Now, I think we should bulldoze the whole property, taking out the subterranean level. The ghosts there need to be released. And then we can sell the property. If I never go back to Las Vegas, it will be too soon."

Shane pulled the last shirt from the closet. It was empty now except for a few hangers.

He folded the shirt, still on the hanger, in half, and placed it in the box. That was it. Everything was packed.

He looked around the room. Boxes piled up just inside

the door. He should go over to the school and grab a few kids and have them haul everything down to his car. It would make the last bit of packing up easier.

This room had been home longer than he deserved. The walls had seen him through too many nightmares. That reminded him, he needed to call Melinda and get her to recommend a therapist in San Diego, hopefully one who would be familiar with his particular quirks. There weren't too many wolves that he knew about down there. Maybe Julia could make some connections. After all she was working on that whole DNA tracking project. That reminded him. He needed to have her send down those DNA kits for the kids and Lucy.

"Looks like you're all ready to go." Morgan leaned against the doorframe.

Shane sighed. "Yeah, this is the last of it. I just need to get it all into the car."

"Do we need to have a chat? You got a station wagon." Morgan gave him a half smile.

He was going to miss him too. But Lucy was on the other end of this move.

"I got a family car, man. I'm walking out of here and into the burbs and soccer practice and homework." He laughed. "I should be terrified."

"But it's everything you could have ever wanted." Morgan finished the thought.

He was right.

"You're gonna need to think of upgrading soon. I can't imagine car seats fitting into the mini." Shane winced as soon as he realized what he had said. "I'm sorry. How's Honey doing?"

Morgan huffed. "She's good. Doc said give it three

months, but Caro said ignore the doc and get busy as soon as she feels up to it."

"Let me guess, she's listening to Caro?"

"Wouldn't you?" Morgan raised his eyebrows.

"Ah, Morgan, there you are." Jinx, the head household manager, interrupted. "Remi was looking for you." She scanned the boxes. "Should I get a few of the boys to haul this downstairs for you?"

Shane nodded. "That would be great. Have one of them pull the car up so they don't have to lug everything down to the garage."

Jinx nodded, then blinked a few times. "We'll miss you around here, Shane." She turned and left.

Morgan stepped into the room and pulled Shane into a hug. "Oh, you almost got some emotion out of Jinx. She really will miss you. The rest of us will too."

"I'm not leaving until the morning. Besides I expect you down there in a few weeks for the wedding." Shane clapped Morgan on the shoulder. "I'll see you at breakfast before I leave."

Of course Honey wouldn't let Shane go with a basic breakfast. She had coordinated with everyone to prepare a little surprise going away for him with a lavish selection of Connie's finest breakfast foods. That meant everything from French toast to fajita omelets and her famous guacamole.

Hugs, kisses, and a few tears escorted Shane to his packed car. Joe had promised to ship his bikes at the end of the week, threatening to possibly drive them down himself. After all, there was no way he was going to miss the mighty ever-single Shane getting married.

By the time Shane hit the road, the sun was high enough to not be directly in his eyes as he headed east before picking up I-5 and heading south. He took a breather before he hit the grapevine. The last stretch of the drive would cover the least amount of distance and take the longest amount of time, thanks to the area traffic in LA and south.

It was dark when Shane pulled into the driveway.

The front door burst open, and Justin came barreling out. He was followed by the dog, Luna, then his sister and finally his mother. Shane couldn't stop smiling. Justin and the dog bounced around the front yard as Shane gathered a few items he would need to take inside for the night. He could unpack the rest of the car in the morning.

The kids and the dog ran back inside. Lucy slid into his embrace. Her arms snaked up his back, and she pressed him against the side of the car.

"I missed you," she purred right before she placed her lips against his and kissed him.

"I was only gone for a few days." Shane ran a knuckle down the side of her face. She was beautiful. Her eyes were lit from within, and her skin glowed.

"Long days without you. But everything is better now; you're home."

She was right, he was finally home.

EPILOGUE 1

S hane wiggled his toes in the cool sand. Lilting music filled the air.

He scanned the small group that had gathered for this. Honey leaned against Morgan, obviously fondly remembering her own wedding. How different this one must seem to her. No large crowd, no tuxedos. In the back Ben Roberts sat under a parasol next to his burly date. Shane had grossly underestimated the man. He was glad of that.

Everyone had gathered to wish them well; even with the short notice, people were here. The Del Coronado had even managed to help them out with a quiet beach location. A copse of palms created a semi-secluded area, perfect for their small gathering.

Lucy had said big and white—well, the dress was white and formal, and the sands were white and warm. The love was big. She accepted this and said everything sounded perfect after Shane had divulged the details of the wedding he and Stacey had managed to plan for her. Well, mostly Stacey. That kid had a talent for pulling an event like this together.

Justin shifted. "This is taking forever," he whined.

Shane put an arm around his shoulder. "It certainly feels like it, but it will be over in a flash, I swear it."

He extended his hand to shake. Justin took it. "I'm glad you're marrying Mom."

"Me too, J-man, me too."

Everyone hushed, and Shane turned to watch Lucretia walk up the aisle toward him. Really just a path between ribbon-decorated spikes in the sand and a few folding chairs. Stacey walked in front of her mother. Stacey was crying, but she had a smile on her face.

Tunnel vision. All he could see was Lucy.

Lucretia was radiant. She literally glowed, though Shane was fairly certain he was the only one to see the light radiate from her. If he didn't know what that glow was, he would have thought she was an angel. He had thought she was a shining star once. She was both for him.

Her dark hair was coiled sleekly against the back of her neck. He couldn't take his eyes from her face. He already knew the rest of her was perfect. She wore a long white wedding dress, just as she'd requested, but the dress and the details were all superfluous. It was his Lucy.

Stacey hugged him, and everyone shuffled into their places before the officiant. Stacey and Jason said their "I do's" as they gave away their mom in the ceremony. Their part over, Lucy handed the flowers she carried to her daughter, his stepdaughter. His daughter. The adoption papers would be signed and submitted on Monday morning.

Lucy slipped her hands into his. His own voice sounded strangled as he repeated the vows and said, "I will."

They had chosen simple traditional vows instead of writing their own. Apparently repeating "I love you" over and over wasn't considered a vow. But it was; nothing else mattered. Shane loved Lucy. She loved him. They would manage everything else. Lucy's voice was barely above a whisper.

Shane's nerves were on fire as he slipped the ring onto Lucy's finger. She was finally his, after all the years of longing, of never believing she would love him with as much ferocity, with as much pure need, she was now his wife. Something he hadn't dared even dream or hope for when she had married before. Shane would never give her cause to doubt him, or ever have to wonder if he loved her. He would always be faithful. Those weren't just words he repeated; he felt every single one of them deep in his soul.

When the officiant said that he may kiss his bride, Shane was more than eager to oblige.

Her lips trembled against his.

"I love you," he whispered against her mouth as he held her close.

The cheers from their small gathering of friends pulled them from their private revelry.

Holding Lucy, Shane turned to look out at the smiling faces of the people he considered family.

Lucy squealed as Shane scooped her up and carried her back down the aisle.

"You're supposed to carry me over the threshold, not away from the ceremony." She laughed.

Shane set her down once they reached the grassy lawn surrounding the hotel. "I want to run away with you and start the honeymoon right this second." He nuzzled her ear.

"We have company and a dinner to attend." Lucy smiled at him.

Morgan clapped Shane on the shoulder with bone-jarring impact. "Welcome to the club."

"It's a good club to be in. I honestly never thought I'd

make it."

Everyone sat around a large table in the restaurant. They had a view of the beach and the sunset, but Shane could only focus on Lucy. Justin had been right; everything was taking forever. Shane smiled and talked and thanked people for coming.

Morgan stood and made an awkward speech, since the best man, Justin, had declined vehemently about talking in front of everyone. Fortunately Morgan kept it short. But still the evening dragged on.

It wasn't until Jennifer and the kids left that Shane relaxed.

He was finally alone with Lucy, his wife.

He repeated his actions of picking her up, and he carried her across the threshold of their hotel room. Two nights here, then home with the kids for a week before he whisked Lucy away for a tropical honeymoon in Tahiti. He didn't get the luxury of taking off three months to be sequestered with his woman. He didn't need it. As long as he could be with her every day, that's all that mattered to him.

Shane sat in one of the side chairs and brushed the remaining sand from his feet. His dress shirt, an embroidered African dashiki with a stand-up open collar, formal without requiring a necktie, lay discarded on the opposite chair.

Lucy stepped from the bathroom, and Shane forgot how to breathe.

She'd exchanged her long white lace dress for matching red lace bra and panties. She also now wore shiny black heels a mile high, and dear God, she carried a riding crop. Shane gulped down the pool of drool that formed in his mouth. This was his wife. How the hell had he gotten so incredibly lucky?

EPILOGUE 2

Bobby sat on the edge of the messed-up bed. Not that it had been made before they had gotten on with tonight's activities, but now it was much, much worse.

A languid, boneless arm draped across his back, followed by the warm press of female breasts.

"Stay. You don't have to go." Kate's voice was sleep drunk and sexed out.

"Not tonight." He lifted her limp form away from him as he stood up, pulling on his jeans. Not any night. That was one of his few rules: never spend the night.

"See you around," he said, picking up his shirt. He shoved his feet into his boots and left, walking out of the apartment as he pulled his shirt on.

The night was warm, and he was still restless. The sex hadn't taken the edge off. The edge that was always there, always in need. Always wanting to run.

The car started with a throaty roar. Damn, he was going to have to look at that. He didn't have a muffler budgeted into his plan this month. He'd have to make sure he included it when he ran his calculations for next month. He could always dip into the AC fund, but he didn't want to risk that. He could drive his car on a crapped-out muffler for a few months. He could not run his business in a Texas summer without air-conditioning. He was already taking a gamble hoping it would limp along until next winter.

The moon was full and high by the time he pulled up next to his house. It didn't call to him, something he didn't understand. Shouldn't a moon this big and beautiful lure him to shift? Shouldn't something so glorious in the sky turn him into a ravenous beast?

Maybe tonight that's what called to him from deep in his restless bones. Usually sex would drive the urge down, suppress it. Not tonight.

As he stripped off he whistled for his dogs. Shaggy, mismatched, and sleepy, the three mutts approached him with lazy wags. Bobby tossed his clothes, followed by his boots, onto the back porch and reached skyward in a stretch that popped his back. He pulled the band holding his hair off and shot it toward his clothes. Shaking his long hair out, he reached forward.

By the time his hands touched the ground, they had already shifted into large fur-covered paws with black claws.

Una, the largest of his dogs, gave a happy yip, and the four of them ran. Bobby outpaced them all, but he circled back to allow Tre to catch up; the old guy wasn't as spry as he once was. Bobby led his ragtag pack north. The dogs scrambled through a hole in the fence that he soared over.

A lowing in the distance urged them forward. Tonight they would terrorize the neighboring herd. And in the morning Bobby would have to remember to fix that hole in the fence, or the steer would come onto his land and return the favor and harass him and the dogs.

They didn't hunt so much as move the cattle around.

Mischief was one thing, destruction something else. And no matter which form Bobby took, he was always in control of his mind. He knew better than to stir up trouble, be seen, or get caught. The last thing he needed or wanted were locals hunting for wolves in his running territory.

After harassing a few of the bigger animals, Bobby led the dogs back toward the house. They loped with a little less enthusiasm than they had started off with an hour or so earlier.

The dogs went straight to their water bowls and slopped up everything before collapsing onto the porch with heavy, happy, exhausted sighs. Bobby lay down on the planks with them, head on paws. He could sleep here; he had done it before. But he still felt restless.

Bobby shifted where he lay, then reached and stretched before rolling to his feet. He cranked the hot tap on the tub, gathered his clothes, and took them inside as he let the tub fill up. He grabbed a beer from the fridge before heading out back. He sat on the edge of the large copper tub lined in white porcelain. A pure luxury, he'd added the tub to his outdoor shower. It was an expense he had budgeted for, and he never once regretted the decision, even if he didn't use it as much as he would like. His free hand dragged through the water. It was hot but not too hot. He slipped into the depths; his hair trailed down his back, sopping up the water. Kicking his feet out, he rested them on the rim in the cool air.

The only thing that would make this moment perfect was if he had someone to share it with.

Well, he could share it with any number of women. He was sure Kate or Chareese wouldn't object to coming out to his house and moving into his tub. They wouldn't, but he would. That's why he didn't bring women home, another one of his rules.

It would take a special woman for him to invite her home.

A meteor lit up the sky before burning out.

"It would take an angel," he said out loud as if he wished on that falling star.

~

Does Bobby's wish on a falling bring him an angel?
Find out in Complete.

If you didn't start reading Legatum from the beginning, it's not too late. Get Protective, Legatum Book 1 now.

Keep reading for a sneak preview of Complete.

COMPLETE, LEGATUM BOOK 5

As far as Bobby is aware, he is the only one of his kind—
a true lone wolf. He fills his days with running his bar, and
his nights with emotionless encounters. After all, hooking
up with the town man-whore is as easy as crashing into his
buggy in the grocery store. Everything changes when he
sees an angel.

The pretty new math teacher in town glows. Bobby
believes she must be an angel sent to save him from his
empty life, someone he can have a future with.

Ramona ran away from a secret relationship gone bad in
the big city, to a small town where football is king, and she
has to make sure the star quarterback passes high school
math. Her plans are to not get involved with any
more men, especially bad boy, heartbreaker Bobby. Her
plans fly out the window when he makes an oddball
request. He tells her that he wants to change from playboy
to decent human being, and asks her to train him how to
have a platonic relationship with women.

Ramona accepts Bobby's challenge. Although he already
seems to be a pretty good guy, he just has to work past his

womanizing reputation. Unfortunately, tutoring Bobby becomes increasingly difficult as she develops feelings for him, and questions moving to Haven.

Bobby needs Ramona to believe him when he shares his shifting secret, and asks her to wear his championship ring, that his feelings for her are real, and that he's not out to take advantage of her affections.

COMPLETE, LEGATUM BOOK 5

Excerpt

Bobby leaned back on the old couch from the living room, his long denim clad legs stretched out in front of him. Brad, stepped over his boots, and handed him a cold brown bottle of beer. Brad dropped onto the couch beside him. The thread bare couch sat on the back deck in front of a dilapidated, half full pool. The deck was mid-remodel. Piles of flag stones sat in a corner waiting to replace the broken up concrete around the edge of the pool. The barbecue pit and outdoor bar were finally starting to look as if they might actually, one day, become a functional outdoor kitchen area. The hose spit water into the pool, so the kids could use it for the summer. Hopefully it would get resurfaced next winter. Wordlessly the brothers clinked their bottles together.

"Oh no you don't Bradley." A shrill voice from behind, carried from out of the house.

A woman with perfectly coiffed shoulder length ash blonde hair, a deep even tan, and pink lipstick stepped out onto the deck where the men sat. She was dressed in all black, her dress fell just shy of her knees. Her name tag was still pinned above her left breast, her feet were tucked into fuzzy pink house slippers. "Don't drink that beer baby, not until you spit in this."

Perfect pink manicured fingers held out a test tube to Brad.

Brad sat up, rolling his eyes up to peer at his wife.

"It's that DNA thing, spit up to the line."

He took the tube and began spitting into it as directed.

Bobby looked at her quizzically.

"Since you and Bradley don't know nothin' about your parents or grandparents, I'm hopin' this DNA test thing is gonna work like they say it does on the web site."

"DNA? What website?" Bobby asked.

Brad handed the spit filled tube back to his wife. "Melissa is doing a family genealogy search. Using one of those ancestor things online."

Bobby shifted his focus from his brother back to Melissa. She nodded. "I'm using that GeneoloTree site, they help you find birth records, and who your great-great-great-granddaddy was. My cousin Cindy has our side of the family back past the Oklahoma Land Rush. Maybe we can find something out about you two. It supposedly finds genetic relatives. DNA matches. I researched it, and this is from one of the few companies that includes Native American DNA. The kids will want it someday. Who knows," she gestured toward Bobby, "you might actually settle down, and your wife and kids would be interested."

Bobby shook his head as his sister in-law stepped back through the sliding glass doors into the house.

"And you just spit in the tube, like that?" Bobby focused on his brother's bearded face.

Brad took a long pull on his beer. "Hey, it keeps her happy. A happy wife makes for a happy life."

"You are happy aren't you?" Bobby asked.

"Bobby, I can't begin to tell you how happy she makes me. Almost twelve years, and I have never doubted marrying her was the smartest thing I ever did."

"No seven year itch? I know you don't even look at other women, she that good?"

"Be respectful of my wife little brother, I can still take you."

Bobby held up both hands in surrender, his thumb holding the neck of his beer. "No harm, no foul. Seriously, you used to be a horn-dawg. What gives?"

Brad chuckled, it rumbled deep in his chest. Both men had smooth low tenor voices and similar looks. Brad wore his thick wavy hair business short, with a close trimmed, full beard. His wife Melissa claimed it emphasized his warm brown eyes. Bobby's eyes were lighter, amber, his jaw was covered in a few day's scruff, and wore his hair long down his back.

"I was nothin' like you."

Bobby titled his head in acquiescence, he had a reputation as the leading womanizer in town, a veritable man-ho. He knew it, he accepted it, he was getting tired of it. "I'm gettin' to where I don't want to be nothin' like me."

"Something about her made me want to change. What really makes it last, it's not the sex, not the love, not the kids, it's she's my best friend Bobby."

"Not the sex?"

"Best I ever had. Seriously. I'm not joking though, I knew something was different the first time I met her. By the end of that first week," Brad shook his head. "I just wanted to hang out with her, be around her. She was waitressing back then. I would go sit at that restaurant every night just to see her, say hi. Anything. Took a while to convince her to go out with me, but she did. I was a perfect gentleman I didn't touch her for weeks, didn't make one single play. Stopped hooking up with other girls. Wasn't interested. Really got to know her. You should try it. You need to find the right woman."

"I'm jealous, I really am. I don't think I'm ever going to meet the right one," Bobby sounded mournful. "It's going to take an angel to put up with the likes of me."

"As long you still have that bag'em and tag'em attitude, ain't nothin' gonna change."

"Hey, I'm just accepting what's being offered," Bobby deflected.

"If you're looking for the right one, she might not be offering. Just saying." Brad gave his brother a knowing nod.

Click HERE to keep reading Complete.

Sign up for Lulu's newsletter to keep up to date with new releases and happenings. And get a free sexy short story.

https://lulumsylvian.com/newsletter/

ALSO BY LULU M SYLVIAN

Check out these other series

Legatum

Paranormal romantic suspense

The World of Wet Waterfalls

Paranormal reverse harem romance

Rockers

Contemporary and paranormal rockstar romance

Holiday Strippers

Contemporary, paranormal, ridiculous, romance

ABOUT THE AUTHOR

Bio-engineered to be the only redhead in a generation of blonds, Lulu feels that "aliens" may actually be the best answer for a life-time of being asked, "Where did you get that red hair from?"

She did not come into writing from years of scribbling words on paper. Her background is rooted in visual arts and making pictures. Encouraged to make those pictures out of words Lulu began writing just to see what would happen. What happened was two full-length manuscripts in three months.

Lulu cannot ride a horse, a motorcycle, spin a hula hoop, or play roller derby. Yes, she has attempted all of those, even if it has been decades since she's been on a horse or a motorcycle. She embraces the crazy that comes with that one little genetic mutation, and attempts to live up to the reputation that proceeds her. Lulu would like to apologize for her contribution to the hole on the ozone layer from her use of hairspray in the 1980s.

For more information, visit:
www.LuluMSylvian.com

www.ingramcontent.com/pod-product-compliance
Lightning Source LLC
Chambersburg PA
CBHW070834280626
47161CB00015B/589